The Silence

Katharine Johnson

"A tender and gripping coming of age mystery."
Sarah Jasmon, author of The Summer of Secrets

"Suspenseful, thrilling and edge-of-the-seat shocking. The Silence will have you gasping out loud."
Tessa Harris, author of The Sixth Victim

Copyright © 2017 by Katharine Johnson
Photography: Photocreo Bednarek
Editor: Christine McPherson
All rights reserved.

No part of this book may be used or reproduced in any manner whatsoever without written permission of the author or Crooked Cat except for brief quotations used for promotion or in reviews. This is a work of fiction. Names, characters, and incidents are used fictitiously.

First Black Line Edition, Crooked Cat Books. 2017

Discover us online:
www.crookedcatbooks.com

Join us on facebook:
www.facebook.com/crookedcatbooks

Tweet a photo of yourself holding
this book to **@crookedcatbooks**
and something nice will happen.

For Mike,
with my love.

Acknowledgments

I must thank the following people for their invaluable help with this book: my family for allowing me to write - I'm sorry for the times I was so wrapped up I forgot to cook dinner! My fantastic publishers Stephanie and Laurence and the whole Crooked Cat community for their advice and support; my wonderful editor Christine McPherson and my six amazing beta readers - Shirley, Eleanor, Tessa, Lucy, Rosie, especially for her advice as a speech therapist, and Jenny for her insight as a GP. I'm very grateful to police firearms expert, Jef, who let me pick his brains and gave me more detail on shotgun injuries than I hope I will ever need to use. Any mistakes are my own. Huge thanks to Emma Mitchell for organising such a brilliant blog tour and all the bloggers who very kindly gave up their time and helped spread the word about the book.

Finally and most importantly I want to thank you the reader - I really hope you enjoyed reading this novel as much as I enjoyed writing it.

About the Author

Katharine Johnson is a journalist with a passion for crime novels, old houses and all things Italian (except tiramisu). She grew up in Bristol and has lived in Italy. She currently lives in Berkshire with her husband, three children and madcap spaniel. When not writing she plays netball badly and is a National Trust room guide.

Follow Katharine Johnson online, at her blog:
katyjohnsonblog.wordpress.com

The Silence

Chapter One

On those rare occasions when Abby allowed herself to think about Philippa, it was never as a pile of bones but as a girl of fourteen. A girl who was very much alive. A girl who could burp the National Anthem (well, the first couple of lines), hurl herself off rocks, catch scorpions with her bare hands, hold her breath until she fainted, and who always slept with one arm straight up in the air.

A girl who rolled her eyes and pulled faces behind people's backs, and spurted her drink over everyone when she laughed. Being with Philippa meant laughing until you were sick, sharing your deepest, most thrilling secrets, keeping each other awake with disgusting jokes and gut-wrenching stories. And, of course, planning the perfect murder.

If she let herself, Abby could still hear Philippa's voice – sweet, teasing and shockingly clear. 'Jump on. It'll be a laugh.'

'Where did you get that?' she heard herself say.

The dark glasses twitched and the freckles on Philippa's nose spread above her unstoppable smile as she shook back spirals of flame-gold hair. 'Does it matter?'

The adult Abby watched her twelve-year-old self move forward and throw one leg over the back of the Vespa.

'Hold on,' said Philippa. 'Not like that. I can't breathe. Stop moving about.'

The bike wobbled as they set off, shouting and laughing. Abby held her breath as they plunged through the tunnel of trees towards the first hairpin. Light flickered through the leaves, darts of heat stabbing at knees and elbows as they hurtled from shadow to blinding light and back into shadow.

'We're going to die!' they screamed, as they bounced over potholes and snapping twigs.

Abby found herself trapped inside a fireball as Philippa's hair whipped around her face. Unable to see, she was acutely aware of smells – dust on wild herbs, melting tarmac, petrol fumes, and coconut shampoo. But the hair tickled her nose and crunched in her teeth. She grabbed a fistful and held it out of the way.

'What are you doing?' Philippa yelled. 'Stay still.'

Seeing they were now skimming the edge of the precipice, she did so. Below them, the land fell away through vineyards and olive trees to a shimmering patchwork of rooftops and bell towers. A flash of metal as a small van rounded the hairpin bend in front of them.

'Move over!' shrieked Abby.

'All right. Keep your knickers on.'

Philippa slewed across the road. The driver leaned out of the window and made a rude gesture. But then, seeing it was Philippa, he turned it into a wave and shook his head, smiling.

Past the church and into the village, through the web of tiny streets, past cages of canaries, geraniums bursting from windowsills, a blur of terracotta moons on sun-baked walls, gargoyles leering over lintels. As they ducked under a line of washing, Philippa reached up with a whoop and grabbed a pair of the woodcutter's voluminous pants. She held them up like a flag before discarding them over a stone cherub.

Abby's teeth rattled as they bounced over the cobbled stones, and her plaits thumped against her back so hard she could feel bruises forming. A woman carrying two bags of shopping flattened herself against the wall. Philippa blew a raspberry at Brutto, who was sunning himself on a balcony. The dog flew at the rails, barking himself into a frenzy.

They cut through the piazza, scattering pigeons in the golden haze, sticking out arms and tongues to catch the drifting spray from the fountain.

'*Ciao*, Armando,' Philippa shouted.

'*Ciao bella*!' called the barkeeper, looking up from

wiping his tables, and setting right the wig that made him look as if he was auditioning for a role as a Medici in a costume drama. '*Dove andate?*'

But they were already gone, under the dark arch at the end of the piazza, past the abandoned convent where Abby used to imagine a chorus of ghost maidens flinging open the shutters and singing out operatic warnings.

If she could stop time, that's where she'd have stopped it. Right there under the arch that first summer, before everything went bad. Looking back, perhaps the whole thing had been inevitable. She had always known she would lose Philippa – it was just a question of how. She wasn't interesting or exciting enough to hold onto her, no matter how hard she tried. She had made pacts with invisible beings, invented rituals – *if I bounce this ball a hundred times without missing; if I touch every one of the olive trees before the song on my Walkman finishes; if I eat this white, blobby cheese on my plate...* But in her heart, she had always known.

She never thought of Philippa as she'd last seen her. How could she do that and carry on living a normal life? How could she finish school, get a degree, go to work every day, marry, do all the things normal people did? So much easier to think it had never happened.

After all, it was impossible to imagine now, just as it was impossible to recapture the blinding heat, the scorching clouds of dust that peppered your legs as you walked, and the incessant nagging of the cicadas that drilled into your skull.

Impossible to think of the place existing without them, of life going on just as it had when they had been there. But it must. People drinking in the bars below the villa or lazing in deckchairs around the swimming pool, must look up into those forested hills hundreds of times in a day and have no idea what they were concealing.

Brambles as thick as Abby's arm must have grown up by now over the place she had last seen Philippa, spreading their fingers around the stones. Acacias with their dagger thorns would have muscled in to form a second line of defence. Landslips would have showered mud and rocks on top, erasing it, erasing Philippa, erasing everything.

'If you keep on lying about something, it becomes the truth,' Philippa had said once.

But perhaps it really hadn't happened. Because if it had, surely by now someone would have broken through the woods, torn down the brambles, pulled apart the stones, clawed back the earth, and they would have found her, wouldn't they?

A girl without a face.

Chapter Two

Something about this place was familiar. She unlatched the heavy shutters and pushed them back as far as the creeper would allow. The rough feel of the stone ledge beneath her hands, the smell of damp wood and foliage, the silky feel of early morning air brushing her face, the muffled toll of the bell swinging in its open tower below, only just visible through the veil of cloud – yes, she'd been here before.

As the first mountain peaks pierced the cloud, she brought a hand up to shield her eyes from the sudden glare of sunlight. Of course, that was where she was – back at the villa. Just for a moment, in spite of everything that had happened there, she felt a surge of wonderment. But there was something else. Her stomach lurched even though she knew she was dreaming.

Bursting out onto the loggia, down the broken stone steps towards the chestnut tower. Skidding down the terraces through the olive trees, the acacia woods, tripping over tree roots, her breath knifing her lungs. She had to get there before it was too late. Had to get to Philippa. She tripped on something soft. Went sprawling.

Philippa sprang up, shaking back those strawberry-blonde ringlets, wiping the mess off her face, laughing delightedly, freckled nose crinkled, holding out her bloodied hands. 'You see? It's paint, you idiot.'

Relief swamped her. It felt so real. If she could only stay in this dream and make it the reality, everything else the illusion… But already the images were jumbling like fragments in a kaleidoscope. Then the mist was sweeping in again and Philippa wasn't there any more.

Abby lay in the darkness, her face wet with tears, heart

slamming against her ribs, going over everything. Of course, it couldn't have happened that way. Philippa's hadn't been the first dead body she had seen, and people didn't recover from injuries like that, did they?

Slowly she adjusted her gaze, took in the room around her – the white waffle bedlinen, polished oak floorboards, sash windows and linen curtains, black and white prints of Paris on the wall, and pictures of the children on the chest of drawers. The books on the shelves, the perfume James had bought her for Christmas.

Outside, she could see the tops of trees swaying in the park opposite, hear the shouts from the football pitch, the shush of traffic on the road below, a pigeon calling down the chimney. This was her life now. The only one that mattered.

The life she had chosen for the woman she had become.

There had been a time when the villa had invaded her sleep quite regularly – sidling in at the end of the high street, over the brow of a hill, round the bend of a bay. For months after she came back to England, she'd wake up to find the sheet soaked, the duvet in a knot on the floor, and her father crouching beside her, his eyes small without his glasses, hair standing up in tufts, face creased.

'It's all right, it's all right. None of it was your fault.'

But how was he to know what had really happened? Although his words could never be adequate, his tone eventually soothed her back to sleep, and the next time she fought harder, kept fighting until her dream-self turned away from the villa.

And after that she had managed to stop the dream altogether. At least she thought she had. In a silent ritual in her bedroom, she had written some words on a piece of paper and set light to it. Watched the flame lick over the ink, turning the paper black. Erasing the words, obliterating the deed. She had opened the window and flung out the charred remains, watching them float away into the night.

So, why hadn't she been able to stop it this time? After so many years, the dream had caught her off-guard. Stupid, she shouldn't have let it happen. What time was it? She lay in semi-darkness waiting for her heart rate to return to normal, focusing on nothing more than how the light in the room changed, turning the wall from grey to rose.

The sheet beside her was empty and voices floated up from downstairs. A clinking of crockery and hissing and shushing. At last, she heard the stairs creak and the tray rattle. She staunched her tears in the duvet and forced her breathing under control.

'Surprise!' shouted Sophia, bursting in.

Lucy elbowed her sister out of the way, frowning fiercely as she carried the rattling tray.

James stood behind them with a bunch of flowers. 'They even remembered to boil the kettle this time,' he said with a grin.

Abby marvelled at the toast soldiers arranged to form the letters MUMMY, the envelopes with shaky writing, and the chocolate heart melting into a squishy mess against the teacup.

'This is wonderful. I can't believe you did this.'

Lucy, beaming her gap-toothed grin, bounced onto the bed, folding her skinny legs under her. Abby hauled Sophia up on the other side. 'Did you really make these cards yourselves?'

Sophia nodded, her face aglow with pride.

'I drew the cat for her because she can't draw cats,' said Lucy.

It still seemed incredible that these amazing little people were anything to do with Abby. But they were. They needed her; she would do anything for them, and surely that was what mattered now.

'What time are we going to Granny's?' she asked.

'I said we'd be there about twelve,' replied James, straightening the curtains. 'Are you sure you don't mind?'

She smiled, settling back against the pillows. 'Of course not. It's her day, too. And Trix's and Jo's. And they'll all want to hear your news. They'll never forgive you if they see it in the papers first.'

Only a few years ago, occasions like this used to fill her with dread. James's family never missed an opportunity to celebrate, but Mother's Day had been the worst. Since she was ten, the event had been a taunting reminder that she no longer had a mother. And in the early years of their marriage it had reinforced her sense of failure to conceive, especially when surrounded by an ever-growing brood of nephews and nieces.

But eventually, Lucy had come along, followed a year later by Sophia. And in their eyes, she was a good person; the best. She was Mummy.

***

Two hours later, they pulled up at the pebble-dashed Edwardian home in which James had grown up. The girls tumbled out of the car, banging on the door and lifting the letterbox. As the door opened, they jumped around their grandparents, babbling news, then tore through to the garden to find their cousins.

'You are good to come all this way to see us,' said James's mum, kissing them both and drawing them inside.

'We wouldn't miss it for the world, Moira,' said Abby, presenting her with a cake she had made.

The house smelled of roast lamb and herbs. From the garden came the sounds of laughter, children shouting, dogs barking, a baby crying. When she'd first come here, she had been overwhelmed by the noise, the chaos, the unpredictability – so different from what she had been used to.

'Get in here, man, you're on the apple crumble,' said James's older brother, hauling him into the kitchen. 'Hello there, Abby.'

'No mums in here,' their father said, barring her way. 'It's all in hand. You take the chance to relax. I bet it doesn't happen very often. Grab a seat in the garden while you can.'

Abby made her way through to the back of the house. Everywhere you looked there were reminders of the family's past – lines marked with names and dates on a doorway to show the children's heights at various ages; photographs of them playing cricket on a Cornish beach, standing on the ramparts of a Welsh castle, and up a mountain in Norway. The boot room was still cluttered with an assortment of coats and Wellingtons in different sizes, wooden surf boards, old tennis racquets, brightly coloured fishing nets, and camping gear. In some ways, it must feel as though James and his siblings had never left home.

Outside, the air had a hint of sharpness and smelled of damp grass. It had rained on the journey down but was brighter now. Camellia House lived up to its name at that time of year, the garden brimming with trees of pink and red blooms.

High up in a corner of the lawn was the tree house Norman had built for his children when James was five, and beneath it a gravestone for a dog who had lived to seventeen and several smaller ones for hamsters.

Norman and Moira often talked about downsizing, but it was hard to imagine them living anywhere but here. To Lucy and Sophia, used to a small suburban lawn, the garden was a magical place.

'Can you be the dragon like last time, Aunty Abby?' asked one of her nephews. He was blond with lots of freckles. One of the twins, but she could never work out which was which unless they were together.

'Hmm, I don't know,' she said, pretending to consider. 'You see, the thing about dragons is that they come out when they're least expected.'

She turned away. Then back with a roar. With delighted squeals, the children scrambled in all directions. Abby chased them in and out of the washing, through the camellias and around the pond.

She saw Sophia straight away, crouching among the tulips but pretended not to. Loud whispers gave away the presence of two of the boys in the summerhouse. She found another in the silver birch branches and, after much searching, the eldest girl squeezed behind the potting shed.

All of them went into the imaginary cauldron, but as she turned away to check her recipe they tiptoed out and charged for safety, screaming and laughing.

Catching her breath, Abby flopped down in a deckchair next to Trix, James's elder sister, who was occupying the striped lounger.

'Can we do it again?' asked Lucy. Her face was flushed and her hair coming away from its ponytail.

'Maybe later. Just let me get my breath back.'

'Sit down – have a drink,' Trix said, pouring her a Pimms. 'You are good. I don't know how you've got the energy. Get a dog, that's my advice. Tires them out eventually.'

Her golden Labrador burst through the lavender, chasing a chocolate spaniel that appeared to be wearing a toffee-coloured wig.

'Hope you've brought your coat. Dom's insisting we eat outside as usual. Bit optimistic, judging by those clouds.'

'Are you ready yet?' one of the children asked, but Trix sent them packing.

'Take your little cousins to see the fairy tree. It's even better now.'

They ran off to a hollow stump with a tiny door set into the bottom, peering at the fairies through the glass panel in the top.

'How's the job?' Trix asked. 'Started at the new practice yet?'

Abby accepted the drink gratefully. 'Yes, it's nice not having to travel so far.'

Tempting cooking smells drifted out through the open window, along with the occasional shout and clanging of pots as James and his brothers argued over different cooking methods. A clatter as something was dropped, followed by a moment's silence and then more voices, a howl of indignation, and a shout of laughter.

Trix rolled her eyes. 'I bet the patients are a bit easier to deal with in your new area, aren't they?'

'In some ways. Better diets and fewer smokers. Less

likely to get violent if I don't sign them off sick. But in this area a lot of time's taken up by the worried well.'

'Oh, let me guess – they've looked up their symptoms on the Internet and all they want you to do is sign the bit of paper.'

Abby felt herself smile. 'Pretty much. And they don't like to be contradicted. A lot of pushy parents demanding I write letters recommending special dispensation in their children's exams. Sometimes there's a genuine reason, sometimes it's just exam nerves.'

Trix laughed. 'Mind you, who'd be a teenager nowadays? So much pressure to get top grades in everything. I don't envy them.'

She was right, of course. And that was only the half of it. Cyber-bullying, eating disorders, self-harm – Abby had seen it all in her job. If only she could find a way to prevent her daughters from going through these things.

A child's cry brought her attention back to the garden.

'One of mine. Better go and see what he wants,' said Trix with a sigh. 'No, don't you get up. Sit and have a read of the paper.'

She plopped it into Abby's lap and strode off shouting, 'Now what have you done?'

The paper was full of stories about a terrorist attack in London, Brexit, and a housing scam. So, unsurprisingly, a macabre discovery at a villa in Italy was given little coverage. If the rental guests hadn't been British, it probably wouldn't have got any at all.

And yet the picture jumped out at Abby. Her hand went to the side of her head. It couldn't be. Her heart was hammering before she even read the text.

Bodies found at Tuscan holiday home

Everything slowed as her eyes slid across the page. Her head pulsed. Fear coiled through her as she read it and then read it again. The news she had been dreading for nearly quarter of a century, and she was reading it right here in a garden with James's family all around her.

And yet a little voice whispered: *why not now? Why not*

here? It wasn't as if there would ever be a good time or place.

Chapter Three

Bodies Found at Tuscan Holiday Home

An English family's dream holiday turned into a nightmare when they discovered two skeletons in the grounds of the Tuscan villa where they were staying.

Miranda and Robert Hamilton, who run an IT business in Orpington, had booked a two-week holiday at Le Rondini, an idyllic-looking villa in a classic Tuscan hill village.

It was the couple's six-year-old daughter who made the grisly discovery while playing in the garden. Builders had been clearing a fallen building but the site had not been fenced off.

'We chose this property because it seemed so peaceful and had lots of space for our children to run around in,' said Miranda Hamilton. 'The last thing we were expecting to find there was a couple of bodies.

'We've been offered alternative accommodation, but our children are traumatised and we're having to think about arranging counselling for them.'

Police say they are waiting for forensic test results before they can speculate on how long the bodies have been there and the manner of death, but they are cautiously optimistic about being able to identify them and are following up on several leads...

Looking up, seeing her daughters peering into the fairy tree, their pretty dresses rippling in the breeze, Abby felt everything dissolving in front of her eyes. The ground didn't seem solid any more, the trees looked artificial, none of the colours looked natural.

She had a sudden vision, so powerful, of the villa as she had known it – a mishmash of stone and render clad in creeper so thick it was impossible to fold back the flaking shutters, the roof tiles held down by stones, the broken stone steps and the fallen balcony. For a moment, she was back there lying in the hammock under the fig trees, watching lizards dart along the dry stone wall. Had it really been that idyllic? No, of course it hadn't.

How much could she really remember? Not much at all. Just scenes. Snapshots. She tried to sort them, but they kept slipping out of her control because of the one that overshadowed everything.

Perhaps she was getting this wrong. There must be thousands of villas that looked similar. And there were several differences, including the name. *Le Rondini* was a good choice. It reminded her of how the sky had filled with swallows on those warm summer evenings. She remembered watching them flit and dive in and out of the little conical nests they had built under the loggia.

They had found one once with an injured wing and tried to nurse it back to health, keeping it in a shoebox. She saw Philippa's hands deftly cutting the worm into pieces to feed the bird. She had wanted to look away but was fascinated all the same to see if it really did turn into lots of little worms, as she had been told. It didn't.

She saw herself sitting at the stone table under the pergola with Philippa and Mina, listening to them arguing about whether curses really existed and if the house could be cursed; keeping secrets for each of them.

Heard her own childish voice, barely a whisper, 'What will you do if I tell?'

But now the villa was slipping away as she had seen it on that last night, peeping behind grubby, tear-soaked fingers. Retreating into the red earth and chestnut trees behind it like a wounded, blind beast as the car bounced away. Dark, closed-up, silent. And yet somehow, she had always known, hadn't she, that she would see it again? It would find her.

No, she was being ridiculous. Surely she was only making connections with the villa because of the dream she had had? Heart hammering, she scanned the picture, exploring every millimetre. She tried to reassure herself, but it was no use. Perhaps having the dream had just made her more alert so that she noticed a picture she would otherwise have flicked past.

The villa stared back, smug in its new disguise. With its smooth, pink façade, decorative friezes, and window boxes of cascading geraniums, it certainly lived up to the newspaper's description 'idyllic holiday home'. But no amount of paint and repairs could fool her.

The creeper had been cleared away, the two enormous Cypress trees that had blocked the windows of the *salotto*, making it permanently dark, had been cut down, the iron balustrade had been repaired, and the shutters rehung. But the stained-glass window Alan had salvaged from the little church that had been damaged in an earthquake was still there, and an inset image showed a close-up of the cherub head doorknockers.

How could looks be so deceiving? She wanted to rip the page into shreds and trample it into the ground. Instead, she slid it out, trying to stop her hands from trembling, folded it, and slipped it into her bag. She took a gulp of Pimms and then another.

Her head squeezed. Her vision shrank and nausea swept through her. Battling to keep it under control, she stood up and stumbled on rubbery legs towards the house. Dodging children, cats, offers of sherry, and invitations to solve disagreements, she climbed the stairs two at a time and shut herself in the bathroom where she sank to her knees and retched over the bowl.

This could not be happening.

She had become so adept at compartmentalising her life, but now boxes were opening. Contents were spilling out. Contents that must never get mixed up. From downstairs, she could hear James and his eldest brother Dom arguing about something pointless. In the garden below, someone was singing. The branches of the ash tree were moving, and a Frisbee flew up past the window and back down. Splashing her face with cold water, she didn't trust herself to look in the mirror.

A board creaked outside the bathroom. Someone tentatively tried the door. Abby ran the tap fiercely and reapplied her eye makeup with shaking hands, then smoothed her hair down, checking her clothes for vomit stains.

Slowly, she slid the bolt across. The stairs were a single steep flight. She thought about running down them, through the front door. She could drive to the airport, catch the first flight available, get away as far as she could. That way she'd never have to see their faces when they found out. But the idea was ridiculous – the life she'd constructed for herself was so conventional she wouldn't last five minutes on the run.

She brought her hand to her throat as Trix, James's sister, stepped out of one of the bedrooms.

'Are you all right, darling? I'm so sorry, I couldn't help hearing. You're not, are you?'

She looked pointedly at Abby's stomach.

Abby felt herself colour. 'Oh God, no – just a bug. There's something going around. Goes with the job, unfortunately – being surrounded by sick people. I pick stuff up all the time. I'm sorry. I felt fine this morning or I wouldn't have come.'

Trix clearly didn't believe her. She tapped her nose with her finger. 'I won't breathe a word. You're absolutely right to be cautious. A girl in our office lost hers at eleven weeks. I'll keep everything crossed for you. But you look horribly rough, if you don't mind me saying. Was it like this with the others?'

She shook her head, too weak to argue.

'Then it must be a boy. Does James know yet? Of course he must.'

Abby shook her head. 'I really don't think it's that.'

'Does James know what?'

The two women froze as James's dark, curly head appeared at the bottom of the stairs. Trix closed her eyes. She mouthed her apologies to Abby as she slipped into the bathroom.

'Is everything all right?' he called up.

Abby held the bannister as she concentrated all her efforts into getting downstairs without falling. 'Yes. Sorry, just not feeling too great.'

He looked concerned. 'Do you want to have a lie down in my old room?'

Yes. No. That would mean being alone with her thoughts.

'No, it's fine. I'll be all right now. You haven't told them your news yet.'

He kissed her nose. 'All right, but if you feel any worse, let me know. I promise we won't stay long.'

It was the usual chaos downstairs. After much debate, someone had made the decision to eat indoors – a good one, judging by the sudden patter of rain – so everything was being carted back through the French doors into the dining room.

Two extension leaves were added to the table. People squeezed past each other to get to their seats, shouted orders to bring forgotten items – a cushion for the chair at the end, another mat to go under the serving dish. There was a clamour among the children for apple juice and a fight over who had to sit on the piano stool. Norman was sharpening the carving knife with a series of swishes. One of the children had their hands clamped to their ears.

When they sat down to eat, polite conversation was maintained for a few moments before the usual banter and one-upmanship erupted, each family member trying to outdo the others in outrage, intolerance, incredulity, and indignation. Daniel, the youngest brother, was recounting one of his revenge tales about a rude passenger on one of his flights.

'...He was giving me all kinds of grief and calling me names I'd better not repeat at the table. He'd taken off his shoes, so as I wheeled the trolley past I picked one of them up. My last sight of him, he was hobbling over the tarmac with just one shoe…'

She tried to focus on what he was saying but her stomach knotted and her throat closed over as she tried to eat. She stared down at her plate, but the words of the article kept playing back in her head and questions kept forming. What exactly had they found?

Two skeletons, the paper had said – one male, one female. One of these was Philippa. It had to be. But whose was the other? How long would it take to identify the bodies? How accurate could they be after so much time had passed? It must depend on so many things – the soil condition; how intact the remains were; whether any hair, or tissue, or fragments of clothing remained.

Presumably, they could trace back easily to find out who had been living in the house at the time. Further investigations would reveal who had stayed there, too – although surely that would take longer. She pressed her curled hand against her mouth and closed her eyes.

She had a sudden vision of Philippa as she had looked on the day she first saw her – her flushed skin, wide-set, green eyes, and thick, fiery hair flying out behind her as she ran down the overgrown path from the house. Wearing those old cut-off jeans with the rainbow patches, and a bright t-shirt with some Italian writing on it. Jumping down the last few steps, landing in front of the car, hands splayed on the bonnet, laughing, her hair falling in front of her face.

She did not want to imagine what Philippa looked like now, but however much she tried to concentrate on other things she couldn't stop the pictures seeping through. She had lost count of how many dead bodies she had seen in her job – cadavers in the medical lab; people who had died in the operating theatre, during her medical training; care home patients for whom she had signed death certificates. But this was different.

'Are you all right, Abs?' asked Dom. 'You look a bit green, if you don't mind me saying.'

'Ever the charmer,' Trix said, slapping her brother. 'Something she's picked up from the patients.'

She gave Abby a wink, which she felt obliged to return with a smile.

'Oh hello, what's this?' said Norman, as James produced a bottle of champagne and set it on the table. As the hubbub died, everyone looked at him expectantly. He cleared his throat with a characteristic cough. He'd gone a bit pink.

'I wanted you to be the first to know – you're looking at the new education secretary.'

Norman gave a shout of laughter, rose from his chair and hugged his youngest son. 'You did it. We knew you would.'

'How the hell did you wangle that?' demanded Trix.

'You? God help the poor children of this country,' cried Dom. 'This from a man who had to take his maths GCSE three times.'

'Twice.'

'And what did you get for your Physics again?'

'Mummy, Uncle James just swore with his finger.'

'It had to be you,' said Moira. 'You're the right man for the job.'

'I don't know about that,' he replied, dabbing at some spilt champagne with a napkin, 'but at least I've had experience of working in schools, which is more than my predecessor had. And I couldn't make a worse job of it than he did.'

'And hopefully you won't die in such humiliating circumstances,' murmured Trix.

'Working in schools? You make it sound as if you were the caretaker,' said his father. 'Your dad was a superhead,' he told the girls.

Lucy frowned in confusion. 'Is that like Superman?'

'Yes, that's right,' James told his daughter with a wink. 'When you were asleep, I used to put my pants on over my trousers, don a red cloak, and fly off to save troubled schools from the big bad ogre.'

'Ogre?' She cocked her head to one side and then the other, considering if this might be true, then thumped him on the shoulder. Clutching it, he gave an exaggerated shout of pain. Then he looked serious for a moment.

'Turns out the reason for the meeting last night was to grill me about my private life. Check I didn't have any misdemeanours that could embarrass the government. I said if only my life had been that eventful.'

'Well, well, Abby. Time to spill the beans,' said Norman.

'I'm sorry?' Her gut twisted. What did he know?

'You know – your misspent youth. The drug taking and debauchery. You're married to him; you have to be above reproach, too, you know.'

'Norman! Just ignore him.'

Abby forced a laugh, but her heart was still thumping. 'No really, Moira, it's fine. Yep, better keep quiet about the forgeries, too.'

James laughed, too, but then his brow furrowed. 'You know what the press are like, especially after what Patrick Cunningham got up to. They'll want to see who's taking over, what my home life is like. Obviously, we need publicity but we can't afford any more of the wrong sort. What I'm saying is, please be very, very careful what you say to people – you don't always know who you're talking to, or who's sitting at the next table, or how it will be interpreted. I've seen what press intrusion can do to people. I don't want it affecting the girls.'

There were murmurs of assent all round the table. Abby's stomach twisted again. Was it possible that digging into James's life could lead to a discovery about her past? Her chances of staying under the radar would plummet if the press were to be involved. James being in the public eye could change everything. Could anyone really use her past to destroy him? It seemed incredible, and yet…

She looked at him sitting back, glass raised to his lips. He had worked so hard, transforming three schools from Special Measures to Outstanding. And he cared, he really cared, about what was happening in education. The evening he told her he was going into politics, he'd been so passionate about wanting to improve people's lives.

If he had faults, they were minor ones like being too tidy, worrying about money, a fear of spiders, belief in a parallel universe, and an ability to ruin a good song by fussing over bad grammar. Nothing that could hold him back from the success he deserved. Her insides curdled at the thought of a reporter catching a scent.

'Don't worry, Squidge. You can rely on me to be discreet,' Trix was saying.

'Dear God, I might as well resign now.'

During the banter, he squeezed Abby's hand and she squeezed back, but she felt turned inside out. In all these years, it had never seemed like she was lying to him. Yet she had let him believe she was the person he thought she was. How could she ever have thought that was fair? One thing she was sure of – he would never have married her if he'd known everything about her. He'd said many times he had no secrets and had complete trust in her. And somehow, she had thought that was all right. What happened all those years ago at the villa had nothing to do with who she was now. Her happiness with James was more than she could have ever wished for and she couldn't risk losing it.

After lunch, when the rain had cleared the children put on a play, setting out the dining chairs in a row in front of the summerhouse. The plot was an evolving one incorporating witches and Cybermen and someone on a horse, but Lucy and Sophia's faces were aglow throughout.

Abby came to her senses as the performance ended, and joined in the clapping with enthusiasm.

'Feeling better?' James asked in her ear.

'Still got a bit of a headache.'

He nodded. 'We should go. The girls have got school tomorrow and Lucy has to practise her spellings.'

During the journey home, the girls sang *The Wheels on the Bus* around fifty times before they finally fell asleep. Casting a look at them through the rear view mirror – Sophia with her head thrown back and mouth open like a baby bird, Lucy lolling forward, clutching her favourite stuffed rabbit – Abby felt a desperate urge to protect them.

They had done nothing; they didn't deserve to have their lives ripped apart.

She cast a sideways look at James. She should tell him, of course she should, but after all this time what would she say?

This is going to come as a bit of a shock. I probably should have mentioned it before...

How would he take it? She couldn't help picturing his face full of dismay and revulsion.

I thought I knew you.

The risk was too great. The anger took her by surprise, creeping up through her limbs and ballooning in her chest. It was all right for Philippa. No-one could touch her where she was. Abby was the one who would have to face it all alone.

Why in God's name did we do it? Because if Philippa hadn't been so impetuous, so vengeful, and so manipulative, then Abby wouldn't be in this position now.

But then again, she told herself as they left the country lanes and joined the motorway, if she hadn't been so impressionable, so easily led, so blind and so stubborn, it would never have happened.

Chapter Four

'I don't understand the problem,' James was saying. 'It's just one morning out of your life.'

He was standing against the marble work surface, mug of coffee in his hand. She looked up from topping Sophia's egg, and pointed to the calendar with the spoon.

'A morning when I have to be in the surgery.'

It was the third date he had given her and it was getting harder to find excuses. She'd barely slept since Mother's Day. If only she could think straight. The first few nights, she had lain awake imagining sirens, the room flooded by blue lights. In the morning, she'd drawn back the curtains expecting to see a barrage of press or even a lone police car stationed, waiting. She had jumped at the sound of the doorbell and greeted neighbours warily, looking for signs of suspicion in their eyes.

It was the same the next day and the next. But by now the fear had settled below her ribs like a swallowed shard of glass. Every now and then it would snag, but usually it just ached like post-operative pain.

Mostly what she felt was relief. Because she hadn't told James. Hadn't put him through the pain and worry for no reason. The more days that passed, the more hopeful it seemed. But now this – the press wanting to do a piece on James's family life, wanting to come to the house and meet her.

It was the last thing she needed, a reporter sniffing around, delving into her past and coming up with awkward questions, but how could James be expected to understand when she was the one who had kept him ignorant?

'You must be able to rearrange,' he said. 'Can't you

swap with someone? It's supposed to be an article on my home life. It doesn't make sense if you're not with me.'

'It's a difficult time at the moment with Sally on maternity leave and Terence's wife being ill. Do I really have to be there?'

'Fine. It will have to be Sunday. Or do you have a problem with Sunday, too? There's nothing on the calendar.'

All she could do was mumble, 'I'm not sure. There might be something.'

He pushed his springy hair back. His usually smooth forehead was creased with lines of vexation. 'I really don't understand why you're being so unreasonable about this.'

She had to try another tack. 'I thought you were worried about press intrusion.'

He sighed patiently. 'Yes, of course I am, but that doesn't mean we avoid all publicity. It just has to be managed. This is a respectable Sunday magazine and I know the editor. I was at school with him.'

He checked his phone, frowned, and replied to a text. If only he'd let the matter drop but she knew he wouldn't.

Lowering his voice, he added, 'If you're not there, people will read something into it. They'll think we're estranged or something.'

'So, let them speculate. They should have better things to do with their time.'

The look of hurt in his eyes was unmistakable. 'Can't you see? We have to get the press on our side at the start. If I give them this interview now, they will leave us alone.'

The toast popped up. She buttered a piece and cut it into triangles for Lucy, who ate it slowly, following them with her eyes.

'Isn't that rather naïve? You can't court the press, everyone knows that.'

Several minutes of awkward silence followed, in which it was clear neither of them would back down.

'Right, well, thanks for your support.' He poured the rest of his coffee down the sink and slung the mug in the dishwasher. He glanced up at the clock as he began stuffing some papers into his briefcase, then stopped, pointing them at her.

'I don't think you understand that they want an article, so they will write one whether or not we co-operate. I would prefer to have some measure of control and take the opportunity to put forward my vision for education rather than have them slap down their own version based on hearsay. And the one thing you can be sure of is that you'll only make yourself more interesting if you refuse to talk to them. They'll wonder what you've got to hide. Any more of this and I'll begin to wonder myself.'

'Why are you arguing?' Lucy's face was confused and anxious, her grey eyes round and her cheeks pink.

'We're not arguing, darling, we're discussing something. And please eat your toast rather than play with it.'

Abby couldn't remember the last time they'd had a row. They were both more given to sulks than tantrums. James was the quiet one in his rowdy family.

'You're disgusting it very loudly,' said Sophia, bashing her egg with her spoon. The egg flew out of the eggcup, rolled across the table and smashed onto the floor, making a gooey mess on the rug. She watched it in silent horror and burst into angry tears. Lucy gasped and stifled a giggle.

Abby closed her eyes. She picked up what was left of the egg, tossed it in the food bin, and stuck another on to boil. This was madness. The last thing she wanted was to provoke people's curiosity – or make James suspicious, even if it was for the wrong reason. Who read these things, anyway? Most people would thumb past to get to something more interesting.

'All right,' she heard herself say. 'One picture. But the interview's about you, not us.'

He drew her towards him and kissed her, wrapping her in his arms. He smelt of the aftershave she had bought him for Christmas.

'I'm sorry I've hardly been around this week. So many meetings. It will get easier once I get into the swing of things. I'll make it up to you, I promise.'

She assured him it was fine, wishing everything was that simple. After he'd gone, she checked the paper but there was nothing that told her anything new. She keyed in the name of the village on Google Earth. There was still a small part of her that thought maybe she was mistaken. But with trembling fingers she found the arch at the end of the square, the fountain in the middle, Armando's bar, and the church with bullet holes in the door. She traced her steps up one of the little paths that radiated from the square, past the tiny church that housed the scary painting, to the villa. There was no mistake.

An Internet search produced a mention in an English ex-pat's blog and a couple of stories in the Italian and Swiss press. But perhaps that would be the end of it. No-one had even mentioned the story to her. And even if they had seen it, what possible connection could they make between the child she had been and her photograph now in a magazine?

Chapter Five

Holiday Villa was cursed

The owners of a beautiful Tuscan villa where two bodies were discovered at the weekend have been shocked to learn that the house is thought by locals to have a curse on it.

According to villagers, there has been a series of unexplained deaths at the property since a 19th century English poet swore revenge on future generations as he lay dying after a duel.

Romantic stories are circulating that the tragedy might have been a lovers' suicide pact or even a tragic accident. Police, however, are refusing to speculate.

The discovery has also been a financial setback for the owners of the villa. The couple from Bern, who had spent the best part of three years restoring the home, to which they hoped to retire one day, now want to sell it but fear buyers will have been put off by the enquiry.

'No-one told us about the curse,' says Maria Schwegler, a lecturer at Bern University of the Arts. 'The estate agent must have known about it. We thought we got the house at a good price, but if we had known we would never have bought it.'

The couple have had to cancel rental bookings until further notice while the investigation is carried out, and fear the publicity will have a long-term effect on future bookings.

'I wouldn't live there for anything,' said pensioner Livio Mansi, who lives in the village below the villa. 'There's something evil about that place.'

The identity of the bodies remains a mystery.

***

It was spitting with rain as Abby pulled in just round the corner from the school.

She undid the car seats and hauled out the book bags and lunch boxes, telling the girls to wait on the pavement while she locked the door.

There were the usual road rage incidents as they walked round the railings to the school gates – parents double parking and blocking the high street, opening car doors and tipping their children out into the traffic. A white van man getting worked up about the delay, as someone with very poor spatial awareness tried several times to back their Chelsea tractor into a tiny space, mounting the kerb in the process.

Sophia ran ahead, her sturdy little legs pounding the pavement. As she reached the playground, she was engulfed by a cluster of friends who dragged her off to play. Lucy stayed with Abby until the last minute. She had always been the shy one, the last to let go of her mother's hand. Almost as if she knew her mother might one day be taken away from her.

Abby felt something prickle up her skin and over her scalp as she turned and walked back across the playground and up the road towards the car. Someone was watching. It wasn't the first time she had felt it. Over the years, ever since she'd come back from Italy, she had had moments of panic when she had wondered if she was under observation. She was suspicious of people waiting in cars, anyone who came and sat next to her on a bus when other seats were available, every pair of eyes she caught looking up from a paper in a coffee shop.

But this was different, surely. She felt it as she unlocked the car and slid inside, checked the back seats, fumbled with the key and pulled out into the traffic. It could be a reporter. Someone checking how James Fenton's own children were brought up, what they thought of the school, his parenting skills, and the new legislation he was driving through.

Of course, it didn't have to be a professional. It could be any one of the two hundred plus parents and carers whose faces were perfectly innocent but who were hoping to make a few pounds from passing on a story or just create a stir by putting out some observations on social media.

But, most worryingly, she couldn't ignore the possibility it could be someone who had picked up a scent for a much more explosive story. Although, how could anyone have made the connection so quickly?

Her heart was in her mouth as she drove. The worst thing was the not knowing – who it was, what they wanted, whether it was just some sad stalker (she had treated a couple), or if the person was a threat to the children or to James.

She should tell James, tell the police. And yet, by telling them one thing so she would have to tell them others, setting in motion a whole chain of events, like pulling one brick out of the Jenga tower. And she would give anything to keep her past secret. Anything to keep her family together and keep them believing in her.

Even put them in danger?

She ignored the whisper in her head as she drove the two miles to the surgery, checking the mirror constantly for any suspicious vehicles. It probably made no difference, but she took a detour anyway through some back streets before pulling in to the surgery car park. She cast a look around her before going inside.

There was nothing suspicious. She had lost whoever it was. But she had to fight back the thought that this was only one morning. There would be others.

Chapter Six

The photographer arrived at nine on Saturday morning. James was dressed in a rugby shirt and jeans, although he hardly ever wore them, the girls in judiciously chosen bright t-shirts and leggings from a catalogue that was aspirational but not prohibitively priced. Sophia insisted on wearing a tiara and a tutu over her leggings. The house had been given an extra clean; each item considered for how it would be viewed in the picture, what it would say about the people who owned it.

The book shelves were weeded and rearranged, the fridge magnet letters that customarily spelled out rude or ridiculous greetings were removed, the wall planner with scribbled appointments giving away their whereabouts on certain days was taken down, but the children's artwork was left up.

Petra, James's PA, arrived white-faced, hair scraped into a knot and glasses skew-whiff, clutching a takeaway coffee and a couple of huge bouquets and garbling excuses about the traffic. By the looks of things, she'd had a late night, and she spent the first twenty minutes huddled in her coat, eyes barely open. But after her caffeine fix she went into action, arranging the flowers and rearranging magazines on the coffee table.

'Better hide this mug – and that one. We don't want anyone taking the wording literally.'

She eyed Abby's top and slim jeans. 'Good choice. Stylish but not ostentatious. Nice colour, too. Are you sure about the shoes, though? Try mine.'

They had one picture taken in the living room, Lucy on James's lap, Sophia on Abby's, with the bookshelves and rocking horse in the background. Sophia's curls, soft as feathers, tickled Abby's nose.

'Can't see you, Abby,' called the photographer a few times. 'Can you lift your head up a bit?'

Then some photos out in the garden – the four of them on the trampoline, and one outside the house with the girls on their bikes. The reporter turned up later and cooed over the pictures. She took herbal tea and refused a brownie. She pushed her glasses up onto her head while asking questions, which made her look cross-eyed and severe.

She'd done her research so she already knew James had grown up in Devon, that he and Abby met at St Andrews, where he had studied economics and Abby medicine. Apart from talking about James's vision for education, she asked questions like, 'So how much child care do you have?' which seemed to be another way of asking, 'how much time do you spend with your children?' and 'when do you get time for yourselves?' which could have been phrased, 'do you lead separate lives?'

But the mood was relaxed, James answered in his usual courteous and self-deprecating way, and there was a fair bit of laughter. Petra busied herself making coffee and keeping the children amused with jokes, but she intervened once or twice to remind James of names or dates, or to steer the conversation in a different direction.

The feature, when it appeared the following Sunday, came out surprisingly well. The main picture was the one taken in the living room with Abby's face partially obscured by Sophia's curls. In the trampoline shot, her own hair hid her face. There were a couple of other stock shots of James at the House of Commons and at a recent party conference, and one of his school cricket team with him as captain.

James's mother rang up to say how delightful the piece was, and one or two patients asked Abby if she had seen it. The feature focused on James as a family man and, that rarest of things, a principled politician who believed enough in the education system to send his own children to the local school. Abby as the independently-minded, well-grounded wife, a hardworking doctor and firm believer in the NHS. She felt guilty for having doubted the reporter's sincerity.

Running her fingers over the face of the thirty-something GP in the picture, she saw superimposed an image of a pale-faced girl with French plaits, large grey eyes, and a few fine freckles. She had been silly to worry. Who could possibly recognise her from these photographs, especially with her name being different these days? And even then, how many people would join the dots?

But Googling for further news, she found another story.

Villa bodies still not identified

Italian detectives investigating the discovery of two skeletons at a holiday villa in Tuscany are disappointed by the lack of information they have received from the public and are broadening the search.

'It's possible that the victims weren't locals or even Italian,' said Commissario Fabrizio Moretti at a press conference today. Police have been trawling the records of missing persons from the mid-1980s to mid-1990s, but have not yet found a link.

One of the reasons the victims aren't remembered might be that very few of the original residents have remained in the village. Like so many of the hill villages in the area, Santa Zita has become a ghost town, especially in winter.

Many of the residents who were living there twenty or thirty years ago have moved down to the town in search of work and more comfortable housing. The village's altitude and steep, rocky terrain makes it a hard place to earn a living.

The village's sad history – it suffered one of the worst reprisal massacres of the Second World War – has deterred people from moving in, according to an estate agent. Many houses have either been left empty, bought up by foreigners who are only there in the summer, or passed down to relations who use them as weekend homes.

'Maybe the victims were here on holiday or just passing through,' says Moretti. 'The property has had several owners since the war and had fallen into a state of

abandonment for many years before the current owners bought it. While we have traced the previous owners, it has been more difficult to identify the various tenants as records were sadly not filed with the Commune, as they should have been.'

'Mummy, what's that smell?' asked Sophia, bursting into the kitchen.

'What? Oh no.' Cursing under her breath, Abby tore open the oven and hauled out the blackened pasta bake, but it was beyond rescue. Fighting back tears, she scraped the pot uselessly. This couldn't go on. She had to pull herself together.

Chapter Seven

1991

Abby sat straight-backed in a window seat on a Boeing 747, declining food and drink with a shy smile, her stomach twisted into a tight, painful knot. She craned round to see how many seats she'd have to clamber over to reach the nearest exit.

The woman next to her had a kind face and Abby would like to have responded to her questions, but she had felt the silence descend as she climbed the steps onto the plane and she knew she wouldn't be able to speak. It encased her like a glass dome, muffling sounds and making everything seem just out of her reach. Only the noise in her head was clear.

Could it really be described as a noise? It was more an absence of sound, the rushing of a vacuum, like an open, waterless tap. Once it started, there was very little she could do about it. Even someone flicking their hand in front of her face could only bring her back momentarily. Afterwards they'd say, 'Where were you? What were you thinking?' but she never knew how to answer.

She tried to make herself concentrate on the safety announcement, fumbling under her seat for the lifejacket. Yes, there it was, but should she get it out and check it? It might have a tear in it or the whistle might be missing. She tugged, but a stewardess bustled up and told her to put it back.

A momentary vision struck her of the plane tipping and falling, everyone scattering, scrambling over each other and screaming. But as they burst up through the cloud, she blinked at the brightness and found herself marvelling at a snowy wonderland. The layer of clouds looked so safe, so solid, it was almost possible to believe it was land. She saw herself step out of the plane and run across the clouds, falling and rolling and laughing, making snow angels, cramming her face with candyfloss. Illogical, she knew, but it helped to force out other thoughts. Like whether this journey might all be part of a bigger plan, a trick to send her away for good.

She'd believed her father was joking the first time he'd mentioned her going to Italy, but he kept bringing it up in the weeks that followed until suddenly time had run out and she'd realised it was going to happen and there was nothing she could do to stop it.

'You'll love it. Beautiful scenery, incredible history, art, architecture… Amazing ice cream. Sounds like a fantastic set-up they've got – an old villa on a hilltop, with vines, olives, the lot.'

She shook her head.

'You remember Aunty Sue – she gave you Susie Rabbit. The girls are about your age – Philippa's a couple of years older, Mina's six months younger. You'll get on like a house on fire.'

He ran his hand through his hair, evidently deciding to try a different tactic. 'We can't go on like this. It's been hard for both of us this last year. Neither of us has coped very well. You know what the speech therapist said: if you go somewhere new where people speak a different language, you won't feel the same pressure on you and you should start to get your voice back.'

She looked down but she could feel her face burning.

'Look, Abby, you've got to start talking again some time. And don't tell me you can't because you're talking to me now. There's nothing wrong with your voice, it's all in your head. It's so bloody rude.'

The truth was, it frightened her, too, sometimes, the grip the silence had on her. At first, she had thought she had some control over it, but gradually it rippled out to affect all sorts of people, even those who least deserved it. Once she felt it wrapping around her head, felt herself sink into its depths, she knew there was no getting away.

'Are you even going to stop talking to me one day?' Her heart clenched at the tiny break in his voice. He removed his glasses to pinch the bridge of his nose. His eyes looked tired and taut as though they didn't fit properly.

'I do try,' she said at last, although her voice was little more than a whisper. 'Sometimes I can't. It's like a scarf round my neck.'

It was the wrong thing to say. He stood up and turned away, hands folded behind his head. 'Jesus Christ, not this again. There is no scarf, Abby. Just forget the bloody scarf.'

But she couldn't forget.

***

Sitting on the plane, she wished she hadn't mentioned the scarf, but it was too late now. That was the trouble. You couldn't unsay things in the way you could rub out a line of writing or a drawing.

She had vague memories of Aunt Sue, her father's sister – stick thin, dark hair, small face, big glasses. A memory swept in of being swung through the air, with one hand in Sue's, one in Mum's. She remembered Sue and Mum talking to each other for hours on the phone and her father, Sue's brother, getting agitated about the bill. Sue had come to stay once when she had needed a break from her husband and the children.

They weren't detailed memories; just two friends laughing and putting the world to rights. But something must have happened. Sue hadn't come to Mum's funeral or done anything to help Dad, her bereaved brother. In the last year, they had only received the odd, hastily written postcard from places she had already left.

When the invitation came for Abby to stay with them, it was her father's fiancée Mel who had said, 'Are you sure it's a good idea? I mean you know what she's like.'

There was a click and fizz as he snapped his lighter and

lit another cigarette. The irritation in his voice was clear. 'Yes, of course I know what she's like. But the alternative is for her to come with us on honeymoon, and you said—'

'I was *talking* about your sister.'

Admittedly, the idea of being with her father and Mel on honeymoon was not a pleasant one. Being on holiday together, let alone a honeymoon, would make it feel like they were a real family. It would bring back memories of the last holiday she'd spent with her parents, when everything was so normal you didn't stop to think about it. They had stayed somewhere by a lake with a lovely view, especially at night when the lights of the town opposite were reflected in the water, dancing like jewels.

A little white train had travelled between the villages, and there was a sunny promenade with brightly painted shops and restaurants where she remembered buying postcards and eating ice creams. On the day they left, her father had disappeared into one of those shops and bought them both presents: a cuddly dog with a barrel round his neck for her, and a silk scarf for her mother.

She remembered her mother shaking it out of the box, and the colours swimming in the light – beautiful, shimmering shades of blue, turquoise, and purple. The way she had stroked the fabric against her cheek, and Abby's father saying the blue was a perfect match for her eyes.

The thing was, though, Abby had seen him buying three items. But when she asked about the third, the thing in the little box, he had got very cross and said she'd been mistaken. No, she hadn't. She'd seen the lady wrap it up and hand it to him. The more she tried to jog his memory, the angrier he got.

And her mother had thrown down the scarf and left the room in tears.

***

Abby blinked furiously. Blood roared in her ears. The blurred text was making her book impossible to read. The story was a good one. Inside the front cover was a picture of Uncle Alan – or Hal Storm, as he called himself on the books. If she was totally honest, she was excited about getting to meet this famous writer at last.

Despite her anxiety, questions bubbled up through her. 'Did you get the idea from games you played as a boy? Did you invent the creatures, or do they come from old legends? Do you believe magic really exists?'

She saw herself having long conversations with him, and him saying, 'You know, there's a lot of Lila, the cave girl, in you.'

The agility, the determination, the resourcefulness – other people might not see it but he would. 'I didn't realise when I wrote about her that she really existed, but now I see it's you.'

She could tell him how she thought the next story should go. And he'd be grateful because he wouldn't have thought of bringing the chimera back in from the second book, or inventing a long-lost twin brother for the main character.

And she might decide not to go home at all, no matter how much her father pleaded. She might even feel she belonged there with this other family. Then he'd wish he'd never packed her off like that.

***

As she stepped off the plane, the heat flew at her, wrapping itself round her like a snake. Everything looked different, smelled different. She felt a buzz of excitement as she shuffled through the passport queue and collected her case, wheeling it along the grey and white marble floor, past posters of vineyards, castles, and regimented beaches.

At Arrivals, the air was filled with shouts and crashes. People jostled for space at the barrier, calling out to passengers behind her, lifting up small children. They jumped into each other's arms, kissed, laughed, argued over who would carry the bags. Dogs struggled in their owners' arms, desperate to get free.

He was standing at the barrier holding up a sign with her name on. She felt his deception like a physical blow. He was nothing like the picture in the book or even the one in her head. The man inside the books was youthful and exciting, the sort of person you'd expect to pen stories of heroic children battling terrifying creatures. Hal Storm, the name he wrote under, made him sound like one of his characters – young, cool, and fearless.

But he was old and crabby; forty at least, perhaps even fifty. Thinning, gingery hair, a beard, and enlarged pores that looked as though they'd been stamped out with a pen He hadn't seen her yet.

There was still time. She could take a step back, melt into the crowd, attach herself to another party and walk through unnoticed. But then what? She could tell people she was orphaned, brought up by a wolf in the forest, and they'd give her a nice home, a new family. It might work. But then again, it might not.

The travellers' cheques wouldn't last long and she wasn't even sure how to use them. She didn't think she'd be good at begging, and she didn't fancy sleeping rough. For a few moments she hovered, wondering which path to take. Then the decision was snatched out of her hands.

'Abby? Over here.'

And she was walking towards him. What else could she do? Perhaps one day she'd look back and wonder what her life would have been like if she had slipped away and never met him or his family. But for the moment, she stood in front of him, twisting her stubby plaits and feeling the familiar tightening in her throat, and all the questions that had been colliding around her head dissolved.

Chapter Eight

'I almost didn't recognise you. You're twice the size you were when I last saw you. Good job your dad sent a photograph.'

She folded her arms across her chest as he loomed in to kiss her. Felt herself jerk back as he ruffled her hair. He took her case, but she clung tightly to her backpack that contained her precious notebook.

'Good flight?' he asked as they weaved through the crowded space, which smelled of coffee and pastries and duty-free perfume. They stepped over dog leads and skirted around suitcases.

She nodded. As they passed through the automatic doors to the car park, the glare hit her again and she wished she had brought sunglasses.

'How's your dad?'

She shrugged and smiled.

'Plane full?'

She nodded. *Say something*, she urged herself. Those first few moments with someone were crucial – either she'd find her voice or she wouldn't. If she didn't speak to him immediately, she would never be able to.

'Meal okay?'

She nodded. But her throat was sealed. Nothing would get through.

'Well, this is going to be a bundle of laughs,' he muttered as he threw her case in the back of the car. He coloured as he caught her eye, evidently realising he had voiced his thoughts aloud. She looked away, a hot feeling of guilt spreading through her.

'It's not locked,' he said. As she reached for the door, he

added, 'Other side.'

He started the engine, and then came the inevitable throat clearing before he said, 'We were sorry to hear about your mum.'

If only she knew how to react to that statement. In all these months, she hadn't worked it out. Were you supposed to thank them for their words just as you would if they were congratulating you? Or to say it didn't matter? Give them permission to move on and forget? Nothing she could have said would have seemed right.

'You look like her, you know.'

She blushed and fidgeted under his gaze. With every question he asked, she slipped further into herself until it was impossible to imagine ever saying anything to him at all.

Eventually, he turned on the radio. She felt a sense of failure but also relief. Fields of sunflowers flashed past as they shot along wide roads. Excited voices babbled, hotly debating something. Yelps of laughter, an old man crooning, a heavy metal band blaring, more chatter.

They slalomed through an ancient town, snaked up and up through silvery trees, into dark tunnels, back out into blinding sun. Was that the sea down there? In and out of villages, past crumbling towers and villas behind giant sets of gates, castles on hills and orchards full of fruit, along a river, past a fairy tale bridge. It went on forever. He seemed to have no idea how close they were to the trees lining the road. She felt sick.

He was telling her how he had got the car – a story about how he'd met a monk who begged him to take it off his hands because it was a sin to love it so much – but she was too anxious to take in what he was saying.

After what seemed like hours, he pointed up to a village clinging to the rock high above them. 'That's where we're going, see? Right up there. You'll love the house – loads of history. It's even got a curse on it.'

He threw the car around a series of impossible bends. The wooded lane was barely wide enough for the car, let alone vehicles coming the other way. Once or twice he slewed to a halt on the edge of a precipice to let another car pass.

Eventually, they squeezed through a dark stone arch, emerging into a tiny square dominated by a fountain. Her head pounded from the sudden glare of sunlight. The buildings all around the square were shuttered against the heat. A group of old men sat under some trees playing cards. A dog raised its head and lowered it again. No other sign of life.

From out of nowhere, a girl with a cloud of flame-coloured hair threw herself onto the car, hands splayed on the bonnet. Was she trying to kill herself? Uncle Alan swore. The girl made a face, laughing, and guided them into a space with exaggerated sweeps of her arms.

She's Lila the cave girl, thought Abby.

'Remember Philippa?' asked her uncle.

'Come on, it isn't far,' the girl shouted over her shoulder as she scrambled back up the hill towards the house, leaving Alan hauling Abby's case out of the boot. She stood there for a few seconds, twisting her plaits, then broke away and ran after Philippa.

Chapter Nine

Tuscan villa bodies – not suicide

The suicide pact theory of the bodies at the Tuscan villa – which has been called the Romeo and Juliet mystery – was given short shrift by the Italian police at a press conference today. 'It's impossible, unless they arranged for someone to board up the cave from the outside,' said Commissario Fabrizio Moretti. 'In any case, we have evidence that the two met a violent end, which points to a third party being involved. And someone went to the trouble of removing anything that could identify them. Well, almost everything.'

He declined to elaborate at this stage, but there is a rumour that an item of jewellery has been found with the bodies, although it still has to be confirmed that it belonged to one of the victims.

Abby's fingers went involuntarily to her throat where the pendant used to hang.

***

Lucy cannoned into Abby in the playground, clutching a piece of paper that had been covered in so many layers of paint it had a hole in the middle.

'Let me see. Oh, this is fantastic.'

'It's the Great Fire of London.'

'Of course it is. And that's a rat. And you? No, Samuel Pepys. Yep, I can see that.'

Sophia had asked a friend round for tea, and the pair of them galloped ahead on invisible ponies. Lucy walked next to Abby, telling her about a story the teacher had read to the class about a king who lost all his clothes in a storm.

As they walked, Abby made herself focus on small details – a washed-out sign for the Year Four cake sale tied to the railings; a child's shoe on a shop windowsill; the brickwork on buildings; the echo of her own boots on the paving stones. Since reading about the discovery of the bodies, she had been on constant alert, which made her senses more acute. Everything around her seemed brighter, clearer, louder. It was disconcerting but also comforting, because it helped force the past back into the shadows, drowning out its whispers.

If she allowed herself to stop focusing on these things, the words of the article would creep back – along with questions, such as, would Armando still be alive? If so, he would remember how the family's post was sent to his bar, and how their phone calls were made from the little kiosk at the back.

The front door shushed as she pushed it through a pile of post. She gave the children some juice and a snack before they went out to play in the garden. It helped to concentrate on small tasks – cleaning the lunchboxes; checking the book bags for letters, party invitations, and forms to sign; putting PE kits in to wash; and laying out homework to go through with the girls later.

She stopped a few times as half-formed memories slid into her mind. Since Mother's Day, she had been bombarded by fragmented scenes that shifted constantly, always just out of her grasp. The moment she thought she understood something, a fresh doubt started to nag.

She had to get clear in her head what had happened and in what order, but the film in her head kept jamming. Scenes jumped about and images distorted. Perhaps she was giving too much significance to some things and not enough to others. Recalling things that had been said by one person and attributing them to another, attaching too much significance to minor events and conflating events that must have happened over the two summers, and merging them into a single occasion.

Gradually, longer episodes were starting to re-emerge, whole conversations and thought processes that were surprisingly detailed, but it was impossible to know which ones to trust.

While the kettle came to the boil, she shuffled through the post. There was some work-related correspondence and one or two bills, but the last envelope had a more personal appearance.

From outside, she could hear the creaks of the trampoline and the children's shouts and next door's baby crying. There was something unusual in the silence inside the house – an air of expectation that she couldn't quite ignore.

With a sense of foreboding, she opened the envelope, noting the pretty, marbled interior, which was strangely familiar. Inside, she found a photograph but no accompanying letter. As she turned it over, icy fingers walked up her spine. Her first instinct was to throw it down, but it was only a picture. It couldn't harm her.

She picked it up and stood taking it in. It was an old print, colour with a border, an unusual size. An innocent enough picture: three children dressed up in vintage clothes, having the time of their lives. The oldest of the three wore a beaded cocktail dress, headscarf, and a feather boa. She waved a cigarette holder in one hand, and she was leaning in towards the camera, gazing insouciantly, blowing an exaggerated kiss. The second, dark-haired, was swamped in a fur coat, and the third wore a wedding dress that was much too long for her.

Abby remembered discovering the carved wooden trunk in the chestnut drying tower, amongst a heap of junk. They had dragged it outside, bumping it over the uneven ground. The musty smell and cloud of dust that had made her choke and turn her head away when she first opened it. The clothes were moth-eaten and tide-marked with age, but they were pulling them out, delighting in their glamour.

'I'll be a film star. You can be the bride.'

'Look at this. What do you think it was for?

'I'll wear these jewels.'

She remembered the dress, the cool, smooth fabric against her skin, the little beads sewn into it. The tower stood behind them. The door was open – a dark hole, like a gaping mouth.

There must have been somebody else there with them, the person who had taken the photograph. Whoever it was had hung onto it for all these years. She tried to see through the window-sized hole that she had cut through her memories, but the field of vision wasn't wide enough and nothing came.

She waited for her heart to stop thumping. She mustn't cry, not now. This house was her sanctuary, part of her new life. She wouldn't have it sullied with the past. She threw the picture in the bin. The first time, she missed. *How?* It skimmed the side of the bin and floated down laughingly, landing face-up on the ground. Cursing, she picked it up and placed it inside.

It was just a piece of paper. It didn't have any power. There was no reason to be afraid of it and she certainly wasn't going to let it control her. She poked it down with a wooden spoon, driving it under the food wrappers.

Philippa's face was the last to disappear. It stared out at her with a cool defiance, as though challenging her to really go through with this. Because that was how things had always been, wasn't it? She rammed the lid shut, wrapped her arms around herself and tried to walk away, but it kept drawing her back. Not understanding why, she fished it back out, gave it a wipe with some kitchen roll, and put it in her bag where she could at least keep an eye on it.

Why send it now? The coincidence was too great. Her phone rang and she heard the odd, high note in her voice as she answered it. It was such a relief to hear James's familiar voice.

'Are you all right?'

'Yes, fine. Just leapt across the room to the phone.'

He laughed. 'I can picture the scene. Look, I'm sorry but I'm going to be late tonight. I've still got a couple of meetings to get through and we're trying to get this speech bashed out for tomorrow. Don't wait up; you get some sleep.'

It was hardly unexpected, but disappointing all the same. She so desperately wanted to be with him, to be in that world instead of the one she was slipping back into. She tried to forget about the photograph, but all evening as she moved about the kitchen, getting the children's tea and then her own supper, it nagged away. She watched a drama on television but afterwards couldn't remember a thing that had happened.

Towards midnight, she stepped into the shower and turned the water up until it was scorching. She waited for it to hurt, until she couldn't stand it any longer. Let the water smash onto her upturned face, erasing all those images in her head. Only then did she add some cold.

Because that photograph meant she had been right about being followed. Someone knew. And they wanted her to know they were watching and waiting.

***

English holidaymakers angry over death villa

The father whose children discovered two bodies in the grounds of a holiday home where they were staying, has hit out at the rental company. He says the villa should never have been let out in the state it was in, and is considering legal action.

The family, who had booked the house over the Easter period, had to be rehoused when it became the subject of a murder inquiry.

'When we got there, the infinity pool we were promised was nowhere near ready to use – it was just a filthy big hole filled up with rainwater and rubbish,' says software engineer Robert Hamilton, 38. 'The whole area was a potential death trap and should have been fenced off.'

The cave was covered in a thick curtain of vegetation and had been hidden by rocks before the builders cleared them away. Many buildings in this area are built against the rock, and the caves used for storage.

'It was boarded over but some of the planks had rotted, leaving a hole big enough for my daughter to climb through. She got in easily enough but couldn't get back out. You can imagine what it must have been like, trapped there in the dark. And then, of course, she saw what she saw. She was in a terrible state when we got to her.

'It scared the life out of me, to be honest. At first, I thought it was some sort of joke, then I thought we'd stumbled on a tomb. Gradually, as my eyes adjusted to the dark, I could see there were too many limbs for one body and there must be two of them. A couple lying there in each other's arms.

'I'll never get the picture out of my head. The bodies hadn't fully decomposed. One of the skulls seemed to be staring right at me. It was wedged up against the rock, which made it look as if the person had just raised its head to see who had disturbed them…'

Abby pressed her hands against the sides of her head. But thinking about it, something wasn't right. She read the piece again. The bodies couldn't have been found in the cave. That wasn't where it had happened. Unless she wasn't remembering it right. She knew there were gaps in her memory, but the cave?

Hope flickered through her. Perhaps, after all, these bodies belonged to an unrelated incident. Or perhaps it was just more complicated than she had thought.

***

'You shouldn't have stayed up,' James said, kissing her on the lips and then the nose, pulling her hips towards him. 'The debate went on for ever and the trains were all over the place.'

She had to tell him before he found out. Before someone told the press and the press told everyone. She hadn't wanted it to be like this, but she didn't have a choice any more about time and place. It wasn't as if those things would really make much difference in the end.

He slumped on a barstool, rubbing his eyes, and started telling her about his day.

'Can we talk?' she asked.

'Of course. What about?' He took a bottle of wine out of the cooler and retrieved two glasses from the overhead cupboard.

'Not for me, thanks.' She had to keep a clear head for this. She'd rehearsed it so many times it was almost as if she was hearing someone else say the words. 'I should have told you this ages ago.'

His smile wavered, and a hint of nervousness sparked in his brown eyes. 'Sounds ominous.'

There was no going back now.

'Look, the only reason I haven't is because—'

His phone bleeped. He turned it off and signalled that she had his full attention. She started again but a thump from upstairs was followed by a howl. Sophia must have fallen out of bed. Abby closed her eyes.

'She might get back into bed. She sometimes does it in her sleep.'

But by now Sophia was at the top of the stairs calling for her.

'Do you want me to go?' said James.

'No. Just don't go away.'

Sophia had lined up so many toys in her bed that falling out was inevitable. After much debate, it was agreed that the elephant could move out onto the chest of drawers for one night, with the squirrel to keep him company. But by now Sophia had that fixed, wide-awake stare, and suddenly remembered a host of important questions that couldn't wait until morning.

'How big is the world? Why can we see the moon in the day but we can't see the sun at night? Why don't fish have hair? What happens when you die? What if our day life is really a dream and our dreams are our real life?'

When Abby eventually got back downstairs, James was

51

on the phone to someone, sounding business-like. He gestured that he'd only be a few moments, but before he'd finished the call Lucy poked her head around the door saying Sophia had woken her up and she couldn't get back to sleep.

Unlike Sophia's abstract worries, Lucy's fears were ones Abby recognised and understood – logical fears that couldn't easily be dismissed. 'What if someone came in the window and took me away? What if you and Dad get divorced? What if I go to sleep and don't wake up?'

Abby should probably be firmer with her, but she could never forget the fear she had felt in the dark as a child. She sat on the bed stroking Lucy's head, waiting for her breathing to lengthen and that magical calm to settle, before creeping out.

'If you don't mind, I'm going to turn in, too,' said James, stifling a yawn. 'I've got to be up at stupid o'clock. What were you going to tell me?'

'Sorry?'

'Before Sophia woke up.'

'Oh no, it's nothing. It will keep.'

He looked surprised but also a bit relieved. 'All right, well, if it comes back let me know.'

She had the sense everything was sliding away from her. And yet it was still there. It would always be there.

Chapter Ten

More clues in Romeo and Juliet mystery
One of the people found dead at the cursed villa in Tuscany was a red-haired teenage girl, according to police. Despite having lain there for a number of years and what the police describe as 'catastrophic injuries', the skeletons are well preserved because of the sealed, dry conditions in which they have been lying.

Forensic analysis has shown that the bones are at least two decades old. The female victim is most likely to have been under eighteen, around 5ft 8in tall, and right-handed. Less is known about the other body, but the victim was an adult male over 6ft tall.

Abby's mouth went dry. How many other red-haired teenagers would there have been in the village at the time? All it would take was for one person to remember and start raising questions. There hadn't been anything in the British papers for several days and she had started to hope it might all go away, but with people booking their summer holidays, the macabre discovery at a Tuscan villa was sure to keep cropping up.

The words echoed in her ears as she pulled up at the canal-side pub. She had the sense again of being watched, but as she stepped out of the car there was no sign of anything suspicious. She checked her phone and made her way round the building to the garden that reached down to a canal, where willow trees dipped their branches and brightly painted boats were moored.

Dog walkers and people with children occupied a couple of the wooden tables. A small girl with bunches and chubby legs was sitting at the top of the slide and shouting at two boys to get out of the way, but they climbed up defiantly and slid back down on their knees.

The man she had come to meet was already there, sitting at the table nearest the lock. From a distance, Connal looked just the same as she remembered from their student days, but as she got closer she could see that his skin was a bit coarser, his waist thicker, his blond-brown hair shorter these days, standing up in tufts as the wind raked through it.

Was she doing the right thing? Perhaps not, but she had to take the chance.

His face creased into a grin as he saw her. 'Hello, stranger.' His voice, at least, was reassuringly the same. Fifteen years down south had done nothing to diminish his soft Scottish vowels. 'Is it too cold out here? We can sit inside if you prefer.'

No. Outside was better. Fewer people. This wasn't going to be an easy conversation. He went inside to get drinks. She sat watching the boats and going over in her head the things she wanted to say.

She thought about leaving. But then he was back, ducking his head to get through the doorway, murmuring his apologies, and squeezing through the group standing just outside the threshold.

'I took the liberty of ordering you the shepherd's pie,' he said, seating himself. 'The only alternative was the chilli and that looked dried up. So, to what do I owe the pleasure? And don't say you just thought it would be nice to catch up, because I can tell something's going on.'

Where to start? In the end, it was Connal who spoke. 'How's James? Is he enjoying being in government?'

She bit her lip. 'To tell the truth, I wish it wasn't happening. The press won't leave us alone. He's the golden boy – especially after that business with Patrick Cunningham. But it's like they're setting him up, waiting to trip him, watch him fall.'

Something flickered in his eyes. 'So, that's what this is about. You want to know if the press have been asking questions, trying to dig out some gossip. Well, if they come to me, I'll tell them he was my best friend. And the bastard who took my girlfriend when my back was turned.'

She started to speak but he held up his hand.

'I won't say a thing.'

They watched a family of ducks waddle along the towpath for a few moments, then he looked at her sharply. 'It's something else, isn't it?'

His body tensed as recognition dawned. 'It's the villa, isn't it? They've found her body.'

Even though she had thought she was prepared, hearing it was a shock. How on earth could he have guessed at it so easily?

'How did you know?'

He blew through his cheeks and gave a half laugh. 'Why else would you want to talk to me after all these years? I haven't told a soul. If someone's found out, it has nothing to do with me.'

She shook her head. 'No, of course not. I knew you wouldn't. Most people would have done. That's how I know I can trust you. Thank you.'

He looked at her quizzically. 'You didn't come all this way to thank me for that, did you?'

She twisted the glass in her hands. 'You see, you're the only person I've told.'

He raised his eyebrows. 'Are you sure about that? Well, I suppose I should be flattered, except you were shit-faced at the time. And you didn't have any recollection of telling me until I repeated it back to you the next day.'

The scene flashed back through her mind. The single bed they had shared in his student bedsit, the blind stuck halfway down the window, the floor littered with clothes, encrusted plates, empty bottles and overflowing ashtrays, the smell of red wine, last night's cigarettes, and a waste bin full of vomit.

Passing in and out of consciousness, moments of clarity in which she'd begged him not to tell, not to judge. Connal shaking her shoulders and saying, 'You're not making sense. That never happened, did it? For God's sake, what have you taken?'

'Yes, I'm sure. It's not a mistake I'd make twice.'

She'd cut down on the drinking in the years that followed, pretending it was a health thing. She needed one now, though. She gulped it gratefully, the acidity burning her throat.

He gave her that half smile she had once taken for granted.

'I told you I could deal with it. But you didn't give me the chance.'

'I'm sorry.'

He couldn't seem to help adding, 'I wish you'd never told me. It ruined everything for us.'

She looked down at the table. 'I know. I'm sorry. But I thought our relationship was strong enough. I thought after all that time—'

'No, you didn't. You didn't think anything. You weren't capable of thinking rationally.'

Neither were you. Come to think of it, not much of their relationship had been spent sober. Connal was a party animal. That's what had drawn her to him. He didn't think too hard, didn't analyse. Which was ironic now, considering what he did for a living. And even though she had known they were wrong for each other, it was never the way she'd have chosen to end things.

A waitress came out with their food. Abby didn't feel like eating anything.

'The funny thing is, I think you know more about it than I do,' she stumbled on. 'You see, I don't remember, not all of it.'

His grey-green eyes met hers then darted away. 'Perhaps it's best that you don't.'

'I used to think so, too. I thought I'd dealt with it, boxed it away. Buried it so deep I was almost able to fool myself it didn't happen. But I can't go on like this. I keep getting these images in my head and I don't know what's real and what isn't.'

'I expect they are real. Look, don't ask me for details if

that's what you're here for. I don't have them. You were too incoherent. We can at least be grateful for that.'

She shivered as a sharp wind cut through their hair and clothes. 'When I woke up again, you'd gone.'

He gave a short, dry laugh. 'It's not an easy thing, your girlfriend telling you she's a killer. Do you know what I wish? That I hadn't believed you. It would have been easier. I sometimes imagine what it would have been like if I'd pretended you hadn't said anything, just carried on as if you'd never told me. But I needed time to get my head around it. And when I looked round, I found you'd gone off with James instead.'

She looked down at the table. 'I didn't think you'd want me back.'

He dragged his fingers through his hair, groping for a lighter note. 'Yes, well, now you know.'

She caught the look of hurt and anger in his eyes. This made everything even more difficult, but she was here now; she had to ask. He sat back in his chair and lit up another cigarette, cupping his hand around it. He offered her one but she shook her head.

'I didn't think so. Very sensible. I'm sure you advise all your patients to quit.'

'I've seen what happens to the ones who don't.'

A woman appeared at the door and shouted to the children in the play area to come and eat.

'Why aren't you talking to James about this?'

She shuddered. 'I can't. Can't risk it.'

He turned his eyes back to her. 'He doesn't know? Jesus.'

'I told you I wouldn't make that mistake again. I lost you over it.'

Laughter erupted from a table inside. Young people from one of the offices on their lunch break. Unaware of how straightforward their lives were.

He met her gaze. 'But you're not prepared to lose him.'

She made one last attempt. 'I'm here because I want your help. I know you must have a waiting list. I don't mind paying more to get seen more quickly.'

The suggestion hung in the air. He took a long drag and blew smoke out of the side of his mouth. 'Let's get this right – you want hypnotherapy? From me? And you're trying to bribe me to bump you up the list?'

'I know people do it.'

'I don't. And I don't see patients I know; let alone ones I've slept with. It's against the code of practice, you should know that.'

He ground out the cigarette. 'What do you want me to say? You blamed me for knowing. As if I was contaminated or something. That wasn't fair. How did you expect me to react?'

How could she explain that he had never been the problem? It was her: her guilt; her inability to trust; her unwillingness to accept that she had ever been a different person. That they could never go back. Seeing his face every day tainted with that knowledge written across it, she would always be reminded. She wouldn't have known how to behave, what to say to him any more. She couldn't have let it go on.

At last she said, 'I thought when you looked back, you'd be relieved. At least I was honest with you, I gave you the chance to leave. Which you took.'

It was more, after all, than she'd given James.

His eyes didn't flicker. 'Thank you, but I'd prefer to have stayed.'

She closed her eyes, perhaps liked him a little less for his stubbornness although she knew how unfair that was. 'Don't you see that it could never be the same? How could you want to stay after what I told you? It's not a normal reaction. You don't go back from a revelation like that to discussing which band to see that weekend or who's been stealing food from the fridge.'

'Perhaps not, but I'd like to have been given the choice.'

And it all came out – the anger, the hurt, the years of self-doubt.

'I'm sorry,' she said at last. 'But I have to know. It will

kill me otherwise. I've started remembering things that don't add up. There are holes in my memory that make it impossible to piece together.'

He appeared to be concentrating on watching the boats in the lock. 'Like I said, you weren't making much sense at the time.'

'But it can't have happened the way I remembered it, that's what I'm trying to tell you. The bodies aren't in the right place.'

He looked around in alarm at the other tables.

'I suggest you keep your voice down.'

'Will you help me?'

He pushed his plate away.

'Hypnotherapy isn't some pier-end trick. I help people lose weight, stop smoking, recover from a trauma. What I don't do is fish out memories for them.'

'But you can.'

He threw his head back. 'You know that's not how memory works. It isn't like taking out a file from a cabinet and finding everything that ever happened to you stored in it. It's a reconstructive process. We change our memories as we go through different experiences. Every time we remember something, we're remembering the last time we remembered it, and we're taking new stuff and recreating what happened in our minds.'

'But it is possible to access hidden memories, isn't it? Ones that haven't been altered because they haven't been examined?'

He exhaled slowly. 'Potentially. But you have to be incredibly careful. The chances of implanting false memories are huge. That's why revelations under hypnosis aren't allowed as court evidence. That's what's given the profession a bad name. Too many crap films made by people talking out of their arses.'

In a softer tone he said, 'Have you really thought about what therapy would involve? And what you would do with that knowledge if you had it? People think they're going to feel better but, to be quite honest, they sometimes feel a lot worse before they feel better – and sometimes they don't even get through that stage.

'I've seen what can happen when things don't go according to plan or when people abandon it too early. Why put yourself through it? To punish yourself?'

She almost laughed. 'Don't you think I've done that enough already?'

'Why then?' He took a long breath. 'Look, I told you at the time and I know you didn't believe me, but whatever happened happened. You were a child, you did something stupid – the consequence of which was terrible. But it doesn't make you a terrible person. And I stand by what I said. You've moved on, built a good life. You save lives for a career, for God's sake. The balance is in your favour. It's in the past. Leave it there.'

'But the problem is…' For a moment, she couldn't speak. 'Someone else knows.'

He stopped, his glass halfway to his lips. He put it down. 'Why do you think that?'

She told him about the feeling of being watched. 'And then yesterday I got this.'

He looked at the picture and inhaled. 'That's you, the small one?'

She nodded.

'And this is whatshername – Philippa?'

'And Mina.'

He studied it for a long time. She couldn't tell what he was thinking. 'You're sure it was sent maliciously? Was there a note with it?'

She shook her head.

'What about the postmark?'

'London.'

'Which tells us nothing. Who took the picture?'

'I've been trying to remember. My uncle, I suppose. He took a lot of pictures.'

'Do you think he sent it?'

She bit her lip. 'I don't know. I don't think it's possible. The other body, you see.'

He couldn't disguise his shock. There was a silence as he let it sink in. At last he said, 'The other body is your uncle?'

She glanced up at him and then away, catching her hair as the wind blew it around her face. 'It's a fifty-fifty chance.'

'Jesus, there are more? How many?'

'One. Maybe two.' But it crashed in on her— the hopeless, helpless sense that she was to blame for something but she didn't know what. Because she didn't remember, not the thing itself. Only odd details, peripheral images, shapes in the mist.

'I get to a point, you see, and then it's all so confused. Whatever I'm remembering isn't right. And that means there's a chance it wasn't my fault after all. What do you think?'

'Honestly? I think you're clutching at straws. Look, I'm not a priest. I have a legal duty to report serious crimes. What you're asking isn't fair.'

It was hopeless. She wasn't going to get any help from him. She stood up, swallowing back tears.

'I know. I'm sorry. Thanks, anyway.'

Humiliated, defeated, she started back across the grass.

She was halfway across the car park when she heard him. 'Wait.'

He stood there with his hands planted in his coat. 'I can't promise I'll be able to help, but we can give it a go if you're sure that's what you want.'

Chapter Eleven

Villa bodies could be British

At least one of the victims whose bodies were found at an exclusive holiday villa in Tuscany may have been British, according to a police investigation. The theory is linked to a fragment of clothing found close to the bodies.

Police are asking for information about missing Britons who may have had connections with Le Rondini, or Villa Leonida as it was previously known, during the 1980s and 1990s.

'We will keep looking,' says Commissario Fabrizio Moretti. 'We are determined to bring the killer to justice.'

Abby climbed up the iron stairs of a brick-built industrial unit overlooking a river with ducks and boats. It was the first time she had seen Connal dressed in a suit. He obviously didn't want her to mistake this for a social occasion.

'Nice part of the world.'

He nodded. 'It's a wonder it's not better known. Part of me wants to rush out and tell everybody – but the other, selfish part wants to keep it quiet.'

He showed her into his consulting room, which overlooked the river on one side and the old high street with a market cross on the other. She sat on the Chesterfield, running her eyes over the books in the bookcase, the painting on the wall, a photograph on his desk of him with a girl skiing.

'So, what happens now?'

He cleared his throat. 'I usually spend the first session getting to know the client – take their medical history, have a chat about what they want to achieve, and whether that's feasible. I explain how the subconscious mind works and put their mind at rest over any misconceptions – most people have a few.'

He was standing, hands in pockets, leaning against the desk.

'I explain how I will put them under hypnosis and what it will feel like. And if they're happy to go ahead, then we set out our goals.'

She nodded. 'That all sounds fine.'

He hesitated. 'Except that I already know you. And I don't want to bore you with stuff you already know.'

'Please. Just do what you normally do.'

He cleared his throat. 'Right, well, the most important thing to understand is that it's impossible to hypnotise someone against their will. It's not about being put to sleep…'

He explained the process in some detail although it was a condensed version, she suspected, of the talk he normally delivered.

'A trance is an altered state of consciousness – you're awake but relaxed. A similar feeling to when you daydream or get lost in a book or a piece of music. And in that state, your concentration is heightened so you're more receptive and gain greater insight…'

He offered her a choice of coffee capsules, and put one into the machine.

'…What hypnosis isn't is a magic wand. It has nothing to do with reprogramming the mind. I couldn't – even if I wanted to – turn you into a different person. I can't tell you nothing happened back in Italy or tell you it doesn't matter.'

She felt herself colour. 'I realise that.'

He nodded, resuming his professional tone. 'The treatment's a mixture of discussion and hypnotherapy. Sessions last an hour and a half. For roughly half of that time, you'll be in a hypnotic state. The other portion is spent in therapy – discussing points that came up during hypnosis. You do the work, you make the decisions. I'm only there to prompt you.'

She nodded. 'Wait. What if I don't like it, can I ask you to stop?'

'Of course, at any time. You're in complete control. Most people find it pleasant and relaxing. In fact, they're often reluctant to come out of it.'

He stopped. Were they both thinking the same thing? Was he nervous, too, of what she would find? Was that why he was reluctant to get involved?

'Do you want to have a think about it and let me know if you're happy to go ahead?'

Of all the people in the world, it shouldn't be Connal she was asking. But there was no-one else, and she needed answers. She couldn't take the risk of telling somebody new who might not keep a secret as well as he could. She took a deep breath.

'No, I don't need to think. I want to do this. I have to get this nightmare out of me.'

Chapter Twelve

Abby had been determined to dislike Villa Leonida, and she wasn't disappointed. It hung above the village like a great grey vulture, spreading its scraggy wings. As they got closer, it didn't look as though it could be inhabited. Half of it wasn't even in use and no attempt had been made to restore it properly.

Large chunks of render had flaked off the face of the building and the doors of the ground floor rooms had rotted away at the bottom. Or been gnawed away by rats. The wrought iron balcony at the front had fallen away. The faded shutters hung off their hinges. Ugly black tear trails fell from the windows.

The air shimmered and danced in the heat, carrying with it the scent of geraniums, lavender, and parched earth. A peg doll with a crop of dark hair, a painted smile, and oversized clothes, came round the side of the house to greet her. Abby just about recognised her aunt. Behind her stood a smaller peg doll who watched Abby steadily. She must be Mina.

'Look at you, all grown up. And so like your mum,' said Sue, holding Abby by both hands and standing back to scrutinise her, those dark eyes flickering as if the sight of Abby was painful to her.

'We were so close. I can't tell you how much I miss her.'

And yet she hadn't been close enough apparently to have come and seen Mum when she was in hospital. Not enough to come to the funeral or to reply to any of Dad's letters, making him wonder if he had lost his sister as well as his wife.

'Come on, I'll give you the grand tour before lunch.'

She had a way of springing along as she walked, which

Mina copied so precisely it was hard to tell if she did so out of scorn or admiration.

The smell inside the house stuck in Abby's nostrils – a mixture of insect repellent and bleach and something old and fusty. It was the smell of decay, of the hundreds of people who must have died in this house over the years. She half expected to see Disneyesque phantoms, skeletons in period costume dining, playing the piano, or dancing through the rooms.

'Don't take your shoes off,' warned Mina, as she made to unlace her trainers. At home, Mel went mad if you attempted to cross a corner of the polished tiles in shoes, and gave you a lecture on bacteria.

'You don't know what you might step on – millipedes, scorpions, we've got the lot.' Mina seemed rather thrilled by the idea. It was hard to tell if she was joking, but seeing the others had their shoes on Abby wasn't going to take the chance. She followed them downstairs.

'*La cucina,*' announced Sue with a flourish, as she swept into the kitchen

The kitchen took up most of the lower floor. Abby had never seen a room so chaotic. Stacks of plates on the terracotta floor, laundry and paperwork piled up on the worktops. At home, the surfaces were always kept clear and Dad and Mel wouldn't dream of going to bed without emptying the dishwasher. Even during those days after her mother's death when Abby and her father had spent most of their time crying or in bed and living off takeaway pizza, the house hadn't looked this bad.

'This floor is where the animals used to be kept,' said Sue. 'Look, we've kept the feeding troughs and tethering rings on the walls.'

Various smaller rooms led off the kitchen, including a workshop and a utility room. The final door was shut.

'Don't go in there,' said Mina, following her gaze. 'It's Dad's study. He goes mad if he's disturbed.'

On the next floor were rooms of much grander proportions with gilded mouldings, but the walls had large sections of bloated plaster and paint flaked off the internal shutters.

The *salotto,* as Sue called the living room, had three tall, arched windows leading out onto a balcony. It was incongruously furnished with a modular Aztec-print sofa and an armchair with a loose khaki cover, that looked like a giant toad squatting in the corner. A grand piano was barely visible under the conglomeration of mugs and magazines.

Looking up at the ceiling, Abby caught her breath. Someone had painted hats and spectacles on the faded cherubs, and one of them had a hook driven into its heart to accommodate a swinging rattan chair.

'Your dad would hate it, wouldn't he?' Sue said with a clear note of pride in her voice. 'It's a bit of fun.'

Not wanting to appear humourless, Abby smiled. Yes, her father would have been appalled by the state the place had been allowed to get into. He was obsessive about maintaining original features and what he called a building's integrity. It was hard to imagine Sue being his sister. How could they have shared an upbringing and be so different? A part of her thrilled at the lack of restraint.

The room she was to share with Philippa could be reached only by an external, stone staircase. An electric fan ticked and whirred but the room still felt like an oven. A cloud of dust motes danced in the shaft of sunlight that crept between the half-open shutters.

'We'll leave you to settle in for a few minutes. Why don't you unpack your things and come and join us outside for lunch?' said Sue. 'We'll be under the pergola.'

Not having a clue what a pergola was, Abby unbuckled her suitcase that Alan had left on the bed, and stared at her belongings. A few minutes? It was going to take longer than that to settle into this place – if she ever did.

The room was sparsely furnished – monastic, Dad might have said – with two iron beds and an oppressively dark wooden wardrobe that reeked inside. She wasn't going to unpack her things into that so she shoved the case under the bed.

She lay on the bed and stared up at the gnarled beams, following a column of ants that crawled along one of them. She rolled over and rooted out her notebook from her backpack. The speech therapist had asked her to record her thoughts when she didn't feel able to talk.

Day One, she wrote in neat, round letters, going over them backwards and forwards while she collected her thoughts.

'I hate it,' she muttered with satisfaction.

Hearing movement, she looked up and saw Mina standing in the doorway, silhouetted against the bright sun.

'Good. We didn't want you here, anyway,' said Mina, backing out onto the loggia, banging the door and leaving the room in darkness again.

Abby's pen hovered over the notebook She didn't always write. There were some words she didn't even want to see, so she just scribbled furiously, letting the pen spiral round and round until it ripped a hole in the paper.

Moments passed without her noticing. Gradually, she became aware of an ache from having sat in the same position for too long. She stepped out onto the loggia, then drew back as low, urgent voices below drifted up with startling clarity.

'It was your brilliant idea.'

'He's my brother. What else was I supposed to do?'

'Perhaps you should have been honest with him in the first place.'

'Don't you feel at all responsible?'

'Oh no, the responsibility's all yours – you promised, remember? You're the one who said it wouldn't get complicated.'

She waited, heart thumping but didn't hear any more. Eventually, she heard her name being called and found them sitting under a ramshackle pile of sticks she supposed was the pergola.

She tried to make amends with her cousin, giving her an apologetic smile.

'Don't even try,' said Mina. 'What did you come here

for? Is it true your dad doesn't want you any more? Did he send you here to get rid of you?'

Everything felt as if it was sliding away. She was falling and had nothing to hold onto.

Chapter Thirteen

'It's the heat,' Alan was saying, giving her a glass of water. 'You were in full sun there. Feeling better?'

She nodded, looking up at the dense leaves above her head. Her head was still pulsing and her limbs felt heavy.

He laughed with relief. 'You gave us a bit of a scare.'

She felt Mina's bright, dark eyes on her during the meal as Alan attempted to make conversation by firing questions that had nothing to do with the conversation around them.

'How did the wedding go?'; 'What's your stepmum like?'; 'What does she do?'; 'Is your dad still an architect?'; 'What's he working on at the moment?'

Speak, Abby willed herself. *Just try.* She shrugged and smiled but no voice came. The sun dazzled off the table, making her eyes water. The plastic cloth was suckering onto her arms and she had to peel them off trying not to grimace from the pain.

'Will you shut up?' Alan asked after a while, in an attempt to jolly her out of her silence. 'You're giving me a headache.'

Abby acknowledged the remark with a smile although jibes of that sort were hardly original – she heard similar every day at school. Realising he hadn't found the magic formula, Alan seemed affronted. He poured himself a large glass of red wine, sat back, and drank it in one go, then poured another.

Mina watched Abby with fascination and eventually asked, 'Why don't you just say something? It's not that difficult, is it?'

Philippa rolled her eyes, shaking her fiery hair back behind her shoulders. 'Perhaps you should try it for a change. Nothing you say's worth listening to, anyway.'

Mina went red but Abby could feel her eyes boring into her even more. She drank some water, despite the fly floating in it.

Her father and Mel would be touching down in St Lucia now. The pictures in the brochure made it look like paradise, with a palm-fringed white sandy beach and a hotel with a swim-up bar. Mel had bought a whole new wardrobe of clothes for 'going away', even though she said she intended to spend most of the time in her bikini.

Alan jabbed at his food. 'What's this?'

The pasta had congealed into a solid mass, gluey in the centre, teeth-shatteringly crunchy on top. He stabbed a lump of it on his fork and brandished it around the table. Philippa stifled a laugh.

'I didn't know how long you'd be,' Sue replied in a voice that sounded too bright.

'The airport hasn't moved.'

He sighed and ate, chewing noisily as though he had to gear himself up to swallow. Abby passed the bowl to Sue but her aunt shook her head, saying she didn't eat cooked food, as if this was something she ought to have known, and piled her plate with lettuce and raw beans. She didn't seem to have noticed the small slug on the lettuce.

'Did you hear Signor Rossi died?' Philippa asked. 'Everyone was talking about it down in the square. Took the hairpin up at the ridge too fast and went right over the edge.'

Her parents looked at each other.

'Awful thing,' her father said. The third glass of wine seemed to have calmed him a little. 'I hear he was' – and he mouthed the word – '*decapitato*.'

Sue glared at him and busied herself with the pepper grinder.

Philippa lifted her eyes heavenward. 'You might as well say it in English; it's practically the same word. But did you hear what happened to his head? His body got stuck in the trees but the head rolled all the way down the terraces into the school playground where his son was playing. Some of the children thought it was a football.'

Her eyes were alight with excitement.

'Oh God, that's so awful,' said Mina, but she let out a little giggle.

There followed a series of jokes about the bank manager losing his head and being off his head, and some more about bizarre football tactics. Abby gripped her glass. Was death funny to some people? Was this how they had reacted to the news about her mother?

She tried to saw her pasta to give herself something to focus on, but a shard flew off and plopped into Mina's drink. She hoped to God she wouldn't notice, but a moment later Mina let out a shriek.

'What's this? You cow!' She launched the glass at Philippa, who retaliated by pouring her glass over Mina's plate. Abby sprang back, cheeks burning, as the sisters fought it out.

'All right, that's enough,' Alan shouted. 'I bet you're glad you're an only child, Abby. We should take a picture as it's your first day.'

She caught an odd flicker in Sue's expression. Through a tight smile, her aunt replied, 'What a good idea.'

It took a while to get the shot set up with the self-timer, Alan hopping backwards and forwards to check the composition. Philippa moved next to Abby. The sun was directly overhead now, needling its way in through the gaps in the pergola.

Sue came round to stand behind the three girls, spreading her arms across their shoulders and said, 'Say 'spaghetti'.'

Abby tried to imagine what the photo would look like. What would she think when she looked back on this excruciating day? What lies would the camera tell, and how would she choose to embellish them?

'One more in case someone had their eyes shut,' said Alan.

Everyone groaned but resumed their positions. A

scuffling in the vine leaves above them. Something dropped. Sue shrieked, and flicked the lizard off her shoulder, losing her balance and sending everyone sprawling, plates clattering onto the stone floor.

Alan stopped laughing. 'Did you do that on purpose?'

Sue said something rude and walked off into the house.

***

The lunch things sat out in the heat, food congealing on the broken plates and flies gathering. Abby picked up her plate as she had been taught to do at home and carried it into the house.

The interior was dark and the doors were all shut. She stood in confusion for a few moments, surrounded by closed doors. The last thing she wanted to do was go into the study by mistake.

At last, after a series of calculations, she twisted a handle.

'Out!'

She retreated, shutting the door with a slam, her heart thumping. She was about to go in the kitchen when she heard voices.

'How long's she going to be here?'

Sue said something inaudible and then, 'We'll just have to make the best of it.'

She slipped outside again and put the plates back on the table. Not sure what to do, she wandered about the garden trying to look purposeful. Once out of the shade of the fig trees, she felt the brutal intensity of the afternoon heat. Her skin prickled and her hair clung to her head. The crisp grass scratched her ankles as she walked, and her shorts felt pasted to her legs.

It wasn't quiet, despite being isolated, and the sounds were alien, like a soundtrack to a jungle film. There was a constant trilling and buzzing, things skittering just out of sight, leaves rustling, shadows darting and slow, intermittent, crackling steps. She tried to tempt an orange lizard onto her finger but it slipped away. She examined a series of holes in the bank of dry earth, poking them with a stick. It produced a shower of earth. Nothing else.

Something prickled the back of her neck. She had a sensation of being watched. She turned and looked back up at the house but the shutters were all closed. She walked on down the garden, picking up the pace to get out of view.

The terrace hung in mid-air. The dizzying height took her breath away. Below, so far below, the collage of old tiles, chimneypots, and little lanes flickered in the heat. Looking out over them, shielding her eyes from the savage brightness, she wondered how long it would take to walk down to the village. There was an occasional flash as the sun hit the roofs of cars climbing the wooded hill opposite. She felt like Rapunzel in her tower, able to see everything but not be part of it.

Something heavy slammed into her from behind and she cannoned forward. For a second she hovered over the sheer drop, drawing in her breath, arms flying up like useless wings.

'Saved your life,' said Philippa, catching her round the stomach and hauling her back. *Where had she come from?*

'What did you do that for?' Abby demanded, catching her breath and rubbing her elbow.

Philippa only laughed. 'So, you do speak. Well, you could scream here but no one would hear you. Listen.'

Abby covered her ears as Philippa howled like a wolf. Her voice bowled around the mountains in an impressive echo. She belted out a song with no embarrassment and little regard for tune.

'You have a go.'

Abby shook her head. To have found her voice with Philippa felt miraculous, but being able to shout or sing – that was another level entirely.

'Suit yourself. But seriously, you shouldn't stand so close to the edge – we get lots of landslips. This whole place will probably end up at the bottom of the hill one day. With any luck.'

74

Abby remembered something. 'Did you know your house has a curse on it?'

Philippa frowned. 'Who told you that?'

'Your dad said so. He told me in the car. What did he mean?'

'Well, he was lying,' Philippa said, hoisting herself into the hammock and swinging her long golden legs up in front of her. 'There's no curse. Nothing so exciting about this dump.'

Abby would have liked to talk more but Philippa had put her Walkman on and her eyes were closed as she moved her feet to the music. Abby watched her for a moment, trying to guess from the tinny sounds what music she was listening to. But Philippa opened one of her golden eyes enquiringly and she backed away.

She wandered over to the shade of the trees, trying to guess what the different fruits were. She picked an orange the size of a small egg, and sniffed it, wondering if it was safe to take a bite.

'What are you doing?' Mina's clear, authoritative voice made her jump. It reflected the expensive school she had gone to in England.

'Don't you usually ask before taking people's things?' Her fleshy lips turned down as she spoke, producing a few bubbles of saliva at the corners.

Abby dropped the fruit.

'You can have one of these,' she said more kindly. 'We're allowed to help ourselves to as many as we want.'

Abby looked at the hard brown object the girl had plucked from the little silvery tree. She took a tentative bite and immediately choked, her mouth filled with bitterness.

Mina laughed delightedly, producing more spittle. 'Don't you know anything? You can't just eat olives off the tree; they have to be soaked in brine for months.'

It was doubtful it would taste any better whatever you did to it. Abby shrugged, tossed it down into the grass, and wandered back into the house, which felt deliciously cool after being outdoors.

The lower portion of the slatted shutters were pushed out, casting prison bars on the whitewashed walls. It was hard to imagine this place ever feeling like home. But then, these days home didn't feel like home.

She climbed into the hanging chair and for a while enjoyed the gentle movement as it swung, trying to imagine the room as it must have been once when those leached colours were bright blue and gold, chandeliers hanging from the ceiling, silk curtains at the windows, the marble floor unstained and without the chips and dents.

The only thing of beauty was the grand piano, although its top was marked with dozens of rings and scratches where glasses must have been stood on it or been dragged across it. Abby hopped out of the swinging chair, lifted the lid, and tried out some notes on the yellowed keys. Mina's voice made her jump again.

'Don't touch it. It's very old and valuable. You don't know how to play. You'll put it out of tune.'

Abby lowered the lid as carefully as she could, but it was heavy and she dropped it with a thud. Ignoring her cousin's sharp intake of breath, she crossed the room and scanned the bookshelves. There were lots of classics her parents had at home, and several thrillers by the same author. Some books on education and psychology, and lots on art.

She could feel Mina's eyes on her but was determined not to show concern. On the cover of one of the art books was a young woman with long braided hair. She looks like Philippa, Abby thought, running her fingers over the picture. Mina shot across and stood in front of her with her hands out.

'Give it to me. Hasn't anyone ever told you, you have to ask before you take things?'

Abby turned away but her cousin followed. 'Why did your mum kill herself? Was it because she was sick of you?' Then she added in a sickly sweet tone, 'Oh, I forgot – you don't speak, do you?'

Abby turned, met her gaze for some moments, then shoved the book at Mina with such force she screamed, staggering backwards, doubling up. Abby turned to go, but Mina flew across the room and grabbed her.

'Put it back. Now.'

Abby struggled, but Mina held her. She sank her teeth into the older girl's wrist until she cried out. Her cheeks glowed as she walked away. She'd probably made things worse but she was glad she'd done it.

Chapter Fourteen

'Why do you think Mina reacted so badly to you being there?' Connal asked.

She heard Mina's voice like breaking glass. *'You're a leech. You suck the life out of everyone and give nothing in return.'*

'She saw me as an intruder, another person competing for her father's attention. All she wanted was for me to leave.'

'So, she seemed quite insecure?'

'At the time, I didn't see it, but looking back she always seemed to be struggling.'

'What for?'

'Affection, I suppose. From Alan, mainly. She didn't get much.'

She was seeing Mina's face. Not the bright-eyed, rosy-cheeked, laughing face she had seen most often while climbing the waterfall, catching the chickens, or sitting on the train on the way to the beach, but the pale, uncomprehending one she had seen staring so blankly the last time she had ever seen her, as they drove away from the house. Like the house itself, everything was shut down, gone. All she could ever see when she thought about her now was that coldness, weariness, and utter emptiness on that last night.

'Why does she frighten you?'

Her first instinct was to say she didn't, but when she thought about it that wasn't true. 'I'm afraid of what she recognised in me. And of becoming like her, of ending up where she is, going into that same downward spiral, being attacked by the same demons.'

'All right, I think we should stop there for today.'

***

From where Abby stood on the loggia that first evening, she could see the smudged outline of the hills receding into the darkness, leaving their crowns of lights hanging in the velvet sky. The air was full of bats and unfamiliar sounds.

It looked as though it wouldn't be too difficult to get down to the square below. Perhaps from there she could get a bus. She had looked up the word *aeroporto* in the phrasebook. Would she be able to change the ticket or would she have to buy another? Would the travellers' cheques cover the cost? She wasn't staying a moment longer in this dump.

The case was heavy and would make a noise being dragged down the steps. She could do without it. It was full of clothes Mel had picked out for her that she'd never have chosen. But she'd need the backpack, which contained her passport and notebook.

At the top of the steps, she paused. Of course, the house would be shut up. Dad and Mel wouldn't be back from honeymoon for another three weeks. She would have to break in, but what if someone heard and reported her to the police?

She heard a noise at the bottom of the stairs and retreated into the room. She jumped back as Philippa flung open the door.

'Let me do a personality quiz on you,' she said, throwing herself onto the bed. She thumbed through a magazine. 'Answer a, b, c or d…'

Abby answered a series of questions, trying to work out what the right answers were but it wasn't always obvious.

At the end, Philippa totted up the scores and announced, 'Friends like you come along all too rarely and should be cherished,' which made Abby feel warm.

'Is it always this hot?' she asked. Her t-shirt felt sticky, and her arms and legs had come up in lumps from mosquito bites. There was no breath of air even though it was well into the evening.

'It's Italy. In August.' It seemed to be all the explanation needed.

'Why do you pretend you can't talk?'

'I don't do it on purpose.'

Philippa grinned, clearly not convinced. 'No? It's driving Dad bonkers. How do you keep it up? Whenever I try, I always forget and get caught out by a question.'

It wasn't a reaction Abby had encountered before. Most people got impatient or angry when she was tongue-tied. They tried to trick her into talking by insulting her or bribing her with money they clearly didn't have. Once, at school, someone had wrenched her arm behind her back further and further to make her scream. Her vision had whited out and she'd seen stars and thought she could feel it being ripped out of its socket, but despite the pain she still hadn't been able to scream.

But Philippa seemed to view it as some kind of talent.

'What's your stepmum like?'

Abby was surprised to hear herself say. 'She's all right. She's just…'

It was hard to put into words.

'Just not your mum?'

She nodded. It sounded daft but Philippa didn't seem to think so.

That first day Abby had met Mel, her father had tried to make the meeting look like an accident. They had been walking over the bridge towards the castle and Mel just happened to be coming the other way towards them. They'd ended up walking together along the river, past the swans and the pleasure boats, and then had coffee in one of the little cafes along the river. It had been nice.

They'd run into her again a week later in town when Abby needed new shoes. Dad had mentioned the film they were going to see and Mel had said she loved that story, and they'd ended up inviting her along. She'd popped round the next day with one of Hal Storm's books for Abby – and Dad had asked her to stay and have a pizza with them. It was good to have a new friend.

But in the morning, Abby had found her sitting in the kitchen, her knees between Dad's, feeding him toast and wiping a smudge of butter off his nose. She'd felt stupid for not realising earlier.

Dad made a point of telling her that he had only got to know Mel in the past few weeks. She made him happy and that was a good thing, wasn't it? He hadn't thought he could ever feel happy again.

'I'm not going to try and replace your mum. No-one could ever do that, but I hope we can be friends,' Mel had said.

But later, when she bent over, Abby saw something glinting between her pillow-like breasts. It was the necklace Dad had bought back at the lake on that last holiday with Mum.

Even so, she'd tried to like her. Mel had offered to take her shopping and Abby had gone to find her and tell her she was ready. But, coming into the sitting room, she had stopped, realising Mel was on the phone to someone.

'I *know!* You know me, I've never wanted children. Well, yes, it was awful and I make allowances for that, of course I do. But she's so *difficult...*'

Abby shifted awkwardly. It was one of those situations where if you didn't make a noise soon, it would seem like you were hiding.

'Mouthy? No, mouthy I could deal with – you know I was hardly an angel when I was young. But she's *silent.* And between you and me, her dad isn't helping – he lets her wallow in it. She's made this little shrine by her bed with pictures and trinkets, bless…

'No, not just shy. I mean, she says nothing at all. Or not to me at any rate. But she watches, you know? She's got these big, grey eyes and they fix on you, follow you round the room. It's *spooky…*'

Abby retreated and slipped upstairs. On the way past her parents' room, she spotted the nail polish on the dressing table and emptied the pot inside the drawer that contained Mel's lacy undies, then lay on her bed, her heart thumping.

But she wasn't going to tell Philippa any of this.

Philippa was knocking on the side of her head and saying, 'Hello? Earth to Abby?'

'She made us get rid of our dog,' she said, brought back into the moment.

Philippa's eyes widened. 'Your dog? Why? That's cruel.'

She had come home from school and found Alfie gone.

'She's allergic to fur, or something.'

'So? The dog was there first. She's the one who should have gone.'

At last, someone who understood.

'We've got something in common then,' said Philippa. 'We both hate our parents.'

Abby wasn't sure it was the same but, having found an ally, she didn't want to argue.

'Do you miss England?' she asked Philippa.

Her cousin shrugged. 'Some things. Not school. Do you like school?'

Abby shook her head. She had once. Primary school had been fun – long sunny afternoons, lessons outside, doing handstands against the brick wall, playing bulldog in the playground, sprawling on the grassy bank and making daisy chains, and being a lamb in the school play.

But the new school was different. That summer after her mother's death was mostly lost in a blur – Dad's alcohol-soaked grief; finding him crashed out on the sofa in the mornings and still there in the evenings; sitting together in silence for hours, watching cartoons meant for tiny children; the two of them locked together in pain and regret.

He hadn't noticed that she missed most of that first term, and when she started the second term she was isolated and behind in everything. At least they had had each other.

But it was different for Dad now. He had Mel to help him feel better, and she had obviously done a better job of it than Abby because she heard him laughing usually in bed late at night. After Mum died, Dad had kept to his side of the bed as though he had no right to occupy Mum's space, but he didn't seem to mind Mel occupying it.

One of the girls at school said Alfie had been turned into horsemeat. The children in her class seemed darkly fascinated by her mother's death, in the way you enjoy a ghost story. They seemed to forget she had been a real person.

'What happened to your mum?' they'd ask. 'What did she look like when you saw her?' But they seemed to enjoy asking the questions more than hearing the answers, so she stopped answering. Everyone knew what had happened. She heard them whispering, passing notes. They found her silence disconcerting, thought she was weird, the girl who never talked. The bullying had started slowly – just a question here, an unfunny joke there. But, at some point, it had become physical.

'Were you bullied, too?' she asked Philippa. 'Is that why you didn't like school?'

But she realised as soon as the words were out that it was a stupid question. Philippa would never let herself be bullied. An odd look flashed over Philippa's face. She looked away.

'Worse.'

What could be worse? Abby felt diminished, as though her story wasn't good enough. Perhaps she hadn't said it right. She should have made it clear it was more than just name-calling, but to add more detail now would make it sound as if she was making it up. It was dark outside now, properly dark.

'I'm glad you've come,' said Philippa. Her eyes fell on Abby's suitcase and she frowned. 'Why haven't you unpacked?'

Abby shrugged and felt herself colour.

'You are staying, aren't you?'

A few hours before, it would have been an emphatic no. Now the idea didn't seem so unappealing after all. Yes, she would stay.

They talked for hours. Well, it was mostly Philippa who

talked, describing her family's travels through Europe, all the countries they'd been to over the past year, parking their camper van on the beach, the roadside, up in the mountains, in farmers' fields, moving on when they were spotted or people's patience ran out.

The scrapes they had got into – snatching scraps off café tables when they ran out of money, never paying for bus or tram tickets. Being held up at knifepoint in Amsterdam, kicked awake by the police after sleeping on the station steps in Venice.

'I liked Switzerland best but we didn't stay there long. Everything was so expensive.'

'How long will you stay here?'

'Dunno. We've been here six months. It's the longest we've stayed anywhere. It would be nice in some ways – to know whether it's worth making friends, joining a school, learning the language, but then it's also nice not to have to bother with that stuff.'

'Don't you worry about not having any qualifications?'

Philippa laughed. 'What's the point? You don't need qualifications to join the dole queue. Or do you believe in the *green shoots of recovery?*'

Abby had no idea what she was talking about but tried not to show it.

'Anyway, I've learnt a lot this past year that I'd never have learnt in school. I can drive the van, plumb in a sink, cook a risotto. Mina can touch-type – she types Dad's manuscripts for him. And we do have books. I can tell you all about Schrodinger's Cat…'

'Who?'

'…Black Holes, the Renaissance, the Vietnam War. I've read Shakespeare, Thomas Hardy, and *Wild Swans…* I learn what I want to, not what someone tells me I have to know.'

'Why did you leave England?'

Something flickered behind her cousin's eyes. 'Why not? There's nothing so great about it, is there? There aren't any jobs and the government doesn't care. They're just making it worse.'

Perhaps not, but there was something else, surely, something Philippa wasn't telling her. There must be a reason why they had left so suddenly without telling anyone. It had taken Abby's parents by surprise. One day they were there, the next they'd left and nobody had any idea where they'd gone. They must have been running away from something.

When at last they got into their beds, Philippa lay with her arm extended as though she was asking a question.

'Why do you do that?'

'Helps me get to sleep. Try it.'

Abby did, but all she felt was an ache down her arm as all the blood travelled south. What if the blood supply was cut off? The arm might die and have to be cut off.

The sheets were itchy. Something scurried overhead, little insects in the beams. A screech tore through the woods outside, some poor animal being ripped to shreds. Were there wolves in the forest? It seemed the kind of place where there would be.

Philippa didn't reply to the question. She was snoring gently. Her arm had dropped and now trailed over the bed. Her hair was spread out around her on the pillow, a brown leg folded around the sheet.

Little showers of dust fell onto Abby's bed, sent down by the industrious chomping of some invisible creature. A mosquito sang by her ear. She hid her head under the sheets but the heat made it impossible to stay there long. In any case, there were probably bugs in the bed, too. Her skin was on fire.

Gradually she became aware of another sound, the grating of stones under a shoe, a tread on the steps outside. Someone was coming up to the room.

The door was unlatched. She shut her eyes tight, listening to the quiet footsteps crossing the room. She could tell the person was standing over her bed looking at her. What did they want? Her heart hammered. Her eyelids flickered.

Whoever it was turned to go. Opening her eyes a crack,

she saw a figure slipping out through the door, but the darkness was so solid she couldn't make out who it was.

Chapter Fifteen

Abby looked up in confusion at the woman who had just entered her surgery. Clearly not Cyril Tomkins, aged eighty-six, suffering from Parkinson's. The woman looked around forty, although perhaps being a few stone overweight made her look older than she was. She had a thicket of dark hair streaked grey.

'Sorry, I think you have the wrong room. This is room nine. I'm Doctor Fenton.'

Ignoring her, the woman said, 'I need something for my memory.'

After double-checking the screen, Abby gave a reassuring smile and said, 'I'm sure we can help but you need to make an appointment first. Are you registered with us? If you talk to the ladies on reception downstairs—'

'I don't need help to remember. I need it to forget. I want whatever you're on. It must be highly effective.'

Something in the woman's cut-glass voice stirred a vision. Something cold crept over Abby. She saw herself back at the villa in Italy. Her heart slammed against her chest. The face was larger, the chin slacker, the forehead etched with worry lines, but those watchful dark eyes were disturbingly familiar.

'Mina,' she said, although she hardly heard herself. 'When did they – I mean when were you discharged?'

'Three months ago.'

This wasn't happening. Couldn't be happening. Those boxes were opening again, getting confused. Two worlds colliding.

'No-one told me.'

'I don't suppose they had to.'

Of course, the photograph. She should have known.

'I'm assuming you aren't here for a consultation?'

Mina clearly didn't think the question worth responding to.

'We can't talk here,' Abby said, trying to gain control of the situation. 'I have a lunch hour between one and two, although…'

'I'm here now.'

Hoping the tremor in her voice wasn't audible, Abby called reception and asked them to hold Mr Tomkins' appointment for a few minutes. She followed Mina's gaze around the room. Saw it fall on the newly-decorated walls, her jacket on the back of her chair, her bag on the floor, her car parked just below the window.

'You've done all right for yourself.'

'It probably looks like that.'

'You own this place?'

'Only a share. The mortgage comes out of my salary.'

'And James has hit the big time. He's everyone's darling at the moment, isn't he?'

Hearing her husband's name being bandied about by Mina made her stomach tighten. So, that was how she had found her. She had been right to worry about the article.

'That's not how he sees it.'

Mina raised her eyebrows. 'Education Secretary not good enough for him? Wants to be Prime Minister, does he?'

'He's very happy to have got where he is. But it's a lot of work. Lot of pressure…'

'Nice big house. Two little girls…'

Abby's fists curled as she followed Mina's eyes to the framed picture on her desk of Lucy and Sophia, gap-toothed grins, red school jumpers. She turned it face-down. 'If you touch my children,' she whispered, although she hardly recognised her own voice, 'if you speak to them, go anywhere near them…'

She thought of them as they had been that morning as she had strapped Sophia into her car seat, made sure they had their lunchboxes, promised Lucy she could have a friend round to tea after school. She wanted so much to be holding them close.

'You'll what?' A glint of triumph in Mina's eyes. 'Respectable job, good money…'

'I only work three days a week. That is, I only get paid for three…'

A sharp laugh. 'Poor you. Whereas, I've never been able to hold down a job. In and out of secure hospitals since my teens. Tormented by demons. But they've left you alone, haven't they? That's hardly fair.'

Abby shrugged but it felt more like a twitch. 'We've obviously dealt with it in different ways.'

'Have we? I don't think you've dealt with it at all. I think you've put it away in a little box in your head and thought you'd never have to look inside.' She dug in her bag and produced a newspaper cutting. 'But now you do.'

The new-look villa stared out at her with a cool insouciance. It was from a different paper – the picture taken from a different angle, showing the loggia at the side. An inset image showed a hole in the ground that looked as though a giant's tooth had been ripped out, and there was an arrow pointing to where the tower used to be and where the bodies had been found.

Abby looked away. 'I've seen it.' She pressed her fist into her brow. 'Look, Mina, it was a terrible thing—'

'It was your fault.'

No, not all of it. She wasn't having that. She might not remember all the details but she knew that much. 'You were as much to blame as I was. I didn't mean for it to happen.'

Mina gave a short laugh. 'Oh no, we both know what you *meant* to do.'

Abby swallowed back bile. She was getting images she didn't want to see. Her fingers digging into her forehead felt clammy but the pain came from concentration, trying to stop the pictures crowding in on her. Mina standing in the chestnut tower wearing a red t-shirt, screaming.

No, it wasn't a red t-shirt.

She was standing there, screaming. Covered in blood.

'Do you ever even think about it?' Mina asked.

Taking a gulp of water from the bottle on her desk, Abby said, 'I dream about it. That last day. You know if I could go back, I'd do everything differently. But I was a child…'

Mina's voice was quiet. 'Last time I looked, thirteen was above the age of legal responsibility.'

In the corridor outside, someone was being helped down the stairs. They could hear the patient thanking the doctor. Abby tried to keep her voice steady.

'Okay, look. If you want me to apologise, then of course I do. I am so sorry—'

Mina looked disgusted. 'Sorry? *Sorry* is something you say when you step on someone's foot, or you've forgotten someone's birthday, or turned up late for dinner.'

'Please. You've no idea how much I hate myself for what happened.'

Mina shrugged irritably. 'You don't hate yourself. Not enough. All these years, you knew where I was. You could have come and seen me.'

Abby looked down at her spread hands, trying to control the trembling. 'We agreed not to see each other.'

She could hear Mina's thirteen-year-old voice in her head.. 'Don't tell. Don't ever tell.'

Of course, she felt bad about the way Mina's life had turned out. She had taken an interest from afar, checking with the hospital on her progress from time to time. Should she have done more?

'You could have written.'

She nodded. 'I could, yes, of course I could. But whatever I said would have sounded inadequate.'

'You still should have said it.'

She could have pointed out that Mina's spells in the secure hospital were nothing to do with what happened at the villa – or not officially at any rate – but there was no sense agitating her further. If she could only reason with her instead.

'All right, go to the police if that's what you want. But it will be a huge waste of time and money, we'll both suffer and you won't achieve anything. It was so long ago and you can't prove anything. I'm not being unkind here, Mina, but with your mental health record…'

Mina smiled. 'Perhaps they can't prove it. But does that really matter? Not to me. I've nothing to lose. And people tend to believe there's no smoke without fire, don't they?'

She was on her feet again, picking objects up and studying them.

'Please don't touch those. They have to be sterile.'

Abby's breathing felt sharp. She needed the loo.

'What would your patients think if they knew? Would they trust you again? Would they want you handling their children?'

Tears stabbed her eyes. 'They wouldn't believe you.'

From somewhere in the building, a telephone was ringing. In the car park, someone was having trouble backing into a space.

'Perhaps. Perhaps not. The question is, can you afford to risk it? And then there's James.'

Lying there that morning, curled up next to him, she had felt so warm and safe. He was the thing she felt surest of in the world. And yet, she hadn't been honest with him. She wasn't the person he thought she was.

'He knows.' She'd try and brazen it out. 'I told him everything before we married. We don't have secrets from each other.'

She felt Mina's bright eyes studying her face and hoped to God she wasn't giving herself away.

'So, he married you knowing what you had done? Rather calls his judgment into question. What about his constituents? Would they be so understanding? And your children – what would they think of you?'

She saw their faces screwed up in confusion. *'But why, Mummy?'*

She tried to control the shake in her voice as she said, 'Do what you like. Now please leave or I will have to call security.'

A burst of bright, brittle laughter. 'Security? You mean the little old lady on reception?'

The internal phone interrupted them. 'Are you able to see Mr Tomkins yet?' asked Doreen from downstairs.

Abby held her breath.

'Once I leave here, it will be too late,' Mina warned.

'I'm sorry. Could you cancel the next few appointments?'

Her head was throbbing as she replaced the receiver. 'What is it you want? If it's money…'

Mina gave a disgusted snort. 'I don't want your money.'

'What then?'

'You're advertising for a receptionist. I assume the old dear's about to retire.'

'You want a job? Here? Are you mad?' She closed her eyes and mumbled, 'Sorry. I didn't mean it like that. But you can see—'

'I want a life. I want to stop living off the scraps people throw me to keep me in my place. But I have to start somewhere, don't I? Have you any idea how difficult it is to get a job with any sort of mental history? I only need to work here long enough to have something to put on my CV. Then, with a brilliant reference from you, I can move on. I'll be out of your hair. You owe me that much. Hardly unreasonable under the circumstances, is it?'

Abby shook her head. 'It isn't as easy as that. This is a partnership. I couldn't employ you without the agreement of the other doctors. And we have very strict criteria that includes previous experience in a surgery.'

'You could persuade them.'

'No I couldn't. I'm sorry. I haven't been here long myself. And threatening me really isn't going to benefit you.'

A silence hung in the air. Eventually Mina shrugged. 'All right then, I'll take the money.'

For a moment, Abby actually felt relieved.

'How much?'

The sum mentioned was one that in other circumstances

would have made Abby laugh.

'Out of the question. I could never get my hands on it.'

Mina shrugged. 'Doesn't have to be all at once. I'd accept monthly instalments. I need enough to get me a new start. I've been thinking I'd like to live by the sea somewhere, open a teashop.'

Abby felt her face tighten. All those years of studying she'd gone through to get where she was, and Mina expected an enviable lifestyle handed to her on a plate?

'And then what? I'm not stupid. You'd want a bit more. And then a bit more. That's how blackmail works, isn't it?'

Her cousin looked offended. 'Perhaps, but this isn't blackmail, it's compensation. You'd never hear from me again. I'm willing to sign a piece of paper, if you want.'

Abby almost laughed. 'Yes, that would be very helpful in court.'

'Then you'll just have to trust me.'

The last person in the world she would trust.

'I can't do it, I'm sorry. It's impossible.'

Mina helped herself to a piece of paper out of the printer and wrote down a mobile number. 'Think about it. You have twenty-four hours before I start talking.'

Abby got out of her chair. 'Wait. Look, even if I could somehow get hold of the money, I couldn't get it to you by tomorrow. I'd have to arrange a loan. Don't you know how these things work?'

Her cousin adopted a reasonable tone. 'Shall we say the end of the week?'

'For God's sake – please. This isn't fair.'

Mina turned to face her. 'Life isn't fair. Get used to it. I have.'

And she was gone, clattering down the stairs. Abby waited for the sound of her opening the door at the bottom, and watched her cross the car park and disappear into the high street. Tears choked her and she sank back into her chair and slumped over the desk. As far as she knew, Mina couldn't prove anything. But that wouldn't stop her from destroying Abby's life.

Chapter Sixteen

'What are you reading?' Philippa lifted the cover of Abby's book and rolled her eyes. 'Boring. You'll turn into a vampire if you sit inside in the dark all day.'

She snatched the book out of Abby's hands and flung it aside.

'Let's go. The market's on today.'

Under normal circumstances Abby would have objected, but it was always more fun when Philippa was around. She would appear out of nowhere with her infectious smile and make the most mundane suggestion seem irresistible – always the 'best idea ever'.

It had taken everyone by surprise, the way Abby and Philippa had fallen into conversation that first evening. Abby didn't really understand it herself, but gradually over those first few days Philippa had admitted her into her world. Now they sat for hours, heads pressed together listening to each other's tapes on the Walkman, practised dance routines, did dares, read each other's palms, and made horror films with Alan's camcorder.

The little piazza was alive with chatter and laughter. The awnings provided welcome shade and the air carried smells of newly-baked bread, roasting chicken, and confectionery. Philippa grabbed Abby's hand and they squeezed through the bustling stalls, dodging old women with trolley bags, young mothers with prams, and old men who stood with hands in pockets surveying everything.

Philippa charmed her way into getting free samples, and they stuffed themselves with prosciutto, cheese, and honey. She grabbed a floppy orange straw hat and balanced it on her curls, turning her head this way and that, making faces.

'Hmm, probably not my colour. You try it.'

It was too big for Abby, falling down over her eyes, making Philippa fall about laughing. They tried other hats in different colours, dresses, jackets, and every style of shoe, staggering around in stilettos, strappy sandals, and gold trainers, to the amusement of onlookers. The woman on the jewellery stall shooed them away when she could see they weren't going to buy anything. A baby lay in its pram kicking its legs. Philippa tickled its feet but it started to cry, bringing the woman from the jewellery stall bustling over to scold them.

Philippa smiled sweetly while saying apologetically in English, 'You really are the most enormous twat', eliciting a good-natured smile from the woman.

They pushed on to other stalls. Although she spoke Italian effortlessly, she sometimes pretended she didn't and translated to Abby what people around them were saying.

'He says your eyes are the same colour as a blind dog's he had once. And he says I have great tits but my thighs are too chubby for shorts.'

She taught Abby an array of swearwords and body parts, but her favourite game seemed to be setting up Mina to go and ask for something and then revealing delightedly afterwards the true meaning of the words she had used.

'Oops, did I say fig was *fica*? I'm sure I said *fico*. You've just called her a cunt.'

This was what Abby would remember about being with Philippa – laughing until it hurt. When Philippa laughed, she couldn't stop. You could almost see it rising up through her and spilling out of control. Her nose crinkled, her eyes streamed, and she'd keep wiping away tears and pushing her wet hair off her face.

She'd go red, wave her hand in front of her face. She could hardly breathe, hardly stand. Sometimes she'd just sink to the ground helpless, fighting for breath. Yet there was always that flicker of alarm that made you wonder how it would end.

As the awnings came down and the vans were packed up

to go, the heat splintered through again. It seemed to have been lying in wait. The girls sat on the wall of the fountain, dangling their legs in the water. Mina came up to join them but Philippa waved her away.

Seeing the look on Mina's face, Abby felt uncomfortable. Mina turned to go but said over her shoulder, 'Don't get too used to it. She only likes you because you're weird; you're a novelty. She'll get bored of you just like she gets bored of everyone.'

'Ignore her,' said Philippa, offering her face up to the sun. 'Did I tell you about my aunt and her pet snake?

'His name was Toby. She treated him like a cat or a dog. He'd curl up on the sofa with her when she watched television. But one day, she noticed he'd gone off his food.

'After a few days, she rang the vet. He told her he was probably finding food that had been left out or perhaps treating himself to the neighbours' pets, so she promised to keep a really close eye on him.

'But it got worse. Weeks passed without him eating. He came and cuddled up to her at night, pressing himself against her as though he was trying to tell her he was in pain.

'She rang the vet. He said, "Get out. Now." Because he realised the snake was sizing her up and fasting so he could eat her. That's what they do in the wild, you see – starve themselves to make room for their prey.

'The vet jumped in his car and raced over but all he found was a very large snake. He'd had his feast.'

That's such a lie, thought Abby. It was obvious by now that Philippa had a vivid imagination. She lied about most things or, at the very least, embellished the truth. You could never be sure how much of what she said was true, but somehow it didn't matter as much as it should.

Sometimes the stories Philippa told her were ones she had told Philippa in the first place, but they were always much more outrageous, gruesome or hilarious in the retelling, so she didn't point this out.

'I'm going to die of thirst,' Philippa announced, jumping

up and leading the way to the bar in the corner of the square. They pushed their way through a wall of smoke. People stared but parted like the red sea to let the girls through.

Above the hubbub of voices, a television blared out music videos. Glasses chinked, chairs scraped, and slot machines whizzed and clattered. Outside, a car engine was revving, the driver shouting for an espresso.

The girls chose ice creams and wandered out to the yard at the back where a group of boys playing table football roared words of encouragement or howled in despair. Philippa elbowed her way in and scored a goal with a whoop of triumph. She beckoned to Abby, and one of the boys stood back to let her in. Looking at Philippa's hand as she manoeuvred her players, Abby noticed something glinting. It was the ring Philippa had tried on earlier on one of the stalls.

'Did you pay for that?' she asked.

'Course.'

Perhaps she had and Abby just hadn't noticed. In any case, there was no time to think about it then. They stayed in the bar all afternoon, playing the machines and accepting free drinks and snacks. Abby would have preferred to have Philippa to herself, but she was beginning to understand that she was one of those people who gathered a crowd around her wherever she went. Whatever she did, others wanted to join in.

Everything came alive in her company. They all wanted to be part of the magic. Even without knowing what she was saying, it was fascinating to watch her as she talked, the way her eyes danced, and her hands made pictures in the air. The way she bent people to her, caught their attention, held them under her spell.

Philippa was never stuck for words, always had an answer, and could win any argument. Surely if Abby kept watching, there was a chance, wasn't there, that some of this fluency would rub off on her? She was used to being an outsider looking in, but with Philippa she was at the centre of everything.

Late in the afternoon, looking up through the veil of smoke, she spotted her aunt standing at the bar. She had probably come to use the telephone as there wasn't one at the house, but now she was standing at the bar, having drinks bought for her. Sue was eyeing up the plumber, complimenting him on his muscles and letting him feel hers. What was it about her that attracted so many men? There must be something in her elfin features and round dark eyes they found irresistible, and she couldn't seem to help flirting with them.

Turning her head, Abby caught Philippa's thunderous expression.

'Let's get out of here.'

She pushed her way out through the crowd. Abby could barely keep up with Philippa striding across the square.

'Did you see her?' Philippa was saying. 'Doesn't she realise what she looks like?'

Not sure what to say, Abby said nothing. The steep cobbled roads took much longer to climb in full sun. It was a relief when they found themselves back in the shadows.

Seeing Philippa was still angry, she said, 'She was just mucking about.'

Abby wasn't prepared for her cousin's reaction. 'You don't know her. You have no idea what she's capable of.'

Chapter Seventeen

It was one of those long, languid afternoons that became impossible to tell apart. They were lying end-to-end in the hammock, which creaked as it swayed. The sun dappled the leaves above them and the village shimmered in a liquid gold haze below.

'What are you doing here?' Abby asked.

A slow smile spread across Philippa's face. 'Well, let's see. Right now, I'm having dirty thoughts about that man who works in Armando's bar.'

'No, I mean why did you come here? Why did you leave England?'

'I killed someone,' Philippa said as casually as if she had just broken a glass.

For a moment, Abby thought she hadn't heard.

'It was an accident. We wanted to become blood sisters. She couldn't cut her own wrist so I said I'd do it for her. But she freaked at the last minute and her arm twitched and the knife slipped…'

She stretched and rearranged the silk cushions behind her head. Her eyes were the colour of a glacial green marble Abby once had, but with the sun glinting on them she noticed gold flecks in them, too.

'They rang for an ambulance. Her face was all white by then. She never came round.'

Was she lying? Abby couldn't tell. She'd asked a few times now and received a different answer each time. Once Philippa had said they'd left because they were being hunted down by a gang she had testified against in court. Another time she said it was because her father had committed a crime and was on the run. Perhaps she had even convinced herself with her lies.

'You don't know, do you?' Abby said at last.

Philippa shifted. Her look was cold and probing. 'Do you?'

She shrugged, but she knew she'd hit a nerve. She went back to writing in her notebook, but she was surer than ever that Philippa was hiding something.

Chapter Eighteen

Days passed in which nothing happened, or nothing significant enough to record in her notebook. When the heat got too much, they spent long hours down at the river beach.

'Shouldn't we wait for Mina?' asked Abby, seeing her watching them from the balcony as they set off.

'Why? She'll only spoil things. She's always trailing after us.'

Abby felt a bit guilty but was also a bit relieved, so she didn't argue. It was so much nicer to have Philippa to herself. Down at the river, Philippa swung the long Tarzan bridge with such violence it seemed it would turn inside out. On the other side, they skittered down the dusty track to the beach, jumping from rock to rock to avoid the thousands of tiny frogs. Or was Philippa trying to jump on them?

'Did you know frogs explode when they get too hot?' she said. 'They swell up bigger and bigger and then... *pow!*'

Clearly another lie, but there was no point arguing with her when she was engaged in one of her wild theories. She always acted like she hadn't heard you. They followed the river until it formed a series of rapids and deep, glinting pools.

Philippa stripped down to her bikini and crashed into the water, kicking up a swirl of silt, and swam across to the other side. There was a flash of turquoise as she scrambled out onto a large rock. Abby followed. The water was heart-stoppingly cold. It seemed to be moving quite fast. She wasn't sure it was safe.

'You're halfway across so you might as well keep

going,' Philippa yelled. 'Anyway, the snakes lie on the bottom.'

Abby thrashed through the water. Reaching the other side, she clung to a rough ledge, breathing in the damp, ancient smell of the rock, shivering in its shadow. At last, she found a foothold and hauled herself out. She slipped on some slimy weed, grazing her shin, and nearly fell back in again but just caught herself in time.

'What took you?' Philippa said when she finally reached the top.

By now, she was stretched out on the rock like an exotic butterfly, sunglasses pushed back on her head, eyes closed, as though she'd been there for hours, hair fanned out around her like a huge fiery halo. Droplets of water beaded on her skin. Her cheeks and lips were strawberry coloured, her gold eyelashes wet and spiky. Every now and then her nose would twitch and she'd extinguish a mosquito with a ringing slap.

Abby said nothing but flumped down beside her, shivering, feeling her wet costume shrink against her skin as the savage heat prickled through. For some moments, they lay there in silence. It could be any time any day – each one drifted into another down at the river – but she had a vague sense at the back of her mind that one day she would be caught out and it would be the last day. The future lay ahead of them unknown, but this moment would always be theirs.

For around twenty minutes, they did all the usual things: listening to the sploshes and shouts of other bathers; drowsily mumbling questions.

What would you do for a million pounds? How would you most hate to be tortured? If you had to have a bit of you chopped off, what bit would you choose?

The sky above was a brilliant, unbroken blue, the air dancing and shimmering in the heat. The sun needled its way through to their bones, forcing its breath down into their lungs for as long as they could stand before they had to give in and jump into the icy water.

After a while, Philippa reintroduced her favourite topic:

the perfect murder. She had the imagination to think up the ways and means whereas Abby, the strategist, would point out the flaws and the what-ifs.

'We could start a detective agency,' Abby said. She rolled over to let the sun warm the backs of her legs.

'Would you kill someone?' murmured Philippa. 'If you had to?'

Abby frowned. 'Dunno. I mean – only in self-defence. Like, if someone was chasing me or something. Wouldn't you?'

'Same. And to protect someone I really liked. I'd kill someone to save you. Would you do that for me?'

She wasn't certain she would, but it would have seemed ungracious to say no.

'Killing someone's easy,' Abby said, 'it's getting away with it that's difficult. You always leave some kind of evidence.'

'You could pay someone to do it.'

'Yes, but then someone else would know about it and they could betray you one day. That always happens in books.'

'You need to make it look as though they killed themselves then,' said Philippa, rolling onto her front. 'So, you need to plant the gun in their hand afterwards.'

'What about fingerprints?'

'Easy – you wear gloves.'

'Yes, but where would you get a gun from?'

Philippa rolled over again and stretched out on her back, adjusting her bikini. 'Everyone has them round here. My dad uses one for vermin. I'll show you, if you like.'

Was that another lie? Abby hadn't seen one at the house but that didn't mean it didn't exist. She reached out for a twig, snapped it into little bits, and fed the pieces into the water below.

'Still risky, though. A gun's noisy – unless you have a silencer. And messy. And they can tell by the bullet what type of gun was used. And there aren't many places to hide a gun where it would never be found.'

'Hmm, I suppose you could make a sharp weapon out of ice so it melts afterwards,' said Philippa. 'Not much good on a day like today, though. Or better still, not to have a weapon at all. You could frighten someone enough to give them a heart attack. Or just bore them to death.'

'That would only work on someone who was very old or very stupid,' objected Abby, and they laughed until they couldn't breathe.

'The trouble is, dead people look like they're asleep so it would be hard to tell if you'd killed them or they'd just nodded off,' Philippa went on.

Abby sat up and picked at a scab on her knee. She felt uncomfortably hot and her head itched. 'My mum didn't look like she was asleep.'

Philippa screwed her face up. 'Sorry. I forgot.'

Abby hugged her knees to her chest and sucked the fresh wound under the scab. 'It doesn't matter. As long as you don't say it wasn't my fault.'

'All right then, I won't.'

Philippa changed the subject, talking rapidly, but Abby couldn't stop the images coming. The truth was, she didn't remember that much about her mother. Less and less each day, and that hurt more than anything. Just little things remained, like holding her hand as they jumped the waves at the beach or skipped along the street, singing something daft like 'We're off to tea with Alice'. The quality of her voice, her soft brown hair, her pink lipstick.

Each day, it was harder to recall her face. Sometimes Abby feared she would forget it altogether. She made herself study photographs but they never seemed to capture the whole person. On more than one occasion she'd woken in the night crying and said to her father, 'I can't remember what she looked like.'

The day her mother disappeared, she hadn't come to collect Abby from school. Not wanting to wait around in the school office and miss her favourite TV programme, Abby walked home alone. She found the spare key in the shed, in the green tin where they kept string. She'd often watched her mother hiding it there.

She watched a programme about a school, followed by a daft cartoon. Then the news came on, so she got herself a glass of milk and some biscuits. An hour later, she went to the front gate and looked up and down the road, but there was still no sign. She was hungry and made herself some toast with jam. When her mother got home, she would be able to tell her that she had had her tea so there was no need to bother. Sometimes tasks like cooking seemed to overwhelm Mum.

The telephone rang. Abby assumed it would be Mum with an explanation. Something that had slipped her mind to mention earlier – a doctor's appointment, or a meeting with an old friend. It wasn't.

Her father wanted to know where she was in the house. 'Stay where you are. Promise me you won't leave the room until I get home.'

If only she had done as he said. But his words made her curious. Why shouldn't she go in the other rooms? She searched them all, in case her mother was asleep somewhere and had forgotten the time. It had happened before. Mum sometimes stayed in bed all day crying but couldn't explain why.

'She's just tired,' her father would say. But how she could be tired when she hadn't done anything all day?

At last Abby found her, standing quietly in the garage in the dark, wearing her jeans and her blue woollen coat. It struck Abby somehow, although she only really thought about it later, that her mother looked taller that day. She thought at first that she had been hiding there, waiting to be found.

'There you are!'

She ran forward and hugged her. The body swung stiffly away. It was only then that she noticed her mother's feet weren't flat on the floor but trailing, her new, kitten heel shoes left empty and useless.

She had used the long scarf her husband bought her on the holiday by the lake. The only really clear memory Abby had of the chaotic aftermath of the discovery was of her father clutching the scarf like a child's cuddle blanket, tears coursing down his face, which was all crumpled like the fabric. That, and him asking again and again why Abby hadn't rung him as soon as she got in. It just might have made a difference.

Thinking about it, Abby felt her face freeze and her whole body shivered. The next few moments were a blank. It happened sometimes, small sections of time that passed without her noticing and made her feel disorientated. Afterwards, she knew some minutes had been cut out of her life, but the pain she had felt leading up to this lost time was anaesthetised.

She lay for a while on her back, watching brilliant colours flicker under her eyelids. Something prickled her skin. A shadow moved in front of her. She opened an eye under the shade of her hand, and between the dazzle and dark blotches saw some boys approaching. She recognised them as the ones they'd trounced at table football at Armando's bar the previous night.

The lead one grinned at her and put his finger on his lips. Before she had a chance to do anything, he scooped Philippa up and hurled her, upside down, screaming, legs flailing, over the edge. There was a pause, and then a smash as she hit the water. The boys cheered and slapped each other's hands.

Abby scrambled back, knees up to her chest, but the first boy held his hands up as he laughed, signalling she had nothing to fear. An old score being settled, that was all.

They waited. The ripples dissolved. Nothing happened. The water threw back a perfect picture of the mountains and the sky. They looked at each other. Gradually, they crept closer to the edge of the rock. She saw the colour drain from the first boy's face. A cold sliver of fear coiled through her.

'*Merda.*'

Nothing. Philippa wasn't coming up.

His friends said something. He snapped back, a volley of sharp, defensive words. Abby started to slither down the rock but the boy dived in from above. She held her breath. Just as he hit the water, Philippa sprang up, splashing and laughing, throwing up an arc of iridescent droplets, her hair clinging around her face like shimmering seaweed.

It was impossible to tell what she was shouting, but it was obvious by the way the other boys raised their eyebrows, laughed and gestured, that they were rude words, even by Philippa's standards. Philippa and the boy fought in the water. She was up now, dragging him under again. He was tickling her. She was shrieking and hitting him. He was laughing and splashing her.

Abby lowered herself into the water to go to Philippa's aid. But as she neared them she stopped. They were standing in the shallows kissing. She saw his fingers creep under one of the turquoise triangles of her bikini. Abby turned away. She swam back, and for a long time clung to the rock, trying to decide what to do. The water was deep and cold and her teeth were chattering.

Then Philippa was swimming back towards her. The boys were scrambling back up to the bridge, making ape sounds and gestures.

'Did you know they'd be here?' Abby asked on the way back.

'Of course not.'

But then, you could never tell. The more lies Philippa told, the more Abby wondered if she herself believed them, which made her a perfect liar. She had watched her, studied the cool, even tone, the haughty expression, the confident, obliging smile, and sometimes wondered if she would have guessed Philippa was lying. She couldn't be certain that she would.

It was starting to sink in that one day she would lose her. Not that day but some day, and there was nothing she could do about it. She would grow up, move on, and find more exciting or sophisticated people to be with. There were so many ways Abby couldn't compete.

***

It turned out Philippa hadn't been lying about the gun, and she was an alarmingly good shot. Abby winced as she watched her skin a rabbit as easily as slipping a jumper off a doll.

'Do you like my glove puppet?' she asked, coming up behind Abby and stroking her cheek. Abby smelled the blood and felt the velvety fur against her face. Her screams, as her cousin chased her round the olive trees with her hand inside the bloody skin, brought Alan running.

'What the hell do you think you're doing?' he shouted, seizing the gun. 'This is not a toy. Don't you ever touch it without my permission.'

They waited until he'd gone before keeling over in silent laughter.

'It's all right,' whispered Philippa. 'I know where he hides the key.'

Chapter Nineteen

Every time she thought about Mina's appearance at the surgery, a new wave of panic rushed through Abby. She kept checking the papers, the Internet, had the radio on constantly. Each time James left the house, she wondered what would be uncovered before she saw him again. How long could she risk leaving it before Mina carried out her threat to expose her secret? There were times when she thought it had all been talk and that her cousin wouldn't go through with it, but other times when it seemed crystal clear that she would.

She ran her eyes over the columns on her laptop. Not that account. She couldn't touch that. Premium Bonds – there were some in her own name and some for each of the girls, but it was nowhere near enough. There was another account in her name, one they never used. She felt sick as her hand hovered over the mouse. It wasn't as much as Mina wanted – not even half. But it would be something. Perhaps enough to stall her.

How likely was James to look at this account? It wasn't money they were intending to use for years. Bit by bit she could replace it. She closed her eyes and clicked. A sudden sharp pain tore at her chest. The air whirled, sending shockwaves through her. Was it too late to change her mind? She sat, looking at the screen, her hand pressed to her mouth. No, she mustn't, she couldn't. She snapped down the lid of the laptop and forced herself to walk away.

***

Abby froze on the steps of the loggia on her way down to

breakfast. Alan and Sue's voices rose up, one low and angry, one high and indignant. She winced at some of the language and took a sharp breath as Alan grabbed Sue from behind, first by the shoulder strap and then with his hand around her stomach, dragging her back out of sight.

'What's new?' Philippa murmured behind Abby. 'Don't worry, she gives as good as she gets. They're as bad as each other. Come to think of it, he's got worse since you arrived. In a few minutes, they'll snog and make up. It's how they do things.'

'What are they arguing about?'

'Builders – or lack of. The place is falling down around our ears and they can't get anyone to come up here and sort out the problems. My dad organised someone to start this morning, but they haven't turned up. They never do. The house looks all right now, but you should see it when it rains – we'll probably all die of TB in a few months.'

There were no clouds in the sky. It was hard to imagine a drop of rain being a problem.

'It gets in everywhere. Down through the roof, up through the floor – even through the walls. And they're forecasting storms for the end of the week. But no builder will set foot up here.'

'Why not? Is it because of the curse on the house?'

Philippa sighed impatiently. 'Why do you keep saying that? People are just lazy. They don't want to get off their arses and walk up the hill when there's plenty of work down in the town.'

But Abby had seen people's expressions down in the village when Villa Leonida was mentioned. There was something about the house, something people were afraid of. She felt it, too, sometimes, a shadowy presence lurking in the corners.

At breakfast under the pergola, she caught Alan staring at her.

'Are you happy here?'

She nodded.

'You would say if you weren't, wouldn't you? I mean,

110

you'd tell Philippa, at least?'

Something in his expression surprised her. It was almost fearful. He seemed to want to say more but busied himself cutting up a watermelon. She was almost certain it was he who came in at night and watched her. It gave her the creeps, but at least he didn't touch her.

She remembered something Philippa had said about his temper being worse since she had come to the house, but couldn't think what she might have done to upset him. There were times when he laughed quite fondly at something she did. At other times, he seemed to be watching her critically. It was as though he expected her to behave in a certain way and was offended when she didn't. As if she was being tested, but had no idea why.

What did he want from her? She wasn't a particularly fussy eater and she didn't think her manners were that bad. It must be something else then. It must be her silence that frustrated him. She knew it unnerved some people, but it wasn't as if she kept quiet on purpose.

His own manners weren't perfect, either – they weren't even good. He pushed his food around on his plate and spoke with his mouth full, barking out criticisms.

'Am I supposed to eat this?'; 'What are you wearing?'; 'Use your bloody brains.'

It was usually Mina who was on the receiving end of his outbursts – for having her elbows on the table, leaving the top off the jam pot, not being able to tell him the Italian word for 'spanner'. A lot of things in the house got broken, and Philippa said it had nothing to do with her so Mina must be the clumsy one.

Very few of the mugs and plates matched, and sometimes things disappeared from one meal to the next, but no-one ever remarked on it and they were never replaced. There seemed to be a conspiracy to deny that the pink cup or the painted chicken jug had ever existed.

It was a shame, because Mina was the one who tried hardest to please her father, always laughing at his jokes and passing him things before he asked for them. She gave up hours each day to type his manuscripts, which she seemed to consider a privilege, but it was clear neither Philippa nor Sue could be bothered with anything like that.

Philippa seemed to get away with things more lightly, but then she didn't tell Alan anything he wouldn't want to hear. Obviously, this was different from telling straightforward lies. It was a method of self-defence. But how would he react if he found she had lied to him about something serious?

***

After breakfast, Abby found Philippa sitting on the top step of the loggia.

'What have you got there?'

'Paint. To cheer up these old beams. It's supposed to stop the woodworm, too. I thought we could paint them different colours so we can look up at a rainbow.'

'We can't do that to an old building.'

She rolled her eyes. 'Why not? Who's going to stop us?'

'Your parents?'

Philippa tossed her hair back. 'I think we've established that my parents don't give a flying fuck what I do. They don't care about anyone but themselves.'

Abby wasn't sure this was true and wondered if the point of the exercise was to attract their attention, but it was liberating, this lack of parental control.

Philippa started taking the tops off the pots. 'We'll have to mix some of the colours. Let me see *Richard of York gave battle in vain*. Who was Richard of York? Was he the same as the Grand Old Duke?'

'I don't think so. Wasn't he the one who shouted, "My kingdom for a horse"?'

'What did he say that for?'

'Don't know. I think it was in the War of the Roses or something.'

Philippa tutted, brandishing her paintbrush. 'You see, that's the useless sort of thing they teach you at school.'

She stood on her bed and began to splash green paint onto the beam above it, unconcerned about the spatters that fell onto her sheets.

'I wonder what your dad and stepmum are up to? What was the name of that place they've gone to?'

'St Lucia. It looks like paradise – white sandy beaches with coconut trees, a swimming pool with a—'

'I wonder if she'll come back pregnant.'

Abby stopped. For some reason, she hadn't thought about this. Not that she didn't like babies, but one that was half Dad's and half Mel's? Where would she fit into the family then?

'No,' she said remembering, 'she never wanted children.'

Philippa dismissed this with a shrug. 'They all say that. But they always feel differently about their own.'

Was that true? Abby was getting an unwelcome image of Dad with his hand on Mel's stomach. *We've got something to tell you...*

'Careful, look what you're doing.'

A splash of red paint had landed on Abby's shoe. As she looked, another dripped onto the floor.

'Sorry.'

There was a soft thud as a green splot landed on Abby's t-shirt.

'Oops.' Philippa covered her mouth, laughing.

'You did that on purpose.'

Without thinking, she flicked some of the red paint back, hitting Philippa square in the chest.

'Right. This means war.' Philippa held out her brush like a fencing sword, stabbing and parrying. Abby shielded her face but felt the wet bristles dabbing her forearms and hands. Squealing, she lunged for her cousin's stomach.

It didn't take long for things to get out of hand. Seeing she was losing, Philippa abandoned the brush, stuck her hands in the red paint, and clamped them around Abby's head, mashing in the paint like shampoo. Struggling to get out of her grip, Abby stepped in the pot and tipped it over, sending a red lake across the floor.

Diving to catch it, they slid over on the wet cotto tiles and lay catching their breath, staring wide-eyed around them at the mess they had made. The place looked like a crime scene. Streaks of red up the walls, handprints on the sheets and the mirror. The empty can rattled across the floor.

'We are in so much trouble,' breathed Philippa. Her face gleamed red. Her hair was matted with it.

Alan erupted when he saw the mess. 'It looks like there's been a massacre. Clean it up. Now.'

Philippa managed to look contrite until he had left, but then caught Abby's eye and collapsed back into giggles.

***

Those lethargic afternoons slipped into magical evenings, but the night always took her by surprise; the darkness fell so quickly. They were sitting in creaky rattan chairs in a pool of golden light under the pergola, watching the fireflies light up like fairy lights. The air was filled with candle smoke and citronella, and stars sprinkled the sky. Things rustled in the vine leaves above. Twigs snapped in the dark undergrowth. They had showered and changed their clothes. The old ones had gone in the bin.

Philippa took out some cigarettes. 'Have one.'

Abby shook her head.

Her cousin rolled her eyes. 'One's not going to kill you.'

'I know that.'

'Well then?' After a few moments, she clicked her tongue and said, 'Suit yourself', but she sounded annoyed.

Sitting back, Philippa lit the cigarette and brought it to her mouth, arching her back and exhaling slowly, letting the smoke envelop over her like a veil. Slowly Abby reached over and plucked it out of her grasp. Philippa opened one eye, smiled, but didn't say anything.

Abby held it between finger and thumb, examining the warmth and taking in the bitter scent of the tobacco. She brought it to her lips.

'Open your mouth then.'

She parted her lips and parked the cigarette between them, getting used to the taste of the paper.

'Breathe in.'

She was afraid she'd make a fool of herself by having a coughing fit, but inhaling cautiously she found it surprisingly easy. The smoke stung her tongue. She felt lighter, happier. Perhaps she took in too much, but a moment later her head was rushing. The thick, scratchy smoke slammed into the back of her throat, travelled down into her lungs. But then it rebounded. She had forgotten how to breathe. Her head hurt. Everything was spinning.

'Are you going to be sick?' Philippa sprang out of her chair.

Abby folded over and retched into a pot of lavender.

Philippa was laughing, covering her face. 'Gross. Have another try.'

'No thanks.'

'It will be easier next time.'

She watched Abby gulp a glass of water, then looked at her curiously. 'You've still got paint in your hair.'

Abby had washed it several times in the shower and re-plaited it, but she hadn't got all the paint out. She'd weaved the plaits too tightly when her hair was still wet and they were giving her a headache. She pulled out the bands and shook them free so that they fell into springy ringlets.

Philippa called to Mina, 'Come and see. Get the polaroid.'

They pressed their heads together laughing. The image, when it appeared, took her by surprise.

'We look like sisters,' Abby said, looking at her curly, red-tinged hair.

'That's because we are.'

At the time, Abby didn't take too much notice. It just seemed like something Philippa would say. She caught Mina looking at her.

'It's only because of the paint,' said Mina. 'Abby has no colouring at all, really; she's like a black and white photograph.'

She stormed off into the house.

Philippa blew a column of smoke up into the air and watched it curl up towards the stars. 'Look, a shooting star. Do you know what night it is? *La notte dei desideri.* Make a wish, it will come true.'

It seemed there was only one thing to wish for – that she could stay longer, perhaps even forever. It was funny how Abby had hated this place when she first arrived. In such a short time, the villa had worked its magic on her.

But when she opened her eyes, she saw Mina's face floating above them in the gaps between the leaves and bunches of lemons.

'That's a shame, my wish didn't come true. You're still here.' She banged her shutters closed.

'What is her problem?'

Philippa shrugged. 'It's probably because she thinks you're more my sister than she is.'

She smiled, not quite seeing the joke. 'Why would she think that?'

'Because I told her.'

Abby felt cold all over. It was the second time Philippa had said it.

'Why? Why did you do that?'

Philippa propped her feet up on the wicker table, clearly gearing up for one of her theories.

'Think about it. Your mum and mine were best friends. Your mum wanted a child, but couldn't have one and didn't want to adopt. So, mine lent your mum her husband. And bingo – you were born.'

Abby laughed. Then she frowned. 'Do people do that?'

'Of course they do. He was happy to go along with it. Your mum was pretty – I've seen pictures. But then your mum died, and suddenly he realised he was your closest living relative.

'That's why he was so reluctant to let you come and stay. And why he's so awkward around you. You can see he's scared to death of you. He doesn't want to admit who you are. But my mum agreed to you coming because your dad's her brother and she feels responsible for you, especially as it was all her idea in the first place.'

Abby processed this for a moment. 'But that's just rubbish. How do you know my parents couldn't have children?'

At the same time, she was remembering the words she had overheard that first night. *'The responsibility's yours. You're the one who said it wouldn't get complicated.'*

Philippa tossed her head impatiently. 'Well, you don't have any brothers or sister, do you? And think about it: what would be the greatest favour a friend could do for another? But then they must have fallen out. I think they thought they could carry on as normal afterwards, but then found they couldn't.'

Abby didn't like the images she was getting. 'You mean my mum and your dad *did it*?'

A babble of muffled voices rose and fell inside the house. Shutters banged. Glass smashed. A scornful laugh, a roar of indignation. She hardly noticed the rows these days.

'Well, they might have used a turkey baster, but whatever happened my dad fell in love with your mum and that was never supposed to happen. My mum doesn't really love my dad but she demands his total devotion.'

'My mum was pretty,' said Abby quietly. She was trying to remember her face, but the image in her head had faded like an old photograph. It was little more than a blur. 'But how can you know all this?'

Although now that she thought about it, her parents had never been really close. Not in the way her father was with Mel. That was one of the things she resented about her stepmother.

'I don't even look like you,' she said. 'Not really.'

Philippa shrugged. 'Why should you? You look like your mum. I look like my dad. Our dad.'

Abby felt a flash of heat. 'He's not my dad. I don't want him to be my dad.'

It had to be another one of Philippa's far-fetched stories,

and yet a tiny doubt was starting to take seed.

'I don't want him to be mine either, but that doesn't mean he isn't. I don't want either of them to be my parents. I wish they'd both fuck off and die.'

Her face was in shadow. It was hard to tell if she was joking.

'Why do you say that?'

She drew up her knees. 'I still hate them for the way they tricked me into coming out here.'

'How do you mean tricked you?'

Philippa ground out her cigarette and tossed it into the lavender pot. As she turned her head, her face gleamed gold in the light from the candles. 'They didn't give me any say about leaving England. Told us we were going on holiday, but they knew we weren't coming back.'

'Did you really mind that much?' By the way Philippa's eyes glittered with anger, it was clear that she still did.

'It's not that bad here, though, is it?' said Abby, looking down over the dream-lit village. It was still warm enough to be comfortable in a t-shirt. The air flowed like silk over her bare arms and her skin still tingled from the heat of the afternoon.

'That's not the point.' Philippa grabbed the matches and struck one, her face glowing manically in the splutter of light. She swiped her finger through the flame, holding it there for a fraction longer each time.

'They didn't care about what we wanted or how it was going to affect us. They never do. They have these stupid ideas and there's nothing I can do to stop them. Mum has this thing about "follow your heart", but she actually means we should all follow *her* heart. That's what I hate.'

She winced as the flame bit into her finger, making it glow red and then black. There was a sizzle and a smell of burnt flesh.

Abby took hold of our arm. 'Don't do that.'

Philippa shrugged her off and leant back against the wall of the house, looking up through the golden leaves to the black sky.

'They sold our house, all my stuff. I didn't have a chance to talk to Josh and tell him what was happening.'

'Josh?'

'My boyfriend.'

A bright, brittle note entered her voice as she added, 'And hers, it turns out.'

Abby thought she hadn't heard right. 'What are you talking about?'

Philippa's eyes were closed, tears beading on her lashes. She wasn't going to trouble to elaborate. But she murmured something that sounded like,

'Don't worry, I'll get my own back.'

Chapter Twenty

Abby came into the kitchen just in time to see James hurl his phone across the room.

'What is it? What's the matter?'

His whole body was shaking. He hauled open the wine cooler and pulled out a bottle of wine, splashing it into two glasses without even asking if she wanted one.

'I've just fired Anoushka.'

'Who?'

'The accountant.'

Her heart dropped into her stomach. 'What did you do that for?'

His expression was so full of anguish she thought he might cry. 'I hardly know how to tell you. Some money's gone. Quite a lot of it, I'm afraid. Look, I don't want you to worry. We'll get it back. I'll take her to court.'

She heard words like 'deceit' and 'cunning' and 'can't let her get away with it'. He pulled her towards him and folded her in his arms. She could feel his heart beneath his shirt. It was tempting to stay in that secure place and pretend none of it was happening. But she couldn't let an innocent person lose their job, be dragged through the courts.

She pulled back. 'No, you can't fire her.'

'Of course I can. I must. You don't understand – we're not talking about helping herself to a few quid for the bus fare home. She's robbed us. Robbed our children of their future.'

He named the sum. The exact sum.

His face was full of pity and anguish. 'It was the money your dad left you, the money we said we'd put aside for the girls' university education.'

'But we don't know it was her,' said Abby helplessly.

He laughed, incredulous. 'Of course it was her. Who else has ever had access to our accounts?' He sank onto a bar stool, put his elbows on the marble counter and dropped his head in his hands. 'I gave her the password for a different account when I wanted her to make that transfer. I should have changed it. She would have guessed it was the same one. I feel such an idiot. I should have been more careful. I trusted her.'

'But anyone could have hacked into our computers,' said Abby.

He lifted his head. In the minute pause, she caught the hint of suspicion in his eyes. 'Why are you making excuses for her?'

'I'm not. I'm just trying to see things rationally.'

But he was staring at her now, his button brown eyes searching hers. His voice sounded different as he said, 'Abby, what's this about?'

Outside, the trampoline creaked and the children laughed and squealed. Inside, the kitchen felt suddenly too bright and too warm.

She swallowed. 'You can't fire Anoushka, because I took the money out of the account.'

Silence crackled between them. His eyes were filled with puzzlement.

'You? You've moved it? Why didn't you say?'

He slid his hands down the sides of his face as the impact hit him. 'God, the things I said to her.'

This was the point where she should tell him. She had rehearsed it enough times. *Look, sorry, I should have mentioned this before...*

But there was no possible way to say it.

'I didn't move the money. I spent it.'

She watched his face. He seemed to be deciding how to arrange his features. His voice was full of incredulity. 'Why? What on?'

What reason could she give? It wasn't as if she went in for designer clothes or jewellery. He would have noticed a flash car. He brows twitched as he waited for an explanation.

'It's my money. The money my dad left me.'

'I know it is – but we've never made decisions like that without consulting each other. Are you at least going to tell me why?'

She had to think, had to say something, and it had to be convincing. He was looking, waiting. She took a deep breath, said the first thing she thought of. 'I needed it. For a patient. I misdiagnosed her, didn't spot the signs. And now she needs treatment she can't get on the NHS. Her only chance is a hospital in the States.'

She could feel the weight of his stare as he assessed what she'd said. He had no idea how to handle this situation she had thrust upon him.

'So, you're paying for this person you barely know to have this treatment?'

'It was my fault; the least I could do. Without it, she'll die.'

His features were contorted in confusion. 'But how much does the treatment cost? All of it?'

'It's not just the treatment, obviously, it's the flights and accommodation.'

This was getting worse and worse. She'd never lied to him before, only withheld truth. But now she was lying. There was no other word for it.

His face was white, a sheen of sweat lying across his forehead. He couldn't have looked more shocked if he'd been hit by a lorry. 'And if it's not successful, what then?'

'At least I'll have tried.'

He wiped his mouth with his hand. He seemed to be having trouble controlling his breathing. 'Are you going to do this every time someone falls ill with something you failed to spot? For God's sake, doctors miss things. It happens every day. No-one's infallible. Or did you think you were?'

He got up and started to pace around the room. 'It's probably a scam, you realise that, don't you? She's lying about her symptoms. She'll have gone off and bought a yacht, for God's sake.'

'No. I've seen the scans.' Now she was having to make up detail. How could she find a way back from this?

James kept shaking his head in disbelief. 'And you didn't think this was something we should have discussed between us?'

She closed her eyes. 'I knew you wouldn't understand.'

A laugh caught in his throat. 'Well, you got that right. Tell me, how are you going to explain to our children when they're ready to go to university that there's no money for them?'

'Most students manage on loans. And I'm going to pay back what I can, a bit each month.'

But he wasn't taking it in. He was still staring at her as though she were some alien creature that he had found impersonating his wife.

'What if this gets out? How is it ethical to help one patient out of so many, probably offering them false hope? You complain about being overworked now. If this gets into the papers, you're going to have people queuing in the street to see you for a handout. And you'll have to turn them away. How will you feel about that?'

'It's not going to happen.' At least she could be sure of that.

She reached out but he drew away. 'I can't believe you'd do this. Surely you could be struck off for it?'

She shrugged helplessly. For some moments, they sat in silence, the weight of her revelation between them.

'Are you sure there isn't another reason?' His voice sounded strangely hollow.

Her heart banged against her ribs. 'What other reason?'

'You're not leaving me, are you?'

He managed to say it lightly, but there was a flicker of fear in his eyes that told her he was wondering if it might actually be true.

The idea was so ridiculous she laughed. 'No, of course not. Why would you think that?'

He flumped down on the sofa. 'Because it's what people do, isn't it – arrange things, move their funds about, get everything in order for a nice clean break?'

She shook her head wonderingly. 'I would never do that to you.'

The look he gave her filled her with shame.

'I want to believe you – but up until this evening I'd never have believed you'd almost bankrupt us for a whim. What is this treatment? Why do you think it will be successful?'

She sat on the sofa next to him. But before she could speak, he held his hand up. 'No, on second thoughts don't tell me. I can't get mixed up in this, do you understand?'

She placed her hand on his thigh, tried to give it a reassuring squeeze but the muscle was taught and unyielding. He stared down at the hand, slowly lifted it off and put it back in her lap. He got up and left the room.

Chapter Twenty-One

Alan shut himself away in his study for most of the day. Abby imagined him feverishly bashing away on his typewriter, trying to catch the words that fed through him before they disappeared, but once when she passed the room and peeped through the half-open door, she saw him just slumped in his chair as though asleep.

As she sat writing in her notebook that morning under the pergola, she could hear through the closed shutters the typewriter keys working furiously, the slide, thump and ring as the ink roll shot across.

It was still warm but clouds were building up, the first she had seen since she arrived. Philippa had told her rain was forecast. She picked up her notebook and walked towards the house.

Something heavy slammed against the wall of the study, followed by a scream. She stiffened, her heart tight inside her chest, then crept up the stairs to her room.

Throughout lunch in the kitchen, Alan sat hunched and brooding over the table, pressing his fist against his forehead. If anyone asked him about his work he got tense, as though they were piling pressure on him out of spite. The large vein at the side of his head bulged when he got angry, as if a sandworm had taken up residence there.

How could her mother ever have slept with this man, let alone fallen in love with him? How could she have killed herself over him? Abby found herself staring at him as he sat there shirtless at the table. His freckled skin was too fair to cope with the Tuscan heat. Bits of scaly skin showered down around him as he rubbed his shoulders.

How could he be her father? She refused to believe it.

But Philippa's theory bothered her more and more. It was absurd, and yet little fragments of doubt had embedded themselves in her brain and dug themselves in like a tick. Her own father wasn't perfect, but he was a much better person than Alan. If only he wasn't so far away.

It was only when Mina turned her head that the swelling showed. An egg-sized purple lump at the side of her forehead. And yet no-one acknowledged it, just as they didn't say anything about the things that broke. Catching Abby's gaze, Mina glared back furiously.

Alan pushed his food around his plate, then shoved the plate away and stormed off back to the study, slamming the door.

'Thank God for that,' said Philippa when he was out of earshot. 'He's like an overgrown toddler with his tantrums.'

'What do you think happened?'

'He threw the typewriter at her. Come on, let's get out of here.'

'Why would he do that?'

'Frustration.'

They set off down the track towards the village. Abby had to run to keep up with Philippa whose legs were much longer. She had been right about the rain coming. Storm clouds had crept in during the morning and the air hung heavy around them.

'He's lost it,' Philippa said, stripping a stick from a tree and tapping the ground in front of her to ward away snakes. 'He's having a breakdown.'

'Why?'

'Writer's block.'

'Are you sure?' asked Abby doubtfully.

'Certain. Hasn't written anything for months. He's supposed to have his manuscript with the publishers by September but he's got nothing to send. He threw the last one on the fire after a huge row with Mum. It was all a gesture – he'd already decided it wasn't working.'

They stopped at the clearing just above the little church and watched the sky above the mountain opposite fill with sheets of colour like a laser show. The storm had reached the neighbouring village. They might just have time to make it to the bar before the rain.

'He can't write any more. He only ever had one big idea, anyway. Mina says he hasn't given her anything to type for ages. And when he does, she types pages and pages, then the next day she finds them all in the bin.'

'Why can't he write? What's stopping him?'

Philippa's face was pale and luminous against the rain-swollen clouds. The village was closing in on itself, the hills lost in the mist.

'Fear of failure, if you ask me. He doesn't want to go back to how he was – struggling, not getting anywhere. It took him years to get published. Mum had to pay for everything back then. She earned the money, so she spent it how she liked and he couldn't complain. He didn't like being penniless, it made him bad-tempered – violent sometimes. That's when Mum first stopped eating.

'But then he got a lucky break – finally came up with the right story and a publisher snapped it up. They commissioned three books and then three more. He's even got a fan club.'

The first few books had been easy, Philippa said. Abby pictured the stories pouring out of him, as though an invisible force was dictating them. All he had to do was surrender to the voice in his head and write.

'But then the trouble started. He should have stopped there, moved on to something different. He always meant the sixth book to be the last. He'd killed off a major character and lost interest in the rest, but his publishers didn't like any of his other ideas. He has this thing about children's books not being taken seriously, wants to be a *proper* author and write for adults. Problem is, his ideas are all crap.

'He resents being tied to the children's series but at the same time he needs the money. He brought us all out here and we're relying on him now. If he doesn't turn things around soon, he won't be able to get my mum to stay.'

'Why not?'

Philippa laughed. 'She's bored to death, can't you see? It's all turned on its head. Out here, he earns the money and he makes the decisions. It was always his dream to live in another country. She doesn't speak the language – at least, not well enough to teach in it. She hates being a housewife, needs adventure. And he's terrified of losing her.'

Abby pictured him waking with half-formed ideas that turned to dust as soon as he tried to wrestle them onto paper. No wonder he was tired and foul-tempered during the day. But it didn't excuse him throwing typewriters at people.

It started to rain, just a pattering on the leaves at first, then large drops that splashed around them making the muddy path slippery. Branches thrashed above their heads. Below them in the piazza, the awning of the bar was flapping in the wind as two young women struggled to reel it in. Tourists grabbed their belongings and herded for shelter inside the bar.

Abby and Philippa skidded, shrieking down the path, needled by the rain, trying to keep their balance.

'In here,' shouted Philippa, coming to a halt outside the little church of Santa Maria del Soccorso.

'It will be locked, won't it?'

'No, it never is.'

She heaved open the heavy door of the tiny church. Inside, it was dark, fusty, and shadowy but at least it was dry. The air was thick with the smell of furniture polish, incense, and candle wax. Their footsteps echoed on the stone floor. A pew creaked but there was no-one sitting there.

'Probably haunted,' whispered Philippa. She fished in her pocket and dug out a coin which she stuck in a slot in front of the altar.

Behind the altar was a murky painting. With a loud click, a light came on and the picture burst into life. Abby drew in her breath as she took in Mary's ferocious features.

'Cool, isn't it?' Philippa said.

It wasn't the usual adoring mother and baby scene. Far

from serene, this Mary was a gigantic figure wielding a club. Her eyes blazed with foreboding. A small child clung to her billowing skirts, cowering. Abby stared at the face for a long time, puzzling over it, rain dripping off her hair and into her eyes. She took an involuntary step back.

'Why's she so cross with the child?'

Philippa laughed. 'She's not cross with the child, *duh* – she's rescuing it from the Devil.'

She pointed to the Devil in the bottom right corner of the picture, a classic black shadowy demon with horns, who had been attempting to seize the child. How could Abby have missed it? All her attention concentrated on Mary's wrathful face, but the painting was so dark the Devil was hardly distinguishable from a stain or shadow.

'Mothers used to abandon their unwanted babies in this church. They were collected by the nuns and taken to the orphanage through there. They thought she would scare off anyone with evil intentions. She scares the shit out of me, anyway.'

A cluster of candles flickered. Philippa picked one up and tipped the hot wax onto her finger. She winced, but after a moment she moulded the wax between her fingers, rolling it into a ball. She slumped into one of the pews, putting her feet up on the rail in front and letting her hair hang behind the back of the seat, dripping a puddle onto the floor.

They lit dozens of votive candles and sat with their feet up, wringing out their t-shirts and modelling tiny figures out of the hot wax as branches scratched against the roof and rain tapped the window like fingernails.

'What are you going to do when the money runs out?' asked Abby. 'If he's not writing any more, it can't last forever.'

Philippa shrugged and stretched. 'Move on, I suppose, like we always do. Perhaps Greece.'

'Do you think you'll ever go back to England?'

Her expression closed over. 'Doubt it.' She squished another piece of wax and made a tiny snowman then stabbed it with her fingernail. She thought for a moment, and then grabbed Abby by the shoulders.

'Come with us. Write to your dad and tell him you're not going back.'

Caught up in the moment, she agreed.

'It's easing up a bit,' said Philippa. 'Shall we make a run for it?'

At the doorway, Abby looked back at the picture. The light had gone out so it was dark and shadowy again, but she could still make out Mary's furious expression and the Devil's outstretched hands.

They left the door to crash behind them as they ran back up to the house, screaming into the wind, sliding in the mud, jumping over slugs and salamanders. The sun appeared through the sheen of rain, gilding the rooftops against the dark sky, but more clouds were advancing over the mountains. An ownerless umbrella danced on the wind, spinning down the wet street towards the piazza where puddles lay like sheets of silver.

The storm unleashed its full force after lunch, confining them to the house. Lightning forked over the hills, followed by enormous cracks of thunder. It rained all day, the kind of rain that soaks you in seconds. Water crept in under the window frames and ran down the wall. The house smelled dank.

Buckets and washing-up bowls were stationed at various points, but even so when Abby walked into the bedroom she slipped over. Brown patches were starting to appear on the ceiling, and the trees outside were whipping around so hard it was surely it was only a matter of time before one landed on the house.

Philippa stood out on the loggia shouting nonsense into the wind. She ran down the steps and staggered around the terrace, lifting her face up to the rain. She was soaked through, laughing, an enchantress commanding the storm.

Abby lay on the bed and sketched out the picture of the Devil trying to seize the baby and Mary fighting him off with the club. She also drew Mina with the mark on her head, rather exaggerated with blood spurting out, and a typewriter on the floor.

It struck her that all of their lives had changed in a short time. Alan had appeared to be the one with the most control of his destiny, and yet he had the least. A few years ago, it must have all looked so rosy for him. Who would have imagined he would be here now in this self-imposed exile, resenting the boy hero he had created for his books, but at the same time realising that without him he was nothing and would return to that pit of obscurity as fast as he had left it?

***

Abby wasn't sure if she was awake or asleep when she heard deep, operatic tones just below the windows. It had rained for three days without a break and the house stank of mould.

'Give me a break,' sighed Philippa with her eyes still closed. 'Must be the new builders. They've come all the way from San Marcello.'

They crept out onto the loggia and found themselves staring at a bronzed, half naked man probably in his late thirties or early forties, sorting tiles. He was well over six foot tall, with long, untidy hair, which he tied in a ponytail, and a lean, muscular torso. No doubt sensing he was being stared at, he looked up and addressed the song to them. They ducked below the wall, giggling.

At least the builders' arrival might put Alan in a better temper. These people from the Pistoia province presumably didn't know or care that the house was cursed. With them working on the roof, Alan would have time to concentrate on re-lining the well and reconstructing the dry-stone wall that was threatening to collapse at one end of the top terrace.

The head builder, it turned out, was called Marco. He engaged the girls in banter, which Abby didn't understand but which had Philippa and Mina in fits of giggles, and he taught them songs. His team included a squat stonemason and a wiry teenage boy, Marco's son Nino, who seemed to be the general dogsbody, always sloping around. He blushed when Philippa spoke to him, which made her laugh.

The squat stonemason gave Abby sweets. He chain-smoked, dropping the butts into an old blue glazed pot on the balcony, which angered Sue who considered smoking a filthy habit. But she didn't criticise Marco for smoking, Abby noticed, and she spent a lot of time out there, chatting and joking with him. Abby saw the way Marco looked Sue up and down as she was walking away from him in her floaty, see-through dress, and wondered if she was aware he was doing it and whether she minded.

'You know,' said Philippa, coming out to join Abby on the loggia, 'I've been asking around and it turns out you were right. There is a curse on the house.'

She sat on the wall, picking the dead heads of the geraniums.

'The woman who lived here centuries ago was beautiful but vain. She was afraid of growing old and losing her beauty. One night during a storm, she got a visit from a traveller selling magic potions. He promised her eternal youth but in return she must give him her first-born son.

'She agreed, thinking this probably wouldn't happen for years and the Devil (for that's who it was) would have forgotten by then. When her son was born, she was determined that the Devil would not have him. The next night, the traveller came knocking on the door and she handed over a bundle, but inside it was not the baby but a piglet. The woman was delighted that she had tricked the Devil but she had a feeling that he would be back.

'She kept the child prisoner in the house, dressed him as a girl, and called him a girl's name. Several times the Devil tried to snatch the child wearing different disguises, but the mother was always too clever.

'But one day, the Devil found a way into the house and turned the sleeping child into a pig. The woman's husband saw the pig running through the house and killed it. They ate it for supper, saying how delicious it tasted, until the

Devil turned up and told them they had just eaten their own child. He put a curse on the house so that every family who lives here has to give one child to him. And since then, one child in every family who lives here has died young.'

She looked around, her eyes wide. 'The question is, which child is it to be?'

It was obviously a lie, but listening to it Abby felt a chill spread up her skin. At night, she dreamed of the Devil in the painting creeping through the room with his arms outstretched.

She woke in a silent scream. Someone really was in the room. A hand brushed her face. Breath caught in her throat and she flailed desperately, pushing the arm away.

'For God's sake, Dad, what are you doing creeping about like a pervert?' shouted Philippa.

Abby pressed herself against the wall, catching her breath, waiting for her heart to stop jabbering. Alan, it was only Alan.

'Nothing. For God's sake, I wasn't doing anything. Just checking she was all right. I think she was having a bad dream.'

Sue's voice from the loggia was icy. 'I should imagine she was fine before you came in and frightened the life out of her.'

'God, he gets weirder every day,' muttered Philippa after her parents had left. She rolled over and seemed to fall instantly asleep.

Abby lay in the dark with her eyes open. At least it confirmed the identity of the night visitor, but it also made Philippa's theory about Alan being Abby's father harder to dismiss.

Chapter Twenty-Two

'You mentioned a trip to town at the end of last session,' said Connal. 'Was there something about that day? Why do you think it had such significance?'

'Because of what Philippa said and what happened later.'

'Do you think those two things are related?'

'I suppose so. I haven't really thought about it before.'

'I'd like to take you back there.'

'All right.'

She was running down wide, paved streets with elegant, scrolled window grilles, stone steps, and enormous dark doors with lion head knockers and carved stone faces above. Some of the doors were open, and as she ran past she glimpsed courtyards with loggias and lemon trees, sometimes even a fountain. She recognised it as the place she had been to on occasions with Sue when she had to go to the bank.

Now she was in a long, winding lane of shops. Every so often she would stop, waiting for the others to catch up, her attention caught by beautifully dressed mannequins in one window, elegant shoes in another. The aromas of fresh coffee, leather, beeswax, and perfume permeated the street.

Now she was chasing pigeons across a wide, empty square, dipping her hands into a huge fountain adorned with stone, carved lion heads, weaving her way through antiques stalls and climbing a clock tower up and up to the top, looking out over old terracotta roofs framed by mountains.

They ate ice creams, sitting on the wide, marble steps of a church, pigeons scratching around their feet. Heels echoed across the stone flags of the square. An occasional bicycle wheeled through.

A young woman passed them pushing a pram that contained a plump baby, cocooned in a padded anorak with a huge, fur-trimmed Eskimo hood, and several layers of blankets. Its eyes were open, staring upwards at the sky in that unfocussed way babies do, blinking, its lips working as though it was about to say something but producing a large bubble instead.

The woman parked the baby outside a shop that was far too small for the pram. They could hear her greeting the assistant warmly. She was in there for a long time, and the women's laughter, surprise, and remonstrations filled the air.

The shop window was full of exquisitely-made children's clothes and shoes. Every now and then the baby's padded, mittened arms raised and then lowered as though batting away a fly. Abby was getting bored now and impatient to move on.

'I dare you to take it,' whispered Philippa. Her eyes were alight with excitement.

There was just a moment when Abby thought she was being serious.

'*Okay* – I was joking.'

They went into the shop, although Abby really couldn't see the point. Philippa held up a pair of tiny shoes and laughed at their tiny, intricate design, measuring them up against her hand. She looked over at the baby a few times and Abby started to get nervous, but then the mother left the shop clutching a bag full of purchases. She stuck them under the pram, gave Philippa a suspicious look, and pushed it away.

The shop owner asked the girls if they were going to buy anything. Without waiting for an answer, she shooed them out.

Back at the villa, Philippa pulled a small parcel out of her jacket pocket.

'Souvenir,' she said, catching Abby looking at her.

Grabbing the bag, Abby glimpsed the little shoes.

'You took them.'

She acted as though she hadn't heard.

That was when the stealing really started to take hold. She never took big, expensive, or even useful items. Just little ones she could fit in her pocket or, on one or two occasions, Abby's backpack. It seemed to be the challenge of getting away with it that appealed to her far more than the items themselves. She kept her little trophies in a box in the little stone tower, where in the past chestnuts had been stored to make into flour. Now and then she would lay them out in front of her on the floor and look at them.

All were small and pretty, from an eraser shaped like an apple to a soap in the shape of a heart, which smelled of strawberries. Although Abby knew it was wrong, she found herself rationalising and excusing Philippa's behaviour.

It probably had something to do with the fact that they never seemed to have anything new. Sue was a firm believer in re-using and recycling, and Abby assumed that they must be very poor. All their clothes were jumble shop finds or from the market in town. They were made to last as long as possible – worn knees were patched, and skirts and jeans were chopped off to make pedal pushers.

On her birthday, they gave her a very used-looking shoulder bag. When she opened it up, she saw that the lining was torn and there was an ink stain in the corner. She had shut it hurriedly and tried hard to look pleased. Perhaps Philippa just liked the idea of things that were new and unused.

In her notebook, Abby drew pictures of all the items.

***

'Present for you.'

Philippa dropped something wrapped in tissue into her lap. As she opened it, a shooting star-shaped pendant fell out. She fed the gold chain through her fingers. There was a diamond on each of the three strands of the tail, which sparkled as they caught the light. She didn't have much experience of jewellery but this looked a very expensive piece.

'It's beautiful. Can I really have it? No, you keep it.'

'It's okay – that's only half. I've got one, too,' Philippa replied, and held up a matching pendant. 'Look, they join together here. Best friends forever, right?'

Abby didn't have to ask how she had got them. She put hers on, but wore it under her t-shirt. A growing sense of unease told her that Philippa's behaviour was going to land them both in trouble one day.

Chapter Twenty-Three

The school phoned. Lucy's had an accident. She's been taken to hospital. Can you go straight there?

Getting into the car outside Connal's, she checked her phone. The screen lit up with texts from James.

Are you getting my messages? I've cancelled my meeting this afternoon but it will take me a while to get up there. Are you on your way?

I'm on the train. Where are you?

There were voice messages, too. 'I'm sure it's nothing to worry about,' James's calm, reassuring tone betrayed just a note of fear.

Her fingers shook as she pressed the numbers. No reply from James's phone.

She rang the school. The receptionist sounded relieved. 'Mrs Fenton, we've been trying to call you. Your husband's on his way from London. Lucy fell off some play equipment. She had a little bump on the head. Miss Baker took her to A&E as a precaution. We thought it better to be on the safe side.'

Abby's heart lurched as she drove the seventy miles back from Connal's. She parked the car and ran down the long corridors. A bump on the head could mean all sorts of things.

But when she got there, Lucy was sitting up in bed, absorbed in a story James was reading her.

'Ah, here's Mum,' he said, getting out of his chair. 'Told you she wouldn't be long.'

Abby bit back tears as she squeezed her daughter to her, kissing her head and then examining it. Lucy suddenly seemed so small and fragile.

'Are you all right? How did it happen?'

'No lasting damage,' said James. 'They did a scan to be on the safe side. They thought she might have had a slight fit. They've kept her in for observation, but we're hoping she'll be discharged when the consultant comes back.'

'A fit? Before or after the fall? How long did it last? How did she fall? What was she doing before? What was she like afterwards?' Abby couldn't stop the questions.

Lucy related the accident with pride – she'd been hanging upside down from the bar and slipped. The whole school had seen her go off in the ambulance.

'Dad bought me this book,' she said.

Abby stared in disbelief. She reached for it slowly, running her fingers over the cover, trying to control the trembling.

'It was left on our step, for some reason,' James said. 'Hal Storm. I used to love these stories, didn't you? You sit here, I'll get us a coffee.'

Left on the step – that meant Mina knew where they lived. She must have come to the house. Abby's stomach tightened. She had felt relatively safe at the surgery, knowing there were people around, but Mina coming to the house was a different matter. What if she hadn't found it empty? The thought of Mina tricking the childminder, worming her way into their home, going through their things, sent a swirl of panic through Abby. What if one of the children had answered the door?

She lifted the cover. Published in 1994. She stared at the date. That wasn't possible, though, was it? Alan couldn't have written this book, not if he had died at Villa Leonida in 1992 on that last evening, as she had supposed; not if his was the second body.

Looking at Alan's picture, she was reminded of how different he had looked from his author picture. She remembered the way he had watched her during meals, his frustration when he couldn't get her to speak. For a while she had been convinced by Philippa's theory but it seemed ridiculous now. But if he had survived, where was he now?

139

Was it possible *he* had left the book?

James came back with the coffees. A nurse came round and they moved aside to let her do some checks.

'Where were you?' said James in a low voice. 'I thought you'd be at the surgery.'

'I was on a visit.'

She caught the look of suspicion in his eyes. 'Reception told me you weren't working today.'

She felt herself go red. 'No, that's right. I was just following up on some things from the other day.'

He seemed to accept it or at least he didn't ask anything else, which she managed to convince herself meant the same thing. When Lucy was eventually discharged, they drove back in Abby's car, James having travelled by train. Lucy was sleeping in her car seat at the back, snuggled under James's jacket.

Abby's phone lit up. She reached for it but James got there first. He frowned.

'Connal. Says he hopes Lucy's all right. Can't see you tomorrow, how about Thursday?'

She kept her eyes on the road. 'Thanks.'

After a pause, he said, 'That wouldn't be Connal Emsworthy?'

'Yes.'

'I see. I didn't realise you were still in contact.'

She shrugged. 'I saw him at that mental health conference recently.'

She tried to change the subject but he said, 'You didn't say.'

'Didn't I?'

After a long silence in which she concentrated on the road and he appeared to be looking out of the window, he said, 'Should I be worried?'

'What about?'

'You seeing Connal.'

She was ashamed of herself for trying the old line. 'Of course not. Why? If I didn't know you better, I'd think you were jealous.'

He bristled. 'Not jealous, no. But given the fact you've been behaving oddly…'

Her heart beat a little faster. 'Have I?'

'Yes. The money. And you jump at every sound, you drop things, you burned dinner the other day. And now it turns out you've been spending the day with your ex which you hadn't mentioned – in fact, I'd say you'd gone out of your way to hide it.'

She closed her eyes. 'You have absolutely nothing to worry about. I'm sorry. Please but you have to trust me on this.'

'I do trust you.'

She wished she could believe him. But he'd said it as though he was trying to convince himself as much as her. If only she could put his mind at rest; it was so unnecessary for him to worry. But she couldn't explain her meetings with Connal without telling him the reason.

In the middle of the night, she lay awake, pressed up against his warm body. She could tell him now, her lips against his skin, and whisper it in the darkness. But it wouldn't do any good.

Chapter Twenty-Four

Abby opened the windows and pushed back the shutters before Philippa was awake. The air was still cold and smelled of wet foliage, geraniums, and raw mist. A gauze of cloud hung over the valley below, muffling the toll of the church bell. The trees glittered with raindrops as the first smudges of light seeped into the sky. Somewhere in the distance, a car rumbled.

Looking down, she noticed two figures sauntering back along the track that led to the front of the house, their silhouettes smudged against the soft, diffused light. As they came nearer, she saw that it was Sue with Marco the builder, Sue having done her usual spot of gardening before the sun got too hot.

There was something in the way they walked so close together that made Abby think they were holding hands, although it was impossible to see from that distance. Certainly, Sue rested her head on his shoulder for a moment when they were laughing about something.

She found herself exploring the possibility that they were having an affair, but she couldn't seriously believe that they would be conducting this relationship so blatantly so close to their families. It must be just another of Sue's flirtations. But still, there was something, a shadowy understanding she couldn't quite ignore.

At a muffled groan from Philippa, she slammed the shutters closed and went back to her bed, getting out her notebook and drawing a scene of two figures holding hands on the track, with the chestnut tower behind them.

'What do you write in that thing?' Philippa asked, propping herself up on one elbow.

She felt herself colour. 'Nothing.'

She slid it under her pillow but Philippa flopped back, flinging an arm over her face. 'It's all right, I'm not going to read it. I doubt it's that interesting, anyway.'

She found herself squashing down the thought that Philippa's respect for her privacy might have something to do with lack of interest. Philippa didn't seem to care that much about anyone, not even herself, and yet strangely enough that seemed to make people try harder to please her. Should Abby test out her theory about Sue and Março? It was tempting, but remembering how Philippa had reacted to her mother's behaviour in the bar, perhaps it would be better to keep quiet about that.

***

'What's this?' The cheque in Mina's hands fluttered in the breeze that played across the park.

It had been Abby's suggestion to meet in the gardens – somewhere they wouldn't be easily overheard, but where they were visible in case Mina turned violent. It was clear her emotional state was fragile; Abby couldn't risk her coming to the surgery again.

For five glorious minutes when she arrived, she had thought perhaps Mina wasn't coming after all. But then she'd seen her, a forlorn-looking figure in a bulky parka and ill-fitting trousers, with her belongings stuffed into a carrier bag, and she'd felt a pang of sympathy. Nonetheless, her hand had closed around her mobile phone inside her pocket.

'It's the best I can do. Take it or leave it but there won't be any more.'

Mina didn't lift her eyes from the cheque. 'Is this all you think my sister was worth?'

Abby kept her breathing steady. She was prepared for this. 'No, but I'm not going to confess to something I didn't do. At least, not in the way you're suggesting. I don't deny I was there and I take some responsibility for what led up to Philippa's death, but you can't blame me for everything. It's impossible to say if it was you or me who killed her, and either way it was an accident. If you want to drag us both through the court then go ahead. But you can't accuse me without implicating yourself, and then your dream of running a teashop by the sea will never happen.'

Mina thought about this for a moment but she wasn't going to be put off.

'It's not enough.'

'Enough to get you started.' She spread some papers in front of her on the bench. 'You could buy any of these – seaside café in Weston-Super-Mare, coffee shop and cake place in Sidmouth, vintage teashop in Hove, sea view sandwich shop, Scarborough. ...They've all got accommodation. This one's even got a forecourt with a canopy for a few tables outside.

'I'm sure you've done your research on setting up a teashop, but I thought this book might be useful. You'll need a business model based on the number of covers, the start-up costs, business rates, energy cost estimates... and you'll have to organise some food hygiene training.'

Mina glanced at the printouts then shoved them back at Abby. 'Where's the rest of the money?'

'I'm sorry but it's the best I can do.'

A couple walked past arm-in-arm. Some teenagers shot through on skates.

Mina's voice shook. 'All these years I've carried the burden. It's your turn. All I want is to take some of it off my shoulders and put it onto yours.'

Abby wrapped her arms around herself. 'You're wrong, you know, if you think it didn't affect me.'

Those weeks after she'd come back to England, she'd drifted in and out of fever, waking screaming from nightmares. Her father had held her, shushed her, and promised everything would be okay, but then the dreams weren't about what he thought they were. She'd wanted to tell him. Her throat had hurt from the effort of keeping the words in, but after a while she had sunk further and further back into that silent world because how could she speak

144

about trivial things when she might let out something so terrible, so enormous?

In the months that followed, when she had stopped eating, everyone had thought she was still reacting to her mother's suicide and probably that had been bound up with it all. One doctor had talked about post-traumatic stress disorder, another diagnosed it as ME. They all thought they understood. She'd spent most of that next term off school, barely able to make it up and down the stairs.

'And gradually I did bury it at the back of my mind, but only because I had to in order to function.'

The truth was she'd been so scared of being dragged back into that dark pit where thoughts built up, crackling like electricity in her brain, threatening to explode at any moment. The only way to stay sane had been to shut it all away and focus a hundred percent on her studies, cramming her mind with information, leaving no room for other thoughts

So, when her aunt had written to her father a few months after she got back to England saying the family had moved on to Greece except for Philippa, who had gone travelling in India with her boyfriend, she had almost believed it.

When she heard Mina was coming back to England to go to a boarding school in Derbyshire, she had freaked out, stopped breathing. But still the connection hadn't been made and she had rammed those memories further still into that dark place in her head where she thought she would never have to see them, and nailed the lid down.

She could have told Mina she had been free to rebuild her life just as Abby had. That if she had married a man who turned to alcohol when his business went down and subjected her to mental cruelty, much as her father had done, that had at least been her choice – but she knew it wouldn't help.

She had heard about the self-harm and the suicide attempts. And she also knew that Mina had attacked a nurse while on a cocktail of drugs, leaving her with brain damage. But none of this was Abby's fault. At least, she had never thought so. Of course, she felt sorry for Mina – how could she not, after all she'd gone through? But it didn't mean she was going to ruin her life for her.

'It's not enough,' repeated Mina. 'I want something else.'

Abby held her breath. 'What?'

'I'll let you know.'

She watched her stride across the grass to the bus stop and tried to compose herself. She must get back to the surgery, but her limbs felt like they had concrete poured into them.

Chapter Twenty-Five

The storm only cooled the temperature by a couple of degrees and she often woke early as the sun beat through the roof. The whine of the mosquitoes drove her under the sheets, and the smell of the paint was giving her a headache and a dry throat.

Eventually she slipped out, leaving Philippa asleep. Creeping down the external steps, she went into the house for a glass of water. But before she opened the door, which was always left on the latch, she heard raised, muffled voices in the kitchen. She hovered outside, wondering whether to wait for the argument to blow over, or slip away. It seemed to be Alan doing most of the shouting. He was clearly very angry about something. The other voice was Sue's. She was trying to calm him. Every now and then she would shout, too, letting forth a volley of equally vicious expletives.

A scream followed by a crash as something, probably a plate, hit a wall. Another scream and then the splintering of china or glass. Abby froze. She turned to go, but before she could do so, the door flew open and Alan stood there glaring at her. She shrank back against the wall as he pushed past her.

'So, that's how I know, you stupid bitch,' he called back at Sue.

Sue sat at the table, very straight, with her back to Abby. She bent slowly to pick up the pieces of smashed crockery. Abby was about to go and help her but, realising her aunt was trying to conceal her tears, she felt embarrassed and just stood awkwardly in the doorway, watching her. Eventually Sue pushed past her out of the room, leaving her feeling useless.

A piece of paper fell from her pocket as she went out of the door. Abby watched as it was buoyed up for a moment by the draught as the door closed and then floated slowly to the floor. She picked it up and was about to go after her aunt with it, but thinking it might just be rubbish, she opened it out. A blush crept over her as she read it.

It was part of a letter, written in English. Her heart beat fast as she realised that this must have been the cause of the argument and was something she definitely shouldn't be reading. At first, she thought Alan must have written it, but as she read on it was clear that it had been written by a much younger person.

...I will never agree with you that you are doing the right thing so don't ask me to forgive you. Those bastards have twisted everything and made it sound like you corrupted me, but we both know that's not true. You know that age and maturity are two different things – you've told me often enough.

She stopped. So, Sue had been having an affair with someone younger than herself. Much younger, by the look of things.

You've always said you can't compare me with other people my age. I don't think like them and I don't enjoy being with them, because they are so one-dimensional compared to you. Everyone seems one-dimensional compared to you. You've taught me so much – in every *way!*

It must have been one of her pupils. He must be mad. How could a boy of presumably sixteen or seventeen ever want to go to bed with a woman in her forties, or vice versa? It was ridiculous but he clearly found her attractive, like so many other men. Perhaps it had made him feel important.

You should see the old bag that's replaced you. No danger of her corrupting anyone!

You talk about needing 'a new start' with your husband, but I don't believe that going away will change your feelings. I know that mine will never change for you, no matter where you are. I beg you not to leave things like this. You've ruined my life…

There were some more lines that made her blush and feel sick. So, that was why they had left the country. To save Sue from being arrested.

A noise from outside made her jump. She couldn't stand there reading the letter. Anyone could come in at any moment, and having it in her possession made her feel ashamed, as though she was part of it. She looked around to see if there were any others but there weren't. Sue would come back to look for the missing page. Stuffing it in her pocket, she slipped outside.

Philippa was still asleep when she crept back into bed. Abby lay in the dark with the shutters closed, heart thumping, trying to make sense of what she'd discovered. The letter explained why Sue had agreed so readily to Alan's idea of moving abroad. At best, she would have lost her job. At worst, what? Prison? Not to mention the scandal. She must have held onto this letter for a long time and Alan had found it.

The letter writer had signed himself Josh. She had heard that name. Philippa had talked about Josh, the boy she hadn't been given the chance to say goodbye to before they left the country. 'My boyfriend. And hers.' Ouch, that must have hurt. But why, how, could Sue do that to her own daughter?

She looked across at Philippa. So, she had been telling the truth that time; had she also been telling the truth about other things?

What would happen now that Alan knew? Would he throw Sue out? Where would she go? She couldn't go back to England and she didn't have any money. They seemed to be stuck with each other. Adults were a mystery. Why did they have to make their lives so complicated?

Had Sue had other affairs? She thought about that morning, seeing her with Marco. That would explain why Alan watched her so obsessively, and possibly also Mina's bewildered inability to win his affection. He swung between taunting and ignoring her, masking his pain with contempt, his doubts dripping a slow poison into the house. Once Abby had heard him refer to Mina as a cuckoo. She suddenly had an idea of what that might mean.

Chapter Twenty-Six

'Whose idea was it to go back that second summer?' asked Connal.

'It was mine. I suggested it. I asked if I could go.'

She hadn't wanted to say it but it was the truth.

'Is that why you blame yourself for what happened?'

She felt the tears slide down her face. 'If I hadn't gone back, if I hadn't been there, she would still be alive.'

'How can you be sure?'

But the words stuck in her throat. She stood up. 'I want to stop this now.'

She had driven the memory back into its box.

'That's fine, we don't have to talk about it today. Do you want to continue with something else?'

She stood halfway across the room. She looked back at him. He lifted his face away from his hand. 'Why do you want to stop?'

'I'm not ready. I thought I was but I'm not.'

He didn't argue. She could walk out now and forget the whole thing. Except, of course, she never would forget it. Slowly, she crossed back to the chesterfield and sat down.

'Last session, you mentioned a secret you kept for Philippa. Can we talk about that?'

***

Returning to Villa Leonida a year later, she found many things had changed. She had been both nervous and excited for weeks about going back. A year of speech therapy, transferring to a new school, and getting good results for her work, had improved her self-confidence although she still felt panicky and tongue-tied in many situations. That summer at Villa Leonida had changed her, made her see herself more positively, made her believe in the future. If someone as cool and exciting as Philippa enjoyed her company, why shouldn't others? However much she tried to forget it, the villa kept drawing her back.

And Philippa's letters had made her even more determined. *You must come. I'm so bored! We're going to have so much fun.*

Abby had written back, updating her on the speech therapy progress. *In the first sessions, I didn't have to try and speak. We just did games and I pointed at things and chose between different colours or words. This term, she brought in some puppets – they're cute, it's like being little again. She asks questions and I make them nod or shake their head. She wants me to make them squeak but I can't. My hand just freezes.*

To reduce the stress, the therapist had invited her to bring along a 'safe person' to the sessions.

I wish you were here – you could be my 'safe person'. But it's nice having Dad there without Mel – a bit like the old days.

Gradually, she had progressed from squeaking the puppet to whispering answers into her father's ear. Then to whispering the answer to him from further away, and eventually whispering to the speech therapist but while still looking at her father.

I said a word in class today.

But it was still a rare occurrence and her body tensed up and resisted just as if she had been asked to run through a burning building. Yet with Philippa, it had seemed so natural, and she'd thought if she could only get back to Italy it would be so much easier. She could feel normal again.

Abby enjoyed the train ride from the airport, cutting through the mountains, emerging from dark tunnels into brilliant sunshine, seeing the little villages perched on top of hills like magical kingdoms, the majestic bridges that spanned the river, and the now-familiar towers and statues.

Her fears about seeing Mina again seemed unfounded. Mina seemed a different person not only in appearance – she was taller and heavier – but she seemed happier, too, and easier to get on with. It was a surprise to see her wolfing down a giant-sized packet of crisps on the train when she had dutifully stuck to her mother's raw vegetables regime last time.

But she also seemed more relaxed, less suspicious. Abby's voice still stuck in her throat but Mina didn't seem to take it personally any more, just saw it as an eccentricity. Perhaps she had forgotten that nonsense about Alan being Abby's father. Perhaps she had spoken to him about it and he had reassured her that it was a figment of Philippa's vivid imagination. Or perhaps she'd just grown up.

Abby had been over it many times back in England. Occasionally, when Dad and Mel were angry with her, she thought it was true and she was glad about it. She was nothing to do with either of them and they had no right to control her life. But most of the time it seemed ridiculous.

It was Mina who spoke most on the journey, regaling Abby with tales of friends she had made and things they had done. Joining a school must have helped her confidence. In any case, it must have helped to escape the stifling atmosphere at the villa. Her laugh was loud and infectious, and at one point she laughed so much that tears streamed down her cheeks, reminding Abby of how Philippa used to be.

Abby found herself smiling although she didn't always know why, because much of the story was lost among the laughter. Philippa sat back languidly, her golden arm resting on the window shelf, her eyes hidden behind sunglasses, but now and then Abby thought she might be looking at her.

'She's dreaming about her boyfriend,' Mina said, nudging Abby with a giggle. 'The lovely Luca.'

It felt like being punched in the stomach. Why hadn't Philippa said something? All those letters and she hadn't mentioned him once. This wasn't fair. It would change everything. How often did she see this Luca? Would he be hanging round with them all summer? Or would he and Philippa want to be alone together? What was she supposed to do then? How would she be able to speak to Philippa if he was there?

It took a few moments for Abby to realise that the burning sensation inside her was jealousy. She told herself she shouldn't really be surprised – Philippa was beautiful and fun to be with – but she sensed it was more than that. She had changed, moved on, away from their world into a new one that Abby didn't really understand and didn't know how to join.

Philippa smiled at the mention of the boy's name, a slow, deliciously secretive smile, but continued to stare out of the window, refusing to be baited.

Abby couldn't let her thoughts show, so she asked her, 'What does he look like?'

'Gorgeous,' replied Philippa with a slight blush, her smile getting even wider. Then she turned serious. 'You mustn't say anything, Abby. My dad doesn't like him. He's been in a bit of trouble, and you know what dads are like. I always say I'm seeing one of my friends, Alessia or Claudia – or just going out with the group. Do you promise you can keep it secret? I can trust you, can't I?'

Abby nodded. She remembered Alan's volatile temper and she didn't want to see it erupt again. She could keep that and any other secret. She liked being trusted. It went some way to re-building the bond between them.

When the train pulled in, they had cold drinks in the little bar near the station while waiting for the bus. It was warm, much warmer than in England, and Abby was impatient to get back up to the house. She felt uncomfortable in her jeans and hooded top her stepmother had made her wear because it had been chilly that morning.

An elderly woman was sitting there, all hunched up. She came to life when Philippa walked in, fingering her hair and exclaiming again and again in almost reverent tones, 'Bellissima! Bellissima!' and something that sounded like 'Botticelli!'

Mina nodded, laughing, but changed the subject impatiently, and said in English, tapping the side of her head, 'Take no notice of her. She's *pazza*.'

The house looked much the same, despite all the work they had done. But it felt different. The magic had seeped away. Philippa was friendly over the next few days, but Abby saw less of her than she would have liked. She had made a circle of friends from the village who used to get the bus into town with her or out to the coast. Abby met them once and they were nice enough, but she couldn't join in their conversation and they probably got bored of asking her questions. Philippa translated something funny every now and then, but often there wasn't time or the joke was lost in translation. Sometimes Philippa forgot to invite her and Abby hung around the house not knowing what to do with herself.

On one of those lazy days during the first holiday, Philippa had asked her to write home and say she wouldn't be coming back. She never said things like that now. Because that Philippa had gone. She was as good as dead.

The heat was worse than Abby remembered. It slunk through the house, climbing up the walls and spilling into every corner, bringing with it a horde of insects – giant ants that crept along the beams and fell onto the bed while you slept; red-backed flies that nested in the shutters and were released in a cloud when you opened them; wasps as long as Abby's little finger; and millipedes that looked like the rubber ones you found in joke shops.

But at least Alan's temper seemed to have improved. He had started writing again, introducing a new character, which opened up a whole new world of possibilities and challenges for the young hero. He still used to shut himself away for long periods, but this summer he emerged in a better mood than when he went in. Mina disappeared with him, a self-important smirk on her face, as though she was dying to be asked what the book was about. Abby never asked.

When Philippa wasn't around, Abby assumed she must

155

be seeing her boyfriend so got used to shrugging or looking blank when anyone asked where she was.

Late at night, Philippa told her in whispers about Luca – what they did and what it felt like. She was lying again, wasn't she? She surely didn't let him do *that* to her? Things Abby had heard about and giggled about, but only half believed anyone really did. And Philippa said she did things to him, too. She said 'for him'. It was sickening.

Yet Abby couldn't stop asking the questions, even though she hated hearing the answers. Perhaps that was why she needed to hear them, so she wouldn't care any more. She was glad that the room was completely dark with the shutters closed, because Philippa couldn't see when she blushed or grimaced. But the one good thing about it all was that she was the only one Philippa trusted enough to share her true feelings with. When you thought about it, even Luca probably didn't really know Philippa, not like Abby did. Her true thoughts about him, for example.

'But why?' she found herself asking one too many times.

Philippa snorted in exasperation and turned over. 'Oh God, Abby. You just don't get it, do you?'

***

The heat ratcheted up each day. There was no way to get cool, to avoid getting on each other's nerves. Once, when Abby asked Philippa what she fancied doing that day, she turned round and shouted,

'For fuck's sake, I don't know. Can't you entertain yourself for once?'

It sunk in, how Philippa saw her – a parasite that she was constantly trying to shake off. Things were so different this summer from how she had thought they would be.

'Don't take it personally,' said Mina, coming up behind her. 'It's what she does.'

She blushed, remembering the way they had dodged Mina last summer. Now she was getting the same treatment. But there had to be a way to win back Philippa's affection.

Chapter Twenty-Seven

Philippa wasn't as passionate about anything now. She was quieter, deflated. It was as if this Luca had sucked all the life out of her. Abby wasn't sure she really knew her any more.

Philippa spent most of the time away from the house, and when she was there she seemed like a ghost of herself. Where she had rarely been still the previous summer, always restless to walk down into the village and spend some money in the bar, hang around the pool, or do daredevil stunts like freewheeling down the steep terraces on her bicycle, she was now often moody, retreating into herself.

She had taken to spending days alone in the chestnut drying tower, which she had turned into a den using the old furniture from the house that had been stored there. On rare occasions, she invited Abby and even Mina in.

'Look at this old trunk – it's full of vintage clothes. Aren't they amazing?'

Seeing Philippa dressed up as an empress or film star, strutting about, commanding her subjects, Abby saw a little of her old spark back. But at other times, she seemed to have forgotten who she was and Abby never knew how she would be greeted. The door would be firmly shut, and if she caught sight of you she would shout, 'Sod off, can't you? Leave me alone.'

Her parents didn't seem to have noticed her changed manner, but then they had problems of their own. Perhaps it was all part of growing up, being a teenager. But she wouldn't be like this if it wasn't for Luca. If only Philippa had never met him. If only he didn't exist. Perhaps he would have an accident, get a terrible disease. Abby found herself fantasising about it all coming to an end, imagined watching the two of them from the loggia, saw herself picking up the blue glazed pot and dropping it on him, crushing his skull, stamping him out. She gripped her head. How had she allowed herself to think that?

***

'I don't think that was the main secret though, was it? Why can't you talk about the other one?'

'Maybe I will, just not yet.'

'What about Sue? In the trance just now, you said you kept a secret for her, too.'

'Sue. Yes. I didn't mean to blackmail her. It just happened.'

***

She had been sitting outside on the steps of the loggia, drawing a picture, her pens and paper spread out around her. The sun warmed her arms and knees as she wrote her story, complete with illustrations, about a woman who lived in the castle above them, and a pact she made with the Devil.

She'd like to have spent the day with Philippa, but when she had gone to join her Philippa had turned and shouted, 'Fuck off. Why do you have to follow me everywhere?'

She could have gone with Mina and some others to the waterfall, but they had gone on ahead too fast and she had sulked and decided to wander back. A breeze furled the corners of her paper, so she found a selection of small stones to weigh it down. Needing more space to spread out her work, she moved up a few steps to the loggia where there was ample room on the stone table.

She heard a muffled noise from inside the house. It sounded like laughter, and then there were cries. In the heat of the afternoon, the windows were open as usual although the slatted shutters were closed. Thinking that everyone had gone out, Abby was curious. Perhaps an animal had got trapped in the house. She crept along the loggia and stood outside the window, listening.

After a few moments, it became obvious what she was actually hearing. Through the gap in the shutters, she caught sight of a pair of naked buttocks pounding up and down, and a pair of female legs stuck in the air, juddering. She caught a glimpse of a breast like a fried egg, a flash of dark pubic hair, and then the buttocks disappeared and there was a head between the legs.

Abby stood there transfixed. She knew what sex was, of course, but she hadn't expected it to be so primal. To her horror, she realised Sue's eyes were open and they were staring directly back at her, wide in shock. She backed away, bumping into a blue glazed planter, grazing her shin as she did so. The planter grated on the tiles as it shifted. There was a moment's silence from inside the bedroom. Someone stuck his head out of the window, shouting what sounded like a volley of abuse at her in Italian.

It was Marco.

Behind him, she saw Sue dart out of view, clutching a sheet around her, although she had nothing left to hide. As Abby slipped down the stone steps, she heard him laugh and say something like, 'What's the problem? She's not going to tell, is she? She doesn't speak.'

But Sue sounded angry. 'She does when it bloody suits her.'

Abby could feel her heart pounding as she walked on through the trees, still clutching her notebook, throwing herself down on one of the grassy terraces and hugging her knees.

Her face burned. She felt embarrassed, stupid, but also angry that Sue had not made more of an effort to conceal this affair. It made Abby look as though she had been snooping, but how was she to know what was going on?

She opened the notebook and doodled over and over again. Two cartoon figures having sex, one with Marco's ponytail and tattoos, and the other with Sue's cloisonné cat earrings. At last, she tossed the notebook down and stomped up the overgrown path, not knowing where she was going except away.

Chapter Twenty-Eight

She went as fast as she dared, while being careful of the dry, dusty mud that suddenly gave way beneath her feet, showering down onto the ledge below, making the pathway ever narrower, and scrambled her way to the lane at the top.

The thought that nobody on earth knew where she was at this precise moment was liberating. She set off up the lane, looking down on a cluster of houses, most of them boarded up and used only at weekends, and up onto the ridge that gave fantastic views of either side of the valley. The land plunged steeply away here, revealing little waterfalls, and a river meandering its way far below; tiny villages, some of which she could identify; dark, cool forests of acacia trees; and the sea.

She walked quickly, trying to erase the images from her head. She had come this way with Philippa once, trying to find an old tower that someone had mentioned, but they had given up before they reached it. Now she thought she would keep going until she got there.

It was ironic that for all Philippa's conjecturing, she had failed to pick up on this affair. Abby would like to have spoken to her about what she had seen, but it was difficult enough to talk to Philippa about trivial things these days.

The snake appeared out of nowhere, rearing up and hissing, its long tongue quivering. She screamed and jumped out of the way, then tore back along the path. She didn't look behind her but she was certain that she could hear it sliding steadily behind her, waiting to stab.

She grabbed one of the acacia trees as she ran. One of its vicious thorns dug deep into her hand but she didn't dare stop and pull it out, so she ran on with it hanging from her.

All the time she was thinking of Philippa's cheery warning that you only had thirty minutes to get to a hospital if you were bitten by a viper, and it took more than that to get to the town.

She remembered that nobody had any idea where she was and there would be no reason for them to look for her here. The old man inspecting his beehives further along the path shot out when he heard her screaming and caught her as she ran. He spoke to her in a flurry of language she did not understand, but she was able to communicate with hand gestures about the snake.

He nodded and shrugged. He inspected her hand, which was bleeding from the thorn and gently pulled it out for her. He then offered to take her home. She knew the word 'casa' but couldn't reply other than to point. He put down his tools and walked with her, reassuring her as far as she could tell that snakes were shy and rarely bit, but she was still shaking.

As they neared the house, he stopped. '*Là*?' he asked. 'La Villa Leonida?' When she nodded, he simply shook his head and said something she didn't understand. He seemed to be saying that he wouldn't come any further, asking if she would be okay from here.

Feeling embarrassed for having been so upset, and also mystified as to his sudden reticence, Abby mouthed a shy 'grazie' and negotiated the last path herself, into the garden of the house.

***

She didn't look at Sue during the evening meal, but she felt Sue looking at her. Surely she wasn't going to say anything? What was there to say? It wasn't as if she'd seen them on purpose.

It had been a shock, certainly, but Abby already knew Sue wasn't above having a fling, and a good-looking builder seemed a better choice than a schoolboy like last time.

She thought of Marco stacking the tiles on the ground

outside the kitchen as he dug them up, his naked back bronzed by a life working outdoors and glistening with sweat, his arms muscular from hard physical work. She thought of his buttocks as she had seen them that afternoon, the way they had been pummelling up and down, those dents at each side and the dark hairs on his thighs.

She could see why Sue would choose him over Alan – anyone over Alan, really. She turned her eyes to her uncle, watched him slurp his spaghetti – bits of the sauce clinging to his beard – and felt almost sorry for him, but he gave her such a hard stare in return her sympathy turned to disdain. He tried to suppress a belch, but was a fraction too late and Abby could smell the sauce and beer on his breath.

When Mina got up to leave, Abby hurried away, too. She avoided Sue as much as she could, but inevitably the moment came. Sue cornered her in the kitchen after a meal.

'Abby, about the other day… I don't know exactly what you saw but I wouldn't want you to get the wrong idea. I know I can trust you not to go telling other people. They could get badly hurt.'

Abby wasn't sure what she was asking. She had no doubt about what she had seen, but did Sue really want her to spell it out? She must say something; she didn't want to be sent home and lose Philippa. She tried several times to speak, remembering the exercises the speech therapist had taught her. At last it came out in a squeaky whisper.

'What will you do if I tell?'

After all, it was better to be in possession of the facts. But Sue seemed to interpret her question differently.

'I see,' she said quietly, nodding. The look she gave Abby made her shrink inside but she held her aunt's gaze. Sue's manner was intimidating, but Abby reasoned that this was probably borne of desperation. She noticed the deep line between her aunt's eyes that made her look tired and sad, and she remembered the smash of crockery during the row over Josh's letter and the bruise on Mina's head.

At last Sue gave a shrug, a snort of impatience or disgust, and said in an icy tone, 'Well, thank you so much,

163

Abby, it's been a real pleasure having you to stay.'

She clearly hadn't meant that. It was annoying when adults didn't say what they meant. It was such a waste of energy having to work it out. For the next few days, Abby was careful to approach closed doors with a certain amount of noise.

The heat crept up another notch. There was a stillness as though the villa was holding its breath. It couldn't go on, surely. If only something would happen to release the pressure – an accident, a forest fire, an earthquake. Why didn't these things happen when you needed them?

'Fancy going down to the swimming pool?' asked Mina.

Abby longed to get away from the confines of the house and plunge into some cold water. But she hadn't brought much spending money and reluctantly had to say no. To her immense surprise, Sue, who was normally so careful with money, slipped some notes into her hand and told her to go and enjoy herself.

'Thanks,' she said uncertainly, not sure if there was some implied deal involved, but decided to take it at face value. As she followed Mina down the hill thirty minutes later, she passed Marco walking up towards the house and realised what it meant.

After that, they visited the pool most afternoons. Surrounded by lush green mountains, the pool with its line of striped sun umbrellas seemed the only sensible place to be, providing an escape from the atmosphere of the house which was becoming increasingly claustrophobic now that she had to be so careful what she said to just about everybody.

At the pool, she could play on the amusement machines or join in a game of table football without needing to speak, because people just assumed she didn't know the language, and lie out on a sun lounger without seeming anti-social. She wondered if she would see Philippa down there with Luca – it would have been quite safe, since neither of her parents ever showed any interest in the pool, and seemed the favourite place for young couples to spend time together.

'Have you ever seen Luca?' she wrote in her notebook and showed it to Mina as they sat eating crisps in the café, watching boys dive off the top board.

Mina shook her head, waving at someone in the distance. 'He doesn't live in the village.'

Abby found herself wondering if he really existed at all, but surely all those things Philippa told her in their night-time chats couldn't be fantasy – and, after all, where else did she go if she wasn't seeing a boy?

Mina didn't seem unduly bothered about her sister spending less time with them. If anything, Philippa's absence had brought her into the limelight. The admirers Philippa had once had now clustered around Mina instead. She was the centre of the group, one of the lads. They chased each other round the sunbeds, pushed each other off the diving board, and ducked each other under the water. As with Philippa, they were drawn to her boldness and her sense of fun, although they perhaps saw her more as one of them whereas Philippa was quite simply a goddess who they worshipped.

At seven o'clock, a strange, gaunt woman with staring eyes shuffled round putting down the umbrellas and folding up the deckchairs.

'She gives me the creeps,' said Mina.

Her claw-like hands gathered up the ice-lolly wrappers, crisp packets, and paper cups from the café tables. She shook her head at the mess people left behind but they never heard her speak. Abby felt sorry for her, but sometimes when she looked up she met the woman's eyes.

It was almost as if she knew – knew something was going to happen.

Chapter Twenty-Nine

Abby's heart dropped as her next patient opened the door. Mina had obviously registered under a different name and this time had an appointment. She could use the panic button, but she wasn't confident it actually worked. Shouting for help would be useless – it would alert the other patients, start gossip; a mad woman the doctor couldn't handle. And what would she say?

'I want a child,' Mina said.

Abby felt her voice harden. 'I told you last time…' She wasn't afraid for her own sake – Mina could do anything she liked to her – but if she hurt the girls…

Her cousin rolled her eyes. 'Not one of yours. I want a baby of my own.'

It was so unexpected it took a few moments to digest.

'All right,' she said slowly. 'Are you asking for my professional help now?'

Her cousin laughed. The smile froze. 'No. I want you to have a baby for me.'

She pressed her curled hand into her forehead. 'I'm sorry, I don't understand.'

'Really? You're the doctor.'

'If you want a baby, why don't you go about it in the normal way?'

Mina laughed. 'I don't have a man. Strangely enough, you don't get many offers when you're eighteen stone and have a mental health record.'

'You could go to a sperm bank.'

'I could, couldn't I? But the sperm isn't the problem. I have an incomplete womb. Makes the chances of a successful birth very slim. That's why I need a surrogate host.'

'I see. I'm sorry. But I don't understand why you're asking me when you don't even like me.'

But she was starting to see. It was punishment.

'Think of it as repaying a debt. For Philippa's baby.'

Abby felt the world closing in. 'I told you before I would do anything to change what happened.'

'Well don't keep saying it. Do it.'

But not this. This was ridiculous. How could Mina even expect her to consider it? It took all her strength to stay calm

'It wouldn't bring Philippa back, would it? It wouldn't be Philippa. It wouldn't be her baby.'

Mina rolled her eyes. 'I'm not stupid. But it's the closest we'll get.'

Snakes writhed in Abby's stomach. The idea of having Mina's baby inside her, Mina inside her, was sickening.

'No. The answer's no. I'm sorry, but I just couldn't do it. For one thing, you'd make a terrible mother. And how would I explain it to James? To the children?'

'That's your problem. I'm sure you'll think of something. Perhaps you can just be honest for once. Say you're helping out a friend.'

'I won't do this.'

Mina stood up. 'Then the deal's off. Think it over.'

All afternoon Abby tried to push it to the back of her mind. She saw a student with probable glandular fever, ordered blood tests for a suspected coeliac, assessed an elderly woman for dementia, sent a young boy to have his finger x-rayed, and referred a middle-aged father to a specialist for suspected bowel cancer. There wasn't time to think about other things. But that evening, as she kissed the girls goodnight, her stomach squeezed. To have another baby inside her – a baby that wasn't hers, Mina's baby – would mean they would be linked forever in the future.

It was unthinkable and yet she couldn't see a way round it.

Chapter Thirty

Abby saw something being lowered into the ground, wrapped in a blanket. As she got closer, she realised what it was. The blanket fell away and she saw the baby's eyes move, just a flicker. Its face screwed up, ready to cry, but it was covered by the next shovel of earth. The hand raised in the air three, four times. The earth shifted, but with each new shovelful it shifted less.

Nobody seemed to notice. She cried out but nobody heard her. She realised she wasn't making any sound. She screamed harder and harder but no sound came. It was that scarf round her neck again. She grabbed it, scrabbling with both hands, but it wouldn't loosen She couldn't make any sound. She tried to push through the people standing around the grave, but they were big and solid as tree trunks and wouldn't let her through. She tugged at their arms and shook them, but still no words would come. They didn't seem to feel her. She was banging on their backs with her fists but nobody turned round, or even acknowledged her.

She sat up, still shaking the image from her head, waiting for the fear to drain away, to feel normal again. The baby looked so real, so lifelike, so unmistakably alive. Could such a terrible thing have actually happened? Of course not. It didn't happen like that. She tried to steady her breathing. But the face – it was his face. She had never forgotten the baby's face.

'All right?' whispered James. He pulled her to him, lifting her leg over his warm body, kissing her sleepily.

She returned his kiss, trying to blot out other thoughts. She must stop. It wasn't a baby's body they had found at the house, it was two adults. And yet it was the baby she thought about mostly. What had happened to him?

If she had stayed, if she'd been brave enough to stay, she would have seen. She could have hidden and watched. She would have seen who lifted him up and checked for any signs of life. Seen whether they pressed him close and gave him a cuddle before laying him gently down again. Or if by some miracle they had found that the baby was alive after all. She would have known all these years what had happened, instead of burying the thought at the back of her mind because that was easier than contemplating the alternative.

***

'We're making progress,' Connal said at the end of another session. He opened the door and then stopped.

'What is it?'

James was standing at the bottom of the steps. She couldn't quite read his expression. 'What's going on?' he asked.

'Nothing. What are you doing here?'

He must have driven like the clappers to get here from London. It was so unlike him. He hated making a scene.

Connal cleared his throat. 'Long time no see,' he said with a forced jollity that made her wince.

James behaved as though he hadn't heard him. 'You said you were at a training day.'

A couple of office workers crossing the car park with takeaway coffees looked up.

'I got the wrong day. Are you following me?'

'I tracked your phone.'

'Why?'

Her heart was thumping. Had Mina told him?

'Why don't you come in?' Connal said at last.

'And catch up on old times? I don't think so, thank you.'

'Look, it's not what you're thinking. She's seeing me in a professional capacity.'

'Is that so? What about?'

'You know I can't tell you that.'

'I was talking to my wife. Who, I presume, can tell me if she chooses.'

The three of them stood in awkward silence for what seemed like ages. Connal looked at his watch. 'Well, I'm sorry, guys, but I have to be somewhere. Come in. Talk. Shut the door when you leave.'

James paced around the room, no doubt looking for evidence of an affair. He picked up a book from the desk, checked inside the desk drawer, then went over to the window and stood resting on the frame looking out.

'Are you all right?' he asked at last, but his voice was still tight.

'I needed to talk through a few things.'

He turned to look at her. 'Are you ill?' A flicker of fear flashed across his face.

'No, it's nothing like that.'

He slumped onto the other end of the chesterfield and rubbed his eyes. 'So, tell me. I'm sorry I blundered in. I'm angry that you lied to me but mostly I'm worried about you. I don't know how there can be something so wrong that you need to see a therapist and yet I know nothing about it. You've told me nothing. So, forgive me if it sounds self-centred, but I can't help wondering if you see me as the problem?'

It was so far from the truth it made her smile. She shook her head, reaching out to touch him, but he remained hunched over, his hands clasped together.

'I am offended that you've chosen to open up to someone you used to be in love with. I'm sure you're managing to keep it strictly professional…'

She felt a stab of annoyance. 'Of course we are.'

'But why him? There must be hundreds of other therapists you could have seen. And why the secrecy?'

She sighed. 'I'm seeing him because he's very good at what he does. And because I trust him.'

'I see. And you don't trust me?'

'You know I do, but it's not like that.'

'So, what is it like? We've always talked about things. What can be so bad you can't discuss it with me?'

Her voice shook as she said as much as she truthfully could. 'I'm under a lot of pressure at the moment; it's all getting on top of me.'

He stared at her in silence, before eventually saying while studying the floor, 'I might not be a professional but I do have an opinion. Do you want to hear it?'

'Of course I do.'

He sat back and took her hand and squeezed it. 'You try too hard. You're working all hours, you're a fantastic mum, but you don't have to be the best at everything. I know I haven't been much help to you lately, I've been busy and stressed and I've said some stupid things, but I'm going to put it all right. I don't want to lose you.'

She took his face in her hands and kissed him. 'That's not going to happen.'

Not if she could help it. Not if she could keep Mina quiet.

Chapter Thirty-One

'Mummy! Can you see me?'

She lifted her head. Sophia was standing on the top level of the soft play equipment. It was Sunday, the girls had had their swimming lessons, and while they were playing Abby and James had stolen a few minutes to drink coffee and read the papers. Since the episode at Connal's he had made a point of setting aside some more time to spend with his family, even though she had told him that wasn't the problem.

She approached the newspapers with a certain amount of trepidation. Negative stories about James were becoming more common now that the honeymoon period was over, and after lengthy negotiations with the teaching unions he was ploughing ahead with his reforms. There had been references to him being pompous and complacent and toeing the party line, and some vicious attacks on social media. But fortunately that morning, other, bigger things were happening in the world.

At one point, she looked up and caught his quizzical smile. 'Have you got something to tell me?'

'I don't know – have I?'

He lowered his voice. 'Something about a baby?'

'Ah.'

Her stomach twisted. Mina must have said something. She hid her hands under the table so that he couldn't see them shaking.

'Well? Is there one? Or did my sister get hold of the wrong end of the stick as usual?'

Of course. Trix. Mother's Day seemed such a long time ago now. She had almost forgotten that Trix thought she was pregnant.

'She did, I'm afraid – there isn't a baby.' She bit her lip. 'Not at the moment.'

He raised his dark brows and said in a bemused tone, 'Not at the moment? I see. Do I get a say in this?'

'I haven't been thinking very seriously.' Her only hope of keeping Mina quiet was to go through with the surrogacy, but she still hadn't come to terms with the idea.

He looked relieved. 'Then can I just say something?' He was obviously struggling to find the right way to put it, 'Look, I didn't want to say this if you were already pregnant. But if there's a choice about it, then I'm not sure it's the best time for us.'

He folded his newspaper over and pushed it aside.

'It's going to be a busy year with these reforms going through and I'm aware we're not spending as much time together as we should. We already have the two most amazing little girls anyone could wish for. That rollercoaster of emotions before Lucy – all the hopes and disappointments – I don't think I could go through that again.'

He drank some of his coffee and gave the thumbs up to Lucy as she ran along the tier above them and dived into the tunnel.

'I'm just loving being with them at the ages they are. I'm not sure I want to go through all the sleepless nights and the nappies and hauling the buggy around again. You said yourself not so long ago that you finally felt you'd got your life back. And, well, you have been finding things a bit tough recently. I don't think a baby would help.'

She nodded. 'You're right, it wouldn't be great timing for us.' She bit her lip. Mina's demand replayed in her head. If she ignored it for too long, the decision would be taken out of her hands. 'But I have been thinking about how lucky we were – what we would have missed out on if we hadn't had them.'

She could hardly believe she was about to say it. 'But I have a friend who's desperate for a child.' She was searching his face, waiting for a reaction. 'She's asked me to consider being a surrogate host.'

The coffee cup froze halfway to James's lips. 'She's asked what?'

'You know – to have a baby for her. With her eggs. It would be nothing to do with me biologically.'

He put the cup down heavily. 'Stop. This is madness. It's a terrible idea. You can't seriously be thinking about it?'

'It's not that uncommon. I've had a couple of patients—'

'But who is she? And why you?' He sat there, taking it in. She could see the panic rising in his face. 'Oh God, she's not another of your patients that you feel responsible for? Are you feeling guilty because you weren't able to arrange IVF for her or something?'

'No, she's a cousin actually. Her name's Mina.'

He looked at her blankly. 'I've never heard of her. Mina – what sort of a name's that?'

'It's short for Jasmina. That's not really the point, though, is it?'

'When did you have this conversation with her? I mean, did you offer or did she ask?'

'She asked, of course.'

'Out of the blue?' His face was screwed up in confusion. 'But why did she come to you? There must be other people, people she's closer to.'

Abby shrugged helplessly. 'Perhaps that was why. I suppose she wanted someone she could trust but also someone who she wasn't going to be bumping into all the time once it was over.'

He started to say something but then stopped. He was still having trouble processing it. Which made her think, if this was how he reacted to knowing about a surrogacy, how much worse would it be if he knew the reason behind it?

She's doing it to punish me for what I did.

He was shaking his head. 'No, I'm sorry, I don't get this. How come I've never heard of Mina?'

There was something more, a hard note of suspicion in his voice, which even his professional training to deal calmly with surprise news, failed to disguise. He wanted to know when the subject had been raised, the exact words Mina had used, the reasons she gave, what Abby had said in return, and what she was expecting to get from it apart from an altruistic glow. He was struggling to keep his voice level.

'Don't you think – sorry, does my opinion even matter to you? Isn't this a decision which will affect all of us?'

'Yes, of course it is, but I haven't even decided what I feel about it yet. I wanted to get my thoughts straight before discussing it with you.'

'Boo!'

Sophia crept round her father's chair. 'Daddy, will you chase us?'

He pulled her up onto his lap. 'In a moment, not just now.' He felt her forehead. 'You're burning hot. Why don't you have a sit-down for a few minutes and have a drink?' He lifted up her hair and blew around her face, making her shriek with laughter.

Under protestation, she gulped some juice, then wriggled off to find a friend. When she was safely out of earshot, he said,

'Have you thought about how it would affect the girls? They wouldn't understand why the baby wasn't staying with us. That's if you were able to give it up. Which I've got to be honest, knowing you, I doubt.'

She smiled involuntarily. That was one thing she was sure of at least. 'It wouldn't be a problem for me.'

He sunk his face into his hands. 'It happens all the time – people think they'll be fine, but when they see the baby, hold it in their arms, they can't let it go.'

He was still working through all the connotations. 'How's that going to look? Everyone would know. The press would spot you were pregnant, they'd be asking about the baby, so we'd have to tell them about the surrogacy…'

'Is that what bothers you? The publicity?'

He looked at her sharply. 'It isn't the main thing, no, but it does matter. You seem to be going out of your way to make things difficult for me at the moment.'

'I'm really not.'

For a few minutes, they didn't look at each other. She flicked through the paper without really registering what was on the pages. He'd obviously been thinking it through, because he suddenly said,

'I'm sorry. Look, I understand why you want to do this. You are such a lovely person, you'd do anything to help others. But you can't save everyone.'

I'm not a lovely person.

'Mummy!' They snapped their heads up. Lucy and Sophia were at the top of the slide. The idea of another child there between them, the shadow of a third child, one she had given birth to but had no right to…

'Doesn't it worry you that you don't know this Mina very well?' James was saying in more measured tone. 'Does she have a partner? How do you know they will be good parents?'

She sighed. 'That isn't really my business.'

'How can you say that? What if he's a drug addict, a wife beater, a paedophile? You'd be responsible for bringing that child into the world. You must care about what sort of home they'd be going into.'

It was hopeless. She was never going to be able to convince him. 'You're right, it was just a thought.'

The relief on his face was clear. 'Promise me you're not going to do this.'

James was obviously happier. For him, the discussion was over, problem solved, another mad moment brushed aside. In a way, she was glad he had reacted that way. He hadn't said anything that hadn't already been running around her head, but hearing it from someone whose judgement she trusted and glimpsing the tensions it would cause between them, reinforced her decision.

But at some point, she'd have to tell Mina it wasn't happening, she wouldn't meet her demand. And there would be consequences.

Chapter Thirty-Two

Abby slid her hand under her mattress to retrieve her notebook from its usual hiding place. It wasn't there. She checked around and under the bed but there was no sign. Something was wrong. She sat trying to visualise exactly what had been on each page. A sick feeling coiled through her.

'Is this what you're looking for?'

Mina stood in the doorway, clutching a ball of screwed-up paper. She started reciting some lines in her familiar, cut-glass tone.

'What are you doing, writing down our conversations verbatim? Are you some sort of spy?'

Abby wasn't sure what *verbatim* meant but didn't want to give Mina the satisfaction of saying so. She just shrugged.

'You're a leech. You suck the life out of everyone and give nothing in return. You live your life through other people's experiences because you're too scared or too useless to do anything yourself.

'And these,' she said, brandishing a page of drawings, 'are disgusting.'

Abby tried to grab the notebook back, but she held them out of her reach.

'You're sick. Why would you want to draw things like that?'

She tore the page up into tiny pieces, letting them fall from her hands onto the ground.

'Have you got any idea what my father would do to my mother if he saw these? You don't know anything about us – anything!' She pushed past and slammed the door, leaving

177

Abby to pick up the pieces and throw them away.

Abby went to find Philippa. She had hardly seen her for days. It was evening, and the air was filled with the sweet smell of freshly chopped wood. The chainsaw whined in the trees. Beyond the chestnut tower, she could see the stack of logs taller than a man. The woodcutter nodded to her and she waved back.

Seeing that the door of the drying tower was open, curiosity got the better of her and she peeped in at the door. She stopped, horrified, trying to make sense of what she saw.

Chapter Thirty-Three

Abby stood still in the doorway of the chestnut tower, watching the pool of blood swim out from under Philippa's body onto the quilt. She had to help, but she had no idea how.

She had seen less and less of her recently, and knew she was spending much of her time in the tower, where Abby had assumed she was meeting Luca. Sometimes she spent the night there, though nobody else seemed to notice.

'Fuck off. Leave me alone!' Philippa screamed, but her words were drowned by the chainsaw starting up again. Her face contorted in pain once more and she rolled into a ball. The next moment she was screaming at Abby to help.

Abby hesitated, meeting her desperate eyes. She made a move, as if to run and fetch someone, but Philippa pleaded with her between gasps.

'Help me,' she begged, and Abby ran to her instead, and let her clutch her hand as she screamed. Was Philippa going to die? Shouldn't she get help? But all Philippa seemed to need at that moment was Abby, and she realised she didn't want to go. She wanted to be there even if it meant watching her die.

'Don't tell anyone,' Philippa said again and again between screams, and Abby reassured her repeatedly that she wouldn't. She let Philippa clutch her as she bore down, making noises that seemed half human, half animal to Abby, as if she were possessed.

After it was over, Abby looked down at the grey, lifeless object that Philippa's body had expelled, which was lying there covered in slime and blood. She was still trying to absorb what had happened and how it could have happened.

There was an eerie silence. Very slowly, Philippa placed some towels over the baby, then sank back. Her hysteria had subsided into quiet, exhausted crying, and Abby, cradling her head as her mother had sometimes done to her, sat quietly and waited for it all to sink in.

She thought she saw the bundle move under the towels and went to pick it up, but Philippa stopped her with surprising force.

'Leave it, Abby. It's dead.'

'It might not…' Abby began, surprised, but Philippa shook her head.

'It's dead. You can see it's dead. It was never meant to live.'

She sat back against the wall, tears falling silently down her exhausted face.

'So stupid. So fucking stupid!' she whispered to herself. And then her voice rising to hysteria, she said, 'Just get it away from me. Cut this thing off.'

She was trying to get hold of the cord, but it was slippery and jumping like a live thing. Abby could barely make herself look.

Philippa said weakly, 'Take the laces out of my trainers and tie them tight. There are some scissors in the trunk.'

Abby fished around for the scissors. The cord had stopped moving but her fingers trembled. Philippa still refused to look at the baby. Abby wrapped the towels around its little body.

'It's so tiny,' she said, peeking at the face, which was the size of an orange, and the tightly-closed eyes. It was eerily quiet. It didn't seem right to leave it like that, though. She thought she saw movement, a twitch of the facial muscles, but she was distracted by a groan from Philippa.

'Take it away. Please.'

Abby froze. Had she heard her right? Blood was still seeping from under Philippa, turning the grubby rug beneath her a bright red. Her face was draining of colour as fast as she was losing blood. Was this normal? She felt useless.

Her eyes kept straying back to the bundle. She kept thinking she heard a cry, but it was so weak and thin it could have been an animal outside, the wind in the trees, mice in the tower, or the door creaking. The situation was so alien to her and so shocking that she wasn't sure what she was hearing any more.

'Where? What shall I do with it?' she asked desperately.

Philippa waved her arm listlessly, her eyes half closed. 'Bury it.'

'I don't think it's dead.' Abby's voice shook as she repeated it. She was sure she had felt him wriggling as she had wrapped him up.

'Of course it's dead. It would be crying. Babies scream the place down, don't they? It's been dead for ages inside me.'

She subsided into more sobs that turned into an animal howl of despair, so that Abby really couldn't tell if she could hear the baby at all.

'Why don't we wait a bit?' Abby asked desperately, but Philippa didn't seem to be listening to her. 'I think it's breathing.'

Philippa's voice was thick and cold. 'It's not breathing, Abby. Just get rid of it. I don't want to see it.'

Then she seemed to gather her senses for a moment.

'Don't let anyone see you. Take it as far away as you can.'

'But I really think…' Abby tried one last time, but she realised she couldn't get through to Philippa in this state.

'Get it out of my sight. Can't you see it's fucking dead?'

Slowly, choking back tears, Abby rose and gathered up the shape in the towels and jumpers. It was very light, much lighter than she had expected, but her own legs felt heavy, numb and wobbly. She thought she heard a snuffling sound but then the chainsaw started up again. Suddenly, she just wanted to get the baby away from there as quickly as possible.

She walked unsteadily towards the door, turned and nodded as Philippa asked in a small voice, 'Come back after, won't you?'

Outside, she pulled the door closed, then set off down the track away from the farmhouse, clutching the baby to her, pulling the blood-stained towels up around his head so that no-one could see what she was carrying and so she wouldn't have to look directly at the little face.

The woods smelled of freshly-cut branches. The chainsaw roared up in the trees. She couldn't tell exactly where the sound was coming from. It was so loud it vibrated through the forest. He was up there somewhere, the woodcutter. She had to make sure he didn't see her.

She didn't feel the light rain that fell as she walked or notice the sun that was setting over the opposite hill, casting a fiery orange light across the ridge. She trod carefully over the roots and brambles.

Philippa had said to get rid of the baby. She meant to bury it or leave it in some bushes far away from the farmhouse, but Abby couldn't do that. She was too afraid of what wild animals might do to it if she left it in the open.

Every now and then she thought she heard a cry, but it was so faint and barely distinguishable above her own crying, the racket the cicadas were making in the trees, the whine of the chainsaw, and the rushing of the waterfall. Every time she stopped and bent her head down close to the bundle, there was nothing.

The little church came into view around the bend. Abby headed for it, remembering the story about the orphan children being left there anonymously. She remembered the glazed terracotta faces of the cherubs in the altarpiece, and she felt at that moment this was the right place.

She pushed at the heavy door. It grated and finally gave way. She looked around her at the tiny room and came face-to-face with the painting of the ferocious Madonna rescuing the child from the Devil. Placing the bundle down very carefully on the floor in front of the painting where it would be watched by Mary, she was tempted to kiss the baby goodbye but was too frightened of what she might find if she looked too closely. In any case, he was still covered in blood and slime.

Instead, because she felt she ought to leave him something, because that was what people did in stories, she took off the necklace that Philippa had given her and placed it on top of his little body.

A creak behind her. Perhaps it was more a change in the air of the sort that makes you sense you are not alone, even if you haven't consciously heard anything. Abby whirled round, her heart beating fast, but she couldn't see anyone. She looked back one last time and fled.

As she closed the door, she thought she heard the thin cry again. No, it couldn't be. She turned back, got as far as the door, but there was nothing. She walked back up the lane, her head filled with cries now as she ran along the path and stumbled up the steps, until they got lost in the other sounds around.

When she got within sight of the tower, she slowed to a walk, suddenly dreading going back inside. When she eventually did, Philippa was still there, curled up in a ball. She had delivered the placenta while Abby was away.

Philippa's eyes opened. 'Did anyone see you?'

Abby shook her head. She stared around her at the mess.

'Good. We've got to clean this up.'

Hating herself, repulsed by what she had done, Abby did as she was told, and bundled up the placenta in another towel and dropped it in a supermarket carrier bag. The bag, when she lifted it, left streaks of blood along the ground. She would have to come back and see to those. Philippa had said 'away from the house', but the further she went with it the more suspicion she would arouse, so she stuffed it behind the woodpile. Philippa said to burn it but she couldn't bring herself to do that; it seemed too violent.

She wrung out the towel with water from the stream outside and staggered back to scrub the terracotta floor with it.

She couldn't let herself think too much about what they were doing. She only knew they had to get rid of every trace, make it all clean again. Her hands shook when she stopped, so she pressed on determinedly, exerting the whole of her upper body so that she could blank out her thoughts.

She kept seeing the baby's face. She scrubbed harder, trying to erase the memory and hide her tears. She promised Philippa she would never tell a soul. What else could she say to someone in such distress?

Walking back to the tower, she realised how much her hands were shaking, and she thought over and over again about the scene she had witnessed. She couldn't think about what might happen the next day, or the next.

Chapter Thirty-Four

'What do you mean, no?'

Abby held her breath. From the surgery window, as she was washing her hands before conducting an examination, she had seen Mina step off the kerb and march through the traffic, looking windblown even though it was a still day.

She heard her clatter up the stairs, followed closely by the receptionist telling her the doctor was with someone and she couldn't just go in without an appointment, but the words didn't seem to be having any effect.

'I'm sorry, you can't just barge in…'

But she was already halfway in.

'Please can you wait outside?' Abby said, hoisting the curtains around the patient who was understandably unnerved, but there was something about Mina today. She was agitated, her eyes filled with a strange energy.

In a low voice, Abby said, 'I can't discuss this with you now, but the answer's no and I'm not going to change my mind.'

She tried to close the door but Mina pushed back.

'Do you want me to call someone?' asked the receptionist.

Other medical staff and patients were starting to linger now. Mina wedged her knee inside the door.

'Will you please just get out?' Abby was surprised by the strength in her own voice. She shoved Mina back far enough so that she could pull the door shut. Mina, caught off-balance, slammed against the wall. She started screaming, bringing another doctor rushing from his room.

'You're not handling this properly,' he said to Abby.

By now, Mina was swearing and shouting accusations. It

took several members of staff to remove her.

'Murderer! She's a murderer. Ask her what she did.'

'I'm so sorry, she's delusional,' Abby said to her patient who sat on the bed pulling her clothes back on.

But Mina's words kept ricocheting around the walls. Abby's fingers shook as she printed out a prescription, murmuring more apologies. But she had a feeling 'sorry' wasn't going to be good enough.

***

When she got back to the house, it was filled with comforting cooking smells. James had cleared up and had dinner under control. The table in the dining space was laid with candles and he was playing some feel-good music. He always did things properly, thought of the little details she forgot. During the meal, she had the feeling life was normal again. They talked about people they knew, laughed about some of the things that had happened to them during the week, he talked about the frustrations of his job, and she talked about hers but didn't mention what had happened with Mina. It was hard to believe it really had happened. She tried to stamp on the memory but it kept going through her head. She kept looking around, imagining Mina's face at the French doors. Were they locked?

'You've gone quiet,' he said.

'Sorry.'

'No, I'm sorry. About the other day. I shouldn't have turned up at Connal's like that.'

She smiled. 'No, you shouldn't. There really is nothing to worry about.'

He looked as if he was about to say something, thought better of it and then decided to come out with it anyway. 'I almost believe you. Except for the way you've been behaving lately. There's too much going on for it not to mean something.'

'Yes, but it doesn't mean that.'

They cleared away in silence. The easy atmosphere was

evaporating despite their efforts to maintain it.

'He still has feelings for you. I can tell.'

She felt herself colour. 'I doubt that's true, and in any case, he wouldn't abuse his position.'

'And what about you? How do you feel about him?'

She sighed in exasperation. 'James, you're the love of my life, the father of my children.'

His expression changed. 'And yet you choose to shut me out and tell all your secrets to someone else.'

This couldn't go on. It was hurting them both too much, making him suspicious for no reason and turning them against each other. She had to tell him or she would lose him anyway. She had run out of options.

'All right,' she said at last. 'I do have something to tell you, but it's nothing like that.'

If only it was that simple. They moved over to the sofa and she sat with her legs curled underneath her, James propped his feet up on the coffee table and put his arms around her.

'I don't care what it is,' he whispered into her hair. 'I just want to know.'

Her heart hammered. It was happening after all this time. In a few seconds, she would know if it was something she should have done years ago or whether it was the biggest mistake of her life. Well, the second biggest, obviously. Her voice sounded strange in her ears as though it belonged to somebody else.

'The reason I've been seeing Connal for hypnotherapy is because of something that happened in my past.'

He stiffened. 'Did someone abuse you?'

'No.' She took a deep breath. 'When I was a teenager, I did something stupid. Someone got hurt. Well, in fact they died.'

She was pinching the fingers of her left hand with the right. Through the blur of tears in her own eyes when she glanced up, she could see the struggle going on in his. This obviously wasn't what he was expecting to hear but he wasn't going to betray his shock.

'I'm listening. What did you do?'

She tilted her head back to stop tears falling. 'I shot her.'

Saying it made it suddenly clear. The air seemed to vibrate around them. He swallowed. 'All right. So, it was an accident. You were playing and…?'

'No.'

He flinched but his voice remained steady. 'Right, tell me from the start.'

Sitting in the over-bright kitchen with the rain streaming down the windows and the fridge humming, she told him everything she remembered, all the stuff she had dredged up over the past few weeks with Connal. And the things that were confused, that still didn't make sense however hard she tried.

As she talked, she was thinking how lucky she was. James had always been there, always supported her and believed in her. She'd been wrong to keep it from him all those years. If she'd just been a bit braver, trusted a bit more, they could have had this conversation years ago.

But the silence that followed seemed to go on forever. He drummed his knee with his fingers. 'Are you serious?'

'Yes.'

His face was contorted in confusion. 'Did I hear you right? One of those bodies in the Tuscan villa is there because of you?'

She barely heard herself say yes. He searched her face. For a long time, he didn't say anything. When he did, his voice sounded cold, as if there was a glass screen separating them.

'And you didn't think I had a right to know this? Before you married me, before we had children together? Before you became part of my family?'

She made a last desperate attempt to get through. 'I'm sorry. I didn't tell you because I wanted to protect you from it, protect what we have.'

'Protect me or protect yourself?'

'All of us. Because it shouldn't be part of our lives. It doesn't matter any more. It has nothing to do with who we are.'

'Doesn't matter? It matters to me. And I'm pretty sure it matters to her family. There's an international enquiry going on and you're withholding vital information.'

'I'm sorry.'

'Yes, so you keep saying.'

She wanted so much to take him in her arms, but there was a coldness about him she'd never encountered before.

'I know it's a terrible shock…'

'You could say that.'

'Look, I know it's awful and I can't change what happened. But what do you think I should do?'

He laughed shortly. 'What do *I* think? When did that come into it? It certainly hasn't figured much in your plans lately.'

'I can't go to the police. Not because I don't have a conscience about it, but because I can't risk being taken away from you and the children.'

He was staring into space, then he flicked his gaze back and she could see hope returning.

'Are you sure this really happened? Sure the therapy hasn't planted false memories? It all sounds a bit melodramatic.'

She shook her head with a shudder. 'It happened.'

The dishwasher bleeped, signaling it had finished its cycle.

'The money,' he said, putting his head up. 'Is that what you've been using the money for? To pay Connal for his quack psychology?'

He was clutching at straws, anything but accept the reality. She could see the struggle going on in his eyes. And why should she be surprised? It had taken her a lifetime to get used to it. He had had to absorb it all in one evening.

'I took out the money for Philippa's sister.'

He let out an incredulous bark of laughter. 'So, you're being blackmailed now? Is that what you're saying?'

She tried to explain that it wasn't strictly blackmail. That in an odd way, despite everything, she knew Mina was basically honest.

'*Mina?* As in Mina, the cousin who wants you to have her baby? Or am I being stupid – did you make that up?'

'No. Her life's been really tough after what happened. She hasn't had the chances I had and she hasn't coped well. She's been in and out of secure hospitals. And… I think it would make me feel better. It would help to—'

He crashed his head back against the wall but didn't seem to be aware of it.

'Oh, as long as it makes you feel better. So, Mina is a fucking psycho and she's been blackmailing you. And you were going to deliver a little baby into her hands *to make you feel better?*'

It was so unlike him. James didn't swear, ever. He got up, walked over to the French doors and stood, looking out into the dark garden. He shook his head.

'I'm sorry, I just don't know how to react to this. I can't sweep it back under the carpet. I haven't had the practice you've had. I'm not sure I even believe it. I think you might be the one who's ill.'

'I'm not ill. I'm a doctor.'

'Doctors get ill.' He was still hoping for an explanation, some medication that could make it all okay again.

He pressed his fingers into his brow. 'I don't know. I just don't know what to think.'

She'd never seen him like this – so hard, unyielding. Perhaps they didn't know each other as well as they thought.

'I know I should have told you before,' she said at last.

'Yes. You should.'

He was terse, not cruel; cruel wasn't in his nature, but his detachment was frightening. He'd always been so kind, so gentle. He was no longer familiar. She went over to him but he held out his hand to stop her.

'Don't touch me, please.'

In just a few short minutes he had gone from best friend to stranger.

She looked into his eyes although she could barely stand

the look of hurt and horror. 'James, I'm still me.'

He turned away, as though the sight of her was painful. 'No, that's just it, you're not, are you? The Abby I knew – or thought I knew – would never have done something like that.'

The clock in the hall chimed. 'It's late,' she said. Perhaps after a night's sleep, it might be easier for him to digest.

He shrugged. 'Go on up if you want to. I'm not going to sleep after this. I'll spend the night on the sofa.'

'You know that's not necessary.'

'I think it is. I can't share a bed with someone who has lied to me for all these years about something so serious.'

'James, please…'

He shook his head and walked slowly out of the room. She watched him. He was gone, and there was nothing she could say to bring him back.

Chapter Thirty-Five

Lying awake, Abby went over everything in her head. She had moments of panic when she thought she had lost him forever, but despite his anger and his pain and her own pain at seeing him recoil from her, there was also a tiny amount of relief. At least she had told him. It would take time for him to get over the shock, it wouldn't be easy, but now that the truth was out they could start to inch forward together and rebuild the trust she had destroyed.

When she came down in the morning, he had already left for work. Sophia, it turned out, had been down before six and they had watched one of her favourite programmes together. She recounted it over breakfast, clearly unaware that anything was wrong.

Abby was on autopilot as she made the girls' breakfast and packed their lunches. After dropping them at their school club, she drove to the surgery where she saw a succession of patients with sore throats, fitted a coil, peered down ears and throats, wrote out prescriptions, and signed letters. All the time the conversation from the night before was replaying in her head.

James was at a conference in Birmingham so wouldn't be back until late. Further discussion would have to be put off until later, but that was quite a relief.

Arriving at school at the end of the day to collect the girls from their after-school clubs, she stood with a knot of other parents – one who insisted on giving her a rundown of symptoms as she'd had trouble making an appointment at the surgery; and the mother of one of Lucy's friends, who wanted to set up a play date.

Children were dismissed one by one into their parents'

charge, their names checked off on lists. Lucy's class teacher looked at Abby in surprise.

'Mrs Fenton. The girls aren't here, I'm afraid.'

She felt the colour drain out of her face. 'What do you mean not here? Who picked them up?'

'It was their auntie, wasn't it?' With a swish of her pony tail, the young teacher turned to another teacher for confirmation.

Abby shut her eyes. Her guts stirred. She was seeing Mina sweep through the playground, a child's hand in each of hers. She had said she wouldn't harm the children, but Abby's blunt rejection of her surrogacy request had angered her. She had known Mina would do something like this.

'The office said they'd had a message from you saying you couldn't get here on time. It's happened before, hasn't it? We'd never have let them go if we'd had any doubt – you know how careful we are,' said the teacher. 'The trouble is, people will change their arrangements without telling us.'

'What did she say her name was?'

The woman was red-faced by now. 'I can't remember. She was dark-haired, quite… quite tall. Is there a problem?'

Abby closed her eyes. She didn't have time for this. She ran out of the gate and up the road, her breath catching as she pulled out her phone. James's voice came through on voicemail. She left frantic messages, one after the other. She sat in the car trying to force herself to calm down and think.

Clinging to the hope, however desperate, that the girls might be safely at home after all, she drove back, barely noticing the traffic or the route.

The house was empty, quiet. She checked the answerphone. The only messages were from her for James. Something caught her eye. A note propped up against the coffee machine.

I'm going to be staying in the London flat. I need some time to think. We probably both do. It's all been a bit of a shock to be honest. I've arranged for Trix to pick up the girls. She's taking them down to my parents for a few days. I think they need to be away from all this.

She fumbled for her phone and pressed his name.

'Abby.'

'What's going on? I had no idea what was happening. I thought something had happened to the children.'

She heard his sigh at the other end. She pictured him in the soulless little flat, a microwave meal on his lap, traffic rumbling below.

'I left you a note,' he said. 'I'm only doing this because of the children. I don't feel happy leaving you with them at the moment.'

It felt as though she was being run over. 'That's ridiculous. Nothing's changed.'

'Nothing's changed? *Everything's* changed. I don't recognise you. I don't understand the things you're doing.'

'But you know it has nothing to do with the girls. I love them. I would never let any harm come to them, you know that.'

His voice broke slightly. 'Do I? I don't know anything any more. You've been threatened by a deranged woman, you've handed over a huge sum of money, you were seriously thinking about giving birth to her baby. You knew she was following you and yet you didn't tell me. Who knows what she might do? I'm seriously worried about your judgement.'

And that was the problem, wasn't it? James was a problem-solver. He hated not being able to see the answer to something. It was what had made him so good at his job. He could move into a failing school and turn it around in months, re-motivate the staff, get the parents onside, persuade the governors, inspire the children.

It was much the same with his current job, albeit on a bigger scale. He could see the problems in the system, he was gathering support, persuading the right people to make the right changes. It was hard going; he was up against entrenched views and determined people. He'd taken a mauling in debates recently, but he would keep going, applying gentle pressure, being polite. Even if he didn't achieve everything in his vision, he would achieve most of it.

But this was different. This was something he couldn't fix, couldn't see a way round.

'You're implying you don't trust me with them,' she managed to say. 'You know that isn't fair.'

'It's not about being fair, it's about keeping my children safe. Anyone would do the same. You snapped once and look what you did. How do I know you'll never snap again?'

He must know this was different. He was retaliating out of spite. But she couldn't entirely blame him.

In a kinder voice, he said, 'I'm worried about you, too.'

'What have you said to Trix?' she asked. It was unbearable, the thought of Trix's eyes open wide in surprise and disgust.

'Just that you're overworked and a bit stressed. She'll bring them back on Saturday morning, and I'll come back so we can spend the weekend as a family. Let's try and keep things normal for the girls.'

'What about school?'

'I've rung the school. It's only three days until they break up anyway.'

She pressed her hand to her head. 'Can't we talk about this?'

'It's all arranged.' His voice lowered again. 'I'm not doing this to hurt you. I love you, I'll never stop loving you, I can't help it. But I can't live with you, not like this.'

The house around her was unbearably quiet after she hung up. She had to compose herself before ringing Trix. What on earth was she going to say to her? But in the end, it was the girls who answered. She pictured them jostling for the phone in Trix's chaotic kitchen.

'We did an Easter trail in the garden.'

'I trained Bailey to hold a biscuit on his nose.'

'He could already do that.'

'And then he throws it in the air and catches it in his

mouth.'

'He was already doing it.'

'And we made you a—'

'No, we didn't. It's a surprise.'

'Oh yes. We didn't do that.'

But they also asked, 'When are coming going home?' and 'Why aren't we going to school tomorrow?'

She bit her lip, swallowing back tears. She couldn't answer those questions. She had no way of knowing what might happen. The girls talked on excitedly, interrupting and shushing each other. They were happy now, but what about tonight? Lucy's stuffed rabbit lay on the stairs, discarded this morning as she rushed off for school.

Abby picked it up and cuddled it to her, and felt everything crashing in.

Chapter Thirty-Six

'I had no idea,' Abby said at last, when she got back to the chestnut tower. She sat down close to Philippa. 'Why didn't you say something?'

Philippa barely opened her eyes. 'I didn't know.'

'You didn't know?' Abby heard her own voice sharper than usual. 'How could you not know you were pregnant?'

She had to admit that Philippa had barely changed shape but there must have been other signs, surely.

Philippa threw her hands up. 'I just didn't want to believe it was happening. I thought I'd made it go away.' Her voice was dull and monotone. 'I tried things – lost a lot of blood once and I thought it was gone. I stopped being sick. I thought that was why. I knew this day would come anyway, but I just wanted to forget for as long as possible. You know what they say – shut your eyes and it will all go away? It really seemed to work.'

'Does Luca know?' Abby asked at last.

Philippa gave a short, brittle laugh, laying her head back against the wall. 'It's got nothing to do with Luca, Abby. It was Marco.'

Marco? Abby felt her chest tighten, recalling the episode with Marco and Sue. 'But Marco can't be your boyfriend,' she said, appalled. 'He's…'

Philippa just shrugged and laughed some more. The laughter turned into crying until Abby had no idea what to think.

'He's not my boyfriend. I slept with him once. To get back at her – my mum. She took Josh from me, remember. I'd had my suspicions, but your notebook confirmed them. I thought it would make me feel better.

'It did for a while, before I realised what had happened.'

They were silent for some time. When Abby looked at her again she was sleeping, her face white and tear-soaked, and there was fresh blood on the rug beneath her. Abby quietly covered her with her coat, and slipped out.

She ran down to the stream and washed her hands and face, trying to regain her composure before seeing the others. Her reflection showed that she had blood in her hair, too. It reminded her of the paint fight. It seemed such a long time ago.

She plunged her whole self into the water, letting her tears flow as freely as the stream and wishing it would carry her away, back in time.

Chapter Thirty-Seven

Abby lay awake in the silent house. For years, she had longed for an uninterrupted night's sleep but this deadness was worse than anything. She got up and wandered through the rooms, feeling as though they belonged to someone else.

She folded up the children's clothes and sorted out their shelves. Tucked down the side of Lucy's bed, she found a collection of sweet wrappers. From under the bed she retrieved a sheet of paper entitled Snail Adopshuns and a list of names. Knowing she'd be unable to get to sleep, she headed to the surgery early and got through some paperwork.

She picked up a newspaper from the garage on her way in. James's face stared out at her alongside a story told by Anoushka about his Jekyll and Hyde personality – how he had turned on her and accused her of stealing, and then made a grovelling apology and tried to buy her silence with flowers which she had put in the bin. Abby put her head in her hands. This was hardly going to help win James back.

'Abby, when did you last have a holiday?'

Geoffrey, the senior partner, popped his head round the door.

'I'm taking time off next week when the children break up,' she reminded him.

He stood in the middle of the room. 'Why not start a bit earlier? Have a bit of time to yourself?'

'But I don't need to. I'm fine. And there's far too much to do here.'

'I've arranged a locum.'

'You've what?'

He looked pained. 'We've had a complaint about that

little episode yesterday. Some of the patients were quite alarmed. And staff didn't feel you handled it as well as you could have.'

Her heart sank. 'Is that what you think?'

He sucked his teeth. 'It wasn't very professional to shout back at someone who clearly has difficulties. And it took up an awful lot of time. We've got a backlog of appointments, which we've had to rearrange. But more importantly, you missed the fact that your patient had peritonitis. If she hadn't taken herself to A&E, you could have lost her.'

A cold wave of shock washed through her. 'I'm so sorry.'

He ran his hand through his hair. 'Look, these things happen and they're never easy. People can change very quickly. You think you can deal with a situation and then you find you can't. But you should have asked for help before it escalated to that stage.'

'I really don't need time off. Please…'

'I'm sorry, but I insist. Take a week to get some rest, in addition to the days you've booked. We'll talk after.'

She could argue but what was the point? How could she do her job effectively, knowing that Mina could come back at any moment and that next time someone might take her accusations seriously?

***

The week stretched ahead of her. There were lots of things she could do but she didn't fancy doing any of them. Flicking through the television channels, it was a shock to see James. He was being given a hard time at a meeting with a teachers' union about the reforms. Despite the jeering and haranguing, he managed to remain calm but she could see the strain on his face. And yet his words 'I don't recognise you' kept going through her head, along with the thought that neither did she really know him as well as she'd thought she did.

Her heart leapt as she saw his car pull up. Perhaps he had

changed his mind. But he looked startled when she opened the door.

'I've just come for some stuff.'

'Oh.'

'I didn't think you'd be in.'

'I'm taking some time off work.'

He looked surprised. 'Are you all right?'

'I suppose so.' She wanted to tell him the truth, that she felt she was breaking up, but that would appear too needy and she couldn't stand to hear his icy response. It was unbearable, this cool politeness. She cleared her throat. 'Look, about—'

'I don't have much time. We said all we had to say the other night.'

She followed him up the stairs, watched him pull out drawers and put clothes into a bag. 'But I don't think you understand. I didn't mean to do it.'

He stopped, a collection of shirts in his hand. She had to get him to believe her. Because in the end, it didn't much matter what anyone else thought. It was James's belief she wanted.

'I'm not sure I can believe you,' he said at last, as he slid the shirts off the hangers and folded them. 'If you had nothing to hide, why the secrecy? And if it was an accident, why did no-one call for an ambulance? Why didn't you go to the police and explain it to them?

'What did you do to put things right? I get that you might not have felt able to tell people there and then, but when you came home you could have told your father. You could have done *something.*'

He shook his head. 'I'm still trying to get used to thinking of you as two different people, the one you were then and the one you are now. Because that's what you've obviously been able to do. And that frightens me. It makes me wonder what else you're capable of convincing yourself about.

It was useless trying to get through. They were reasonable questions and she didn't have an answer. She hoped he might stay so they could talk properly, but he was in a hurry to get out. In a few minutes, he was heading down the stairs. They almost kissed out of habit, then remembered and pulled apart. He twisted his head away. She watched him climb into his car and disappear.

Chapter Thirty-Eight

It was a strange weekend. They maintained an appearance of normality for the girls, taking them to Legoland on the Saturday as they had been promising for months. It proved a good choice as they had to ride in separate cars – one adult and one child – for most rides, so didn't have much opportunity to talk to each other. During those moments in between – in a boat on the Fairytale Brook, on the train, and watching the puppet show – they were distracted by other things.

There was a moment when they stood in front of the photographs at the end of the Pirate Falls ride. The family captured together laughing and screaming in exhilaration as a wave drenched them. She smiled but caught James's cold, reproachful stare.

In a café at lunchtime, a well-built, purple-faced man started berating James over the government's immigration policy and became irate at what he took to be evasive answers. When James asked him not to swear in front of the children, he looked as though he was about to headbutt him but a member of staff managed to restrain the man. It left James shaken and the children confused and subdued. So much in their lives was changing and out of their control.

On Sunday, they took the girls to their swimming lessons, dropped Sophia at a party, and went for a walk with Lucy. There were times when Abby was able to convince herself everything might be all right, and other times when it seemed hopeless.

James waited until Trix arrived to collect the girls before heading back to London.

'Don't worry about them,' Trix said to Abby after he'd

gone. 'They're absolutely fine and as good as gold. But what about you? Are you really all right? I don't blame you for throwing him out. I've told him he's a shit. But don't let her do this, she's not worth it.'

'Sorry, who isn't?'

'That Petra woman, of course. You can't hush it up, I'm afraid. It's in all the papers today.'

It felt as though she was being run over.

'Such a bloody awful cliché, shagging his PA. And getting into a fight for God's sake, probably that woman's partner. It's all gone to his head.'

Her stomach dropped. James and Petra? Surely Trix had got that wrong? And James in a fight? He had given no hint of either of these things over the weekend. She hadn't seen a paper, but then they had agreed this was family time and she'd used her phone only to send texts about their position in the queue for a ride or suggest where to meet for the next one.

'I can't think what got into him. He has no idea how to defend himself. I know – I used to beat him up myself, and he was useless then. Mind you, he was half my size in those days.'

Abby laughed weakly but she was still reeling. So many thoughts surged through her head. James and Petra – she really hadn't seen that one coming. Her insides turned to water. Had James used her confession as an excuse to get away, or had her words driven him into Petra's arms?

Afterwards, she checked her newsfeed. There it was in the Sunday papers – a picture of James looking dishevelled and bleary-eyed with his arm around Petra, their heads together. And, although the details were short, a reference to a 'skirmish' with an old friend, Connal Emsworthy. Hands trembling, she pressed James's name on her phone.

The voice that greeted her was cold and brisk, reminding her that any hope she had formed over the weekend about things returning to normal was very much illusory, a show put on for the children, their friends, anyone who might be watching.

'I can't talk now.'

'I just want to know if it's serious. I have a right to know what's going on.'

After a pause, he said in a slow, quiet voice, 'Did you really just say that? That's a bit rich, isn't it?'

She started to object but he cut her off. 'Nothing I've done – *nothing I could ever do* – compares with what you did.'

He had changed again into that person she barely knew.

The last person she expected to see in her living room when she looked up from her phone afterwards was Philippa. Admittedly, the face that stared blindly out at her from the television was unlikely to be recognised by most people Philippa had known, but from the reported hair colour, the age and height, this was as close a representation as they were likely to be able to produce.

Abby stood there holding the control like a wand. With one press of a button she could make Philippa disappear, and yet she couldn't quite do it.

'Take a look at the second victim, a teenage girl believed to be under eighteen,' the presenter was saying. 'Helen, these two representations look extraordinarily life-like. Of course, you can't be a hundred percent accurate, this is just an impression. But how much do we know for sure?'

'Unfortunately yes, a lot of it has to be guesswork,' said the woman. 'Sadly, due to the suspected nature of the injury, a significant amount of bone was missing from the skull of this second victim, although the jawline was still intact which has helped us get a good idea of her age and we will be able to compare dental records. We also know for certain that her hair was red.'

She talked viewers through the reconstructive process, explaining how the skulls had been scanned and the tissue added on screen, based on calculations made about the bone and the victim's age.

'Do we know how these people died?'

'Yes, unfortunately we believe they were both shot – almost certainly in a different location and their bodies moved to the cave.'

The more Abby looked at the girl, the more she began to fuse her own memory of Philippa with this representation that gave her a stillness and sweetness she had never possessed. The snubbed nose was wrong, the rosebud mouth too dainty, and the hair less curly. The eyes had no colour, but the shape and width were convincing.

'From a clothing fragment, we know she was wearing a t-shirt like this one, which we know was sold by Monsoon in England in 1990,' said the presenter.

Abby felt a chill spread through her as she recognised Philippa's dolphin campaign t-shirt.

'So, do you know of a teenage girl who went missing in the early 1990s who had some connection with Santa Zita, this little village in Tuscany?' asked the presenter, as a map came up with the area highlighted. 'Can you connect her with this man, believed to be in his forties?'

The other representation was harder to identify. Without Marco's hair and aquiline nose or Alan's beard and freckled complexion, the face could belong to either of the men, although it had never seemed to Abby that there was any similarity between them.

'It may be that she was there on holiday, or she might have been living in Italy. Perhaps you were in Italy yourself at the time? However, please don't ring us just to tell us you've seen a girl who looks like this or someone who owned a t-shirt like this, because I imagine we'd get hundreds of calls. We're looking for a connection between the girl and/or the man and the villa, or at least some connection with Italy during the early 1990s...'

The camera closed in for what seemed like an eternity on a picture of the shooting star pendant that had been around Philippa's neck. They were making a big thing about it. Abby's fingers crept involuntarily to her throat again, even though hers hadn't been there for years. Sometimes she still felt the weight of it pressing against her in the way that an amputee might experience pain from a missing leg.

Staring at the faces, Abby felt as if all the blood had been drained out of her. She switched channels and tried to lose herself in a pointless reality TV programme, but her mind wouldn't settle. Who would be watching the crime programme? Philippa's old school friends? Her teachers? Suddenly, it didn't seem unlikely at all that she would be identified. It was a certainty.

She stood up on shaky legs, desperate to be busy. She wandered round, tidying up needlessly. The television flickered away in the corner of her eye. The ghost of the face stayed on the screen behind all the other faces – only this time it was the real Philippa. Philippa laughing, talking, blowing kisses, smoking, shouting, pleading. Even when Abby turned off the television, the imprint of the face remained on the black screen.

As she lifted a sofa cushion, her eyes fell on a book Lucy had left behind. Alan's book. Almost without realising she was doing it, she picked it up and hurled it at the television. It skimmed the screen and smashed into the French doors behind, the panel exploding into glass fragments.

The air vibrated in the silence. She had never done anything like that. It was strangely enjoyable. But then it hit her – this was something a mad person would do. She sank down the wall and sat gazing around her at the mess, then dropped her head in her arms and cried properly for the first time since she had read the newspaper story. At first it was just shaky sobs into the back of her hand, then throaty screams, fists clenched by her sides. Then full-on crying that she hadn't experienced in years, releasing a pain and rage that came from deep within her, guttural roars of anger and frustration, her head thrown back. She grabbed the remote and turned the television onto maximum volume to drown out the noise.

Eventually, exhausted by it all, she snapped the television off and felt the silence swim around her as she waited for her breathing to return to normal. The evening air and birdsong crept through the broken glass and she felt the cool air brush her face. She couldn't quite believe what she'd done, the violence of it. She hadn't even heard the phone ring, but the missed call sign was blinking. Her heart leapt thinking it might be James.

But she mustn't play it. She'd be tempted to beg him to come over. He'd get the shock of his life seeing her in this state with all the broken glass. It would be all the confirmation he needed that he had been living with a mad woman who wasn't fit to look after their children. She could end up sectioned and living in a place like Mina's. What would she think about a patient who had done this?

She blew her nose. She had to get it together. She couldn't leave the doors like that. It left her vulnerable. If Mina were to come to the house now, she could just step in.

Abby tried to pick up the bits of glass outside but tripped and felt shards embed themselves in her arm. She felt the pain now – a crawling, throbbing, searing sensation.

Picking her way over the fragments on the floor, she held her arm under the cold tap. She felt panic rise as the blood washed out, staining the basin red. There was too much of it. The cold water numbed the pain. The room started to swim.

She couldn't give in to this. Some of the cuts were quite deep, but on closer examination she decided they didn't need stitching. She took a tea towel and bundled it tightly around her arm. With the other hand, she poured a large glass of wine although she had trouble keeping her hand steady. Drops splashed onto the marble. She downed it and poured another.

When would this stop? She had thought that if she gave into her thoughts it would all become clear, but it had stayed just as jumbled, distorted, and relentless. Philippa was dead. There was nothing Abby could do to help. Although it seemed barely likely, there was a chance that the baby had survived, and if he had she must find him. She had to know if he had lived.

The knocking was timid at first. Then it became more insistent. She hesitated in front of the door and then opened it.

'Connal.'

He stood awkwardly. 'Is everything all right?'

'Fine, yes thank you,' she said with as much composure as she could muster. 'What are you doing here?'

'I heard noises.'

'Must have been the television.'

He didn't move. There was a look of confusion in his eyes. He was peering over her shoulder. She tried to block his view of the room, hoping he couldn't see the broken glass.

'Why are you here?' she asked again.

'I came to see if you were all right. What did you do to your hand?'

She could feel the blood soaking through the tea towel. 'Knife slipped. I was chopping vegetables. It's only superficial. But it's such a long way for you to come.'

Ignoring her, he pushed past heading for the living room. She saw his face flood with alarm. 'Jesus, what have you done?'

He made her sit down while he cleared up. 'Dust pan?'

'In the cupboard.' She started to get up, but he pushed her shoulders back down with just enough force. She saw his eyes stray over to the bottle and the absence of any prepared vegetables.

She sat listening to the clatter of glass as he swept. None of it seemed real.

'You have to get this fixed, it's a security hazard.'

He set about creating a temporary measure with tape and some hardboard from the garage.

'Where's James?' he asked.

'London.'

'And the girls?'

'With his sister.'

The wave that had been building inside her broke. 'I told him. I told him everything. I shouldn't have. You were right. I never should have started this.'

He pulled out a chair and sat beside her. 'Hey, don't be silly. The way James is at the moment, you didn't have a choice.'

'What about you? Are you all right?' she asked. 'The papers said you'd had a fight.'

'Me? Oh God, yeah. Couple of cracked ribs. I'm all right as long as I don't laugh.'

'Not much danger of that at the moment, is there?'

He smiled. 'Ah now, don't get me started. It didn't happen the way they're reporting it. He didn't hit me. It was more of a shove. I took a tumble down the steps. Could have been nasty. There were some people around, unfortunately. One of them must have recognised him.'

He helped her put dressings on her hands, waiting for directions. At one point, he stood up and leaned over the sink, pinching the skin between his eyes. 'Sorry. I'm not great with blood. Last person you want in an emergency.'

'I'm so sorry about everything.'

He sighed. 'It's partly my fault.'

'No, it was mine. I asked for your help.'

'And I should have said no, should have been stronger. I knew no good could come of this.' He held out his arms. 'Can I give you a hug?'

The unexpected touch, the warmth of his skin brought tears to her eyes.

'James'll come round. I did, remember?'

She bit her lip. 'Yes. But it's a bit different when you've been married for ten years. When you have two little children.'

She pulled away. 'Why did you really come here this evening?'

He ducked his head, cleared his throat. 'To tell the truth, I was going to tell you I couldn't do this any more. I don't need the aggro – James in my ear the whole time, and now the press poking their noses in, jumping to conclusions. It's putting my job at risk, making me look unprofessional – like some creep who hits on his clients. And I've probably just lost a girlfriend over it.'

She nodded. 'I see, I didn't realise. No, that's fair enough.'

His eyes slid over to the doors where he'd repaired the

glass. He exhaled deeply. 'No, it isn't. I can't leave you like this.'

'You can. Go on.'

Why had she ever thought it was a good idea to involve Connal in this? She saw the relief flash across his face, but it was quickly replaced with something that looked like furious resentment.

'No, I need to see it through. Tell me what happened to the baby.'

Chapter Thirty-Nine

All night, eyes open, she lay waiting for Philippa. Every now and then she jumped at a sound, but each time it was a false alarm. She kept playing the events over in her mind. All that blood. Philippa had lost so much blood. A dead baby. Or had it been alive? Its rubbery, grey little body. Those tiny, thin cries that must have been in her head. Were they in her head? She thought she saw it move. It had, hadn't it? Surely she had felt it moving when she was carrying it to the church? But it hadn't moved when she put it down in front of the altar under the painting. It was dead then, surely. That meant it had died while she was holding it. She could have got help, but she had let it die.

And Philippa – was she dying, too? Would Abby find her dead when she went down there tomorrow? How would she explain any of it? She could have told someone, ignored Philippa's pleading. It might have saved her life. If she died, would that make Abby a murderer for not getting help?

Before anyone was awake, she crept down the external staircase and ran through the wet grass to the chestnut tower. She had to get there before any of the family saw her. The woodcutter was already out there stacking logs. He greeted her and she managed a smile back, although her heart was thumping. For him it was a normal day.

Cautiously, she opened the door of the tower, trying to prepare herself for what she might see. Philippa sat slumped where Abby had left her. Very slowly, she walked towards her.

Philippa's face was swollen and marked with tear trails, and her jeans showed a large, dark patch of blood, but she was breathing. She was shivering. Just asleep then. There was an odd smell, which Abby didn't recognise but was determined to ignore. For a long time, Abby sat there, hugging her knees, trying to decide what would be best to do. She was aware of the woodcutter moving around outside. She had brought some rolls and a bar of chocolate, and set these down gently beside her cousin.

If only she'd brought a blanket to put round Philippa's shoulders. There must be something in the trunk she could use – the fur coat or the velvet jacket. The lid was heavy and made her arms shake, but she rested it carefully against the wall. When she looked inside, she felt as though someone had sprinkled cold water down her neck. It was clear that, despite what Philippa had said, she had on some level been planning for this. There were clothes, blankets, towels. Abby spotted some small orange tubes nesting in a blue velvet hat and she wondered what they were, but there wasn't time to think about that now.

She hauled out the fur coat. Something fell out onto the velvet jacket beneath – something long and heavy. Abby's heart beat faster as she pushed back the velvet. The shotgun. She ran her fingers over it, remembering with distaste the skinned rabbit.

'Leave it alone.'

Abby sprang back. Philippa was staring at her with hostile suspicion.

She swallowed. 'I brought you these. Everything on your list.'

Philippa glanced at the things and nodded. She clutched Abby with surprising force. 'Please, I need you to do me a favour. Just one more. I want him back.'

Abby froze. 'But you said…'

'I know, I know. But I was so frightened and confused. It was all such a massive shock. I'd been telling myself it wouldn't happen and then it did. It was all so sudden. And I was sure he was dead because I'd been thinking it for weeks. But you said – didn't you? You said he was alive?'

'I don't know about that. It was probably a mistake.'

'But you said…'

213

'I thought he was moving but it was probably just the air ruffling the blanket.'

'What did you do with him?'

'I took him to the church. The one with the painting. They'll know what to do with him there.'

Philippa cradled her head in her hands. 'No, no, no. I have to see him. I have to be sure. I want to hold him. Even if he's dead. I didn't even touch him last night. I don't want someone else burying him. I want to do it myself. I'm his mother.'

Abby stared at the floor in disbelief. It had been a whole night. It would be too late. 'I can't. I can't go back. Please don't make me.'

Philippa's eyes were wide, desperate. 'Abby, I can't go myself. Please do this one thing for me.' She clutched Abby by the arms. Abby could feel her nails digging in.

She stood motionless, anticipating every step of the way but she couldn't, wouldn't visualise the end of that journey. She shook her head slowly. Philippa's crying got louder and louder.

'Be quiet.' Abby looked round desperately. 'Please, someone will hear.'

She tried to calm Philippa but it just made her worse. Someone would come and find out what had happened, and they'd go and find the baby and bring it back dead, and Abby would have to explain why she hadn't done something to help save its life instead of abandoning it in front of that scary painting.

At last, because she couldn't stand it any longer, she got up slowly and walked towards the door.

'Abby,' Philippa called after her.

She turned. Perhaps Philippa had understood at last.

'Please hurry.'

***

She walked swiftly but in a daze back down the path, the sick feeling knotting harder in her stomach. She had no idea what she would find this time. The baby's little alien face had been cute and she had had to hurry away last night. She had made sure he was away from the draught, although she didn't think he was really capable of feeling the cold. But a whole night had passed and babies needed feeding, didn't they?

She stumbled on towards the little church. A part of her was curious now, to see if by any chance he might still be alive. She couldn't hear any crying. The closer she drew, the more silent it seemed. She twisted the iron ring and pushed her weight against the heavy door, filled with a sudden longing to see the baby again.

The church was empty. She checked the pews and behind the altar, looked for another room or crypt where he may have been moved, but there was nowhere. It was a tiny place. She looked up at the painting, the Devil creeping forward with his hands outstretched.

She ran outside, walked all round the building. No sign. Feverishly, she looked for a freshly-dug grave but there were no graves, no cemetery here; there was nothing, just an absolute sense that the baby had gone.

She sank down onto the step in front of the door, bringing her trembling hands up to her mouth and then the sides of her head, trying to breathe. She stared into space, her heart jabbering. Minutes must have passed, perhaps half an hour, perhaps longer. Philippa would never forgive her.

She felt those ice green eyes on her and the cold contempt in her voice. Abby had failed her. Later – an hour perhaps – she was still sitting there, paralysed with indecision and part-blinded by tears that collected but didn't fall. Everything had stopped.

To return without the baby would be almost as terrible as returning with a dead baby. No, it would be worse. A dead baby would be the end of the matter. Philippa would have to accept it. But this emptiness would make her more desperate.

Down in the piazza, Armando could be seen setting up his tables. Somewhere in the distance a siren clanged. Panic rising, Abby got to her feet. If only she had the courage to break the news to Philippa, but she didn't. She couldn't go back. She would avoid the tower, stay away. She could run down to the piazza, jump on the bus, leave all this behind. But there was no getting away from the fact that when Philippa felt stronger she would come and find her. For the first time, Abby realised she was scared of her.

But she couldn't stay here. Someone might see her. She walked slowly, mechanically, on down the path, trying to think of something, anything, she could do or say to make the situation better.

And then she saw it. Like a gift, it stood waiting for her.

***

A pram outside a house just below the church on the steep path leading down into the village. The baby must have been put outside for a sleep. The pram was positioned under a tree to give it protection from the sun. The tree blocked the view of the house. As Abby gazed at it over the wall, the baby looked so serene and beautiful, its hands resting above its head. For a moment, she almost wondered if it could be the same one, but it wasn't.

The idea crept in. Once, a few years ago, she had looked after her friend's hamster while the friend was on holiday, and the hamster had died. Her father had driven round all the pet shops in the area and eventually found a replacement, and the friend had never realised. When you thought about it, this wasn't so different, was it?

Executing the plan was slightly more complicated. She looked around. There was nobody in sight, but how could she be certain no-one was watching from inside the house behind the shutters? It was no good, she couldn't think about that. She reached into the pram. The baby held up its arms to help her, as if it knew, as if it was giving her permission, asking to be taken.

She tugged and pulled. Something was stopping him from coming up. She felt around under the blanket. Of course, a strap. She fumbled with a buckle. Her breathing rattled. She kept looking up at the house. The upstairs shutters were closed, the lower halves of the downstairs ones pushed forwards. The baby twitched and screwed up its face. She thought she heard a noise. She yanked on the strap. Suddenly, it was easy. She lifted him out, cuddling his body to her as she walked quickly up the path.

The baby stopped crying almost immediately and she was able to carry it round the bend before it made any more noise, but then it started coughing and spluttering again. Shushing him, she whipped round but there was nobody coming up the hill.

The baby was wearing only a nappy, and his smooth skin made him difficult to grasp. He was stronger than the other baby and much more wriggly. But then something occurred to her. How did she even know it was a boy? She stopped for a moment under some bushes, crouching down with the baby on her lap. She fumbled with the nappy, with the little body bent awkwardly backwards over her knee. She peeled the tabs back from the nappy, slipped it off, and threw it away. It snagged on the bush but she kicked it as far as she could into the undergrowth.

It was a boy. She exhaled. Almost immediately, she felt a warm wetness over her arms and stomach. She held the baby out at arm's length in disgust but that made him cry more loudly, so she hugged him against her soggy t-shirt, crying with frustration and fear as she stumbled blindly on up the overgrown path.

In the shadow of the trees at the top, she looked closely at the baby for the first time and felt blood drain from her face at the hopelessness of the situation. How could she possibly expect Philippa to believe that this was the same one she had given birth to the night before? He was bigger for a start and his crying was furious, as though he knew what was happening to him.

Oh, God. What *was* happening to him? What was she doing? What was she thinking? Perhaps it wasn't too late. She could still take him back, say she had found him on the path. This was her last opportunity to stop, turn round. But she wasn't going to do that.

How could she? They would have noticed him gone by now. They would be there, looking in the pram. They would see her with him and they would think she was a kidnapper. *That's what she was.*

She had to get away before they came looking for her. She had to deposit the baby as quickly as she could. By the time she reached the tower, he was crying even more loudly, although the noise of the trees being cut drowned the cries, just like the evening before. She hovered for some moments, caught in indecision, looking down at the red little face. And then it struck her.

What would Philippa say to her when she saw what she had done? She would be furious. She would make her take it back. She didn't want just any old baby.

No. She had to go back now. It might not be too late after all. She would say she found him. Someone else had taken him. She was just bringing him back. Of course, that's what she should do.

But looking at the little window at the side of the tower, she realised the chance was lost. Philippa's hand was pressed flat against the glass, her eyes huge. A moment later, she flung open the door, her face wet with tears. She gave a little cry and grabbed the baby out of Abby's arms, folded slowly onto the ground, rocking back and forth, whispering to him.

Abby stood watching her for a few moments with an awful anticipation. It would only be a matter of time before Philippa noticed. But she didn't say anything. What was happening? It was unbelievable that Philippa had accepted him. To Abby, he was already so different. What was wrong with Philippa?

It isn't yours, Abby wanted to say. *Look at it!* But she couldn't.

Before Philippa could ask any awkward questions, she turned and fled. Without the baby, her arms felt heavy and useless. They shook as she raised them to push the hair back from her eyes. What had she done? It had seemed so simple, obvious at the time, but was just beginning to sink in how stupid she had been.

Although it also occurred to her that, just possibly, because of Philippa's state of despair and confusion, she might get away with it. Drawing nearer to the house, she saw a movement up on the loggia. As she walked in the door to her room, Mina was standing there smiling sweetly.

'Where have you been?'

Chapter Forty

Abby got up although it was still dark. It had taken her a couple of nights to realise that the normal timetable no longer applied. She had no job to go to, no children to get ready for school. The bed felt vast and cold without James. Lying there only reminded her of everything that had gone wrong.

Stumbling into the kitchen that didn't need cleaning because no-one had eaten there, she felt lonelier still. She filled the kettle, watching the steam rise and disperse over the glass splashback. There would be no last-minute panics over missing PE kits or clothes that hadn't been washed, no sudden announcements about having to rustle up an Easter bonnet for a competition or bring money for a school trip. There had been times when it would have seemed like heaven to have a whole day without having to bother about these things.

But she couldn't sit around in an empty house waiting for events to catch up with her. She might as well use the time to do some research, get answers to some of the questions that had been colliding around her head since the bodies were discovered.

***

'It's not something I've ever talked about, to be honest.'

It had only taken a few phone calls, infiltrating the past pupils' Facebook group, studying the school photograph for the year in which Philippa's family left England, and a trawl through LinkedIn to track down Joshua Lake, director of a kitchen design showroom in Ruislip.

They sat in a dark little pub in the high street. Abby had seen him as she passed the window of his showroom with its gleaming contemporary kitchens – he was wearing a suit, had closely-cropped, receding brown hair and an angelic face which lit up when he saw her, but fell when she confessed she wasn't there to buy a kitchen. Although he claimed not to remember Philippa at first and panic flashed across his face when he heard Sue's name, he eventually agreed to talk as long as it was somewhere other than the showroom.

It was getting late for the lunch crowd, so they were able to find a table in a quiet corner. It felt odd, this clandestine meeting with a man she had known for so long as the name on the letter. Josh was polite but cautious.

'I don't see how I can help you, but I'll try.'

As far as he was concerned, she was a relative trying to trace Philippa and Sue. Perhaps it was unfair, but she had to get clear in her own head how much of what Philippa had told her was true.

'It's just one of those things, isn't it? When you're seventeen you take any offer that comes your way.'

'Would you say you were in love with Sue?'

'Love?' He looked at her sharply, as though he didn't see what relevance this had to the missing person's enquiry or what business it was of hers, but in the event decided to answer the question anyway. Perhaps it was relief that someone else knew about it.

'I was infatuated certainly. I'd never had feelings as strong as that before – not sure I have since.' He tucked his legs under his chair and hunched over his beer.

'This is strictly confidential?'

She assured him it was.

'My wife doesn't know. If I told her, I'd have to tell her other things and that would bring all kinds of crap to the surface. Stuff I've never dealt with. Can you understand that?'

She suppressed the urge to smile. 'I think so, yes.'

He was quiet, casting his mind back. 'Wow, this isn't

what I expected to be talking about today. At the time, I believed it was love. Perhaps it was different for her. I thought I was mature but I wasn't. What did she see in me? I don't know.'

On the other side of the bar, the office staff broke into a chorus of Happy Birthday followed by some laughter and chinking of glasses. Outside, the traffic had stopped but was moving again.

'You might not believe this, but it was never my plan to sleep with mother and daughter.'

She shrugged to let him know it wasn't her business but he seemed keen to explain.

'I met Philippa when I was sixteen. She was thirteen, but she told me she was fifteen and I believed her. It was never anything serious. We were mates who ended up fooling around. She was one of the lads but sexy with it, you know? She could drink me under the table. We smoked, tried stuff out together, did a lot of things we shouldn't – shoplifting, graffiti, joy riding… Wouldn't think it to look at me now, would you?

'At heart, though, she was still a kid and I didn't see us being together in the future. The things we used to do, you can't have that kind of relationship when you're middle aged, can you?

'And then one day they disappeared. I've never really thought about what Philippa might be doing these days. To be honest, I'd have thought she would either be in prison or dead by now.

'I couldn't imagine her living in the suburbs being one of the yummy mummies. She'd talked about joining the New Age travellers. I think that life would have suited her.'

He bit his lip, tapping the side of glass with his fingers. 'The Philippa I remember was fearless, funny, maddening… She used to scare me sometimes, some of the stuff she came out with. I never knew what she was going to do. Her mum was unpredictable, too – but somehow in the right ways. I don't know if I'm making any sense. I'm probably not saying it right.'

Abby motioned for him to go on.

'I never wanted to hurt Philippa. But when you're that age and an older woman pays you attention, it's exciting. I didn't boast about it. My mates wouldn't have understood. It was like an adventure, a secret, there was the thrill of the unknown but it wasn't sordid. At least, it didn't seem it.'

He drank some of his beer and shook his head. 'But then I look at my son and I think if some teacher ever hit on him, I'd want her strung up.'

The birthday group were moving out now, calling their goodbyes to the bar staff. Someone was collecting up the glasses.

'I'd been with a couple of girls my age, but with Sue it was different. She was exotic, intelligent, well-read – all the things I wasn't. When I was with her, I felt I was being transported into a different world, like the one you see in films. I suppose I was playing at being grown up.

'Our ages were never the issue. Anyway, she didn't look her age. She was lovely – she reminded me of that French actress in the *Three Colours Blue* film.'

'Juliette Binoche?'

'That's the one. She had this smile, this way of looking at you. We used to make love for hours. The first few times, I cried.' He coloured slightly. 'Sorry, you probably don't want to hear this.'

She signalled for him to continue.

'It wasn't like in the stories – she didn't guide me, tell me what to do. She wasn't in the mother, teacher role. We were lovers in the true sense. It felt equal. I never felt I was being used.'

Outside in the street, an incident was unfolding. One of the drivers had got out of his car and the other was gesticulating out of the window of his van, shouting obscenities.

'You can imagine the shock when I found out she was Philippa's mum. They knew about each other but not their identities. She'd never even told me she had children.

'I'd already decided I couldn't go on deceiving Philippa.

I wanted them both but if I had to give one up, well, it couldn't be Sue.

He swallowed the rest of his drink. 'Same again?'

She had a moment of panic, thinking it might be a ruse and he wouldn't return, but then she saw him up at the bar. A girl with a ponytail wiped down the menu board. She smiled at Abby. Then Josh was back.

'The day it ended, I was heartbroken. I thought her husband must have found out. In a way, I was relieved. I hoped they'd break up over it and she'd come and pick me up in her car and take me away somewhere. I saw us living in hotel bedrooms, sleeping in the back of a van or under the stars. You see what I'm saying? I wasn't as mature as I thought I was.

'Turns out another teacher had spotted us together. My dad would have killed her if the police hadn't got to her first, so I suppose she did the best thing by leaving. But it took a long time to get over. I had to leave school, because by then all the kids knew about it. I went off the rails a bit. Blew my chances of going to university. Still, it's worked out in the end.

'But I was afraid for what Alan might do to Sue. I'd heard stories from Philippa about his temper. I couldn't stop thinking about it.'

'Did you ever look for her?'

He looked startled. 'Why are you asking me that?'

She wasn't sure herself, but his reaction piqued her curiosity.

His expression closed over. 'How do I know you're not the police?'

She assured him she wasn't, but he took a bit of convincing. At last, he shrugged.

'I just had this idea that if I could only talk to her, I could persuade her to come back. I was coming up to seventeen and she wasn't at the school any more so it was none of anyone's business.'

Abby's heart speeded up. 'What did you do?'

He gripped his head. 'I've lived with this for so long. I

224

couldn't tell anyone because I know how it would have looked. I can't be involved in this, do you understand?'

Her heart was racing now, but she wasn't going to tell him anything she didn't need to.

He sagged in his chair. 'I went out there. I should have grown up and moved on, but my life wasn't going anywhere. All I had was memories, and I'd convinced myself Sue didn't want to be apart from me, either. She wrote to tell me to stop, but I kept picturing Alan dictating the letter to her, checking it over. I was sure she needed rescuing.

'Then the letters stopped. I was worried about what he might have done. It took a while to save up the money. I was working in my dad's garage, saving for driving lessons. Anyway, eventually I had enough to book a flight. I was still thinking I could persuade her to come away with me.'

Abby felt a needling sensation. This wasn't what she had expected.

'I didn't have the address, but I knew the name of the village and the bar where I had to send letters to. I thought it would be easy to find the house.'

He looked out across the street, no doubt revisiting his memories.

'It didn't go according to plan. When I got there, she didn't want to know. We had a row, Alan found us and beat the living crap out of me. He threatened to shoot me if I came near again.' He looked down at the table, tracing something in a drop of beer. He cast a look up from under his brows. 'That's why she must have done it. Sue must have killed Alan after I'd gone. I guess Philippa got in the way.'

Abby held her breath. 'You think Sue killed Philippa and Alan?'

'The Tuscan villa where they found the bodies. It's in the news, you must have heard.'

Her heart pounded. 'But why haven't you been to the police?'

He looked wretched. 'How can I? I'd have to tell them

the whole story. At best, they wouldn't believe me. At worst, they'd think I did it. I was the jealous lover. Even if I was able to prove it wasn't me, it would get everyone talking. I have a family, a business, people who depend on me. I'm sorry, but I'm not going to do it.'

She released her breath in increments. 'And perhaps you still love Sue?'

He shot her a furious look.

'I understand,' she said hurriedly.

'Once – it must have been just after she'd done it, she came to find me. She was very strange, very nervous. Called me at the garage from a cheap hotel. Said she had to be with someone. In the morning, she told me I'd never see her again and she left.'

Abby only asked as an after-thought, 'Do you know where she is now?'

He paused, finishing the beer and staring into the empty glass. 'I've never spoken to her but I've kept an eye out. I can't help it. I followed her down to Padstow the morning she left. I've kept my promise, never contacted her again, but I sometimes check up on her. She's in St Ives now, has a little art and pottery studio. She uses another name – Suki Rhodes. I went in there once a few years ago. She had no idea who I was and I didn't introduce myself. I've changed more than she has. I just wanted to see her. Wanted to break the spell.'

Abby's heart was aching now from overwork. 'And did it work?'

His mouth twisted into a smile. 'Yes, in a way. She still looks good for her age but my life's moved on. I just want to forget about it.'

'Where is this studio? Can you remember the name?'

He took a long breath. 'It had something to do with cats. It's a little whitewashed place near the harbour. She lives in a flat upstairs.'

Abby thanked him. She felt bad about leaving Josh to suffer in ignorance, but she was the closest she'd ever been to finding the truth.

Chapter Forty-One

Third body in Tuscan villa mystery

Police investigating the deaths at a Tuscan holiday villa are considering whether there might be a connection with a body found in the area in 1992. The body was found hanging from a tree. It was thought to belong to an itinerant man who had been selling items door-to-door. The police have not said whether he is being considered as another victim or as possibly involved in the crime.

***

It was just getting light when she arrived in St Ives. She parked the car and walked down to the harbour. One or two people were already walking on the beach. The tide was out and brightly painted boats lay stranded on the gleaming herringbone sand. It brought back memories of childhood holidays, exploring rock pools with a coloured net, collecting shells in a bucket, building sandcastles with her mother.

It didn't take long to find the Black Cat Art Gallery tucked away in the maze of little cobbled streets; a whitewashed stone cottage with a black cat for a doorknocker and a view over the harbour.

She took a moment to get herself together before pushing the door. It would probably be a big anticlimax. Sue would have moved on years ago, even if it really had been her that Josh saw.

The interior felt surprisingly spacious, with white walls, glass shelves, pale wood and textiles. The walls were hung with watercolours of local scenes, although none so lovely as the view from the window.

It seemed incredible that Sue had been holed away here for years. Heart thumping, Abby passed paintings of local bays and fishing villages, and a series of black and white photographs of sand patterns, sea drift and shells.

There was movement at the back of the shop. A couple were mulling over the hand-made silver jewellery. The woman helping them choose had her back to Abby, but there was no mistaking her aunt's clear vowels.

'This one would suit you. We have some lovely earrings to go with that one, too.'

Anxiety spiked her chest. This was a mistake. She thought about turning round, getting out before Sue realised she was there. But no. She had come this far, she must see it through.

Noting someone standing there as she walked back towards the till, Sue said, 'Are you happy browsing?'

Her face paled as her eyes met Abby's. The cropped hair was silver now and she wore narrow frameless glasses instead of the owl ones, but apart from a few wrinkles she looked startlingly familiar.

Sue managed a smile. 'Sorry, for a moment you reminded me of someone I used to know.' And then doubt flickered in her eyes. 'Unless… Abby?'

Sue's face was tight. For a moment, she seemed to recover, saying, 'I'll be with you in a moment' but Abby caught the nervousness in her bright voice and the darting looks as she gift-wrapped the jewellery.

Once she'd shown her customers out, she flipped the sign on the door to Closed, and in slow motion turned to face Abby.

'For a moment then, I thought you were your mother.'

Abby felt the old, familiar tightening of her throat and for some seconds wasn't sure if she would be able to speak. Then the words came out in a rush.

'I haven't come to make trouble. I just want to know if it's true – was Alan my father?'

For a few moments, Sue didn't say anything. She walked

stiffly over to the till where she sat down, lifting some boxes off a faded blue armchair and inviting Abby to sit.

'What have you been told?' she asked at last.

It didn't seem real sitting in that little studio, the last place on earth she'd have imagined finding her aunt. Sue's eyes grew rounder at the mention of Philippa's theory about her parentage.

'Oh no, Abby, she got that wrong. Is that what she told you, that it was some sort of transaction? In some ways, I wish it had been.'

'I'm sorry?'

'It wasn't love, either.'

'What then? Lust?'

She had to ask the question even though she didn't want to hear the answer.

'Lust – that's a strange word. I don't think it's the right one for what existed between them.'

Sue looked down at the table, tidying up brushes, putting lids back on tubes of paint. 'The truth is your mother and I were inseparable since the day we started school together. I think that in some way I introduced her to my brother because I wanted to keep her close. Perhaps I flattered myself that she loved him because he and I were so alike – he was like the other side of me.

'In any case, when she came to stay Alan was fascinated by our closeness. He wanted to know if we'd ever let it spill into something physical. I could see the idea titillated him and I suppose I played along.'

Outside, a couple of small children were digging in the sand and a young mother dragged a pushchair across the beach.

'It was one of his obsessions – well, it is for most men, isn't it? Erin and I thought it was funny. We might have ramped it up a bit when he was around, holding hands and sitting with our legs draped over each other.

'He and I used to discuss our fantasies. I knew he was attracted to Erin – most men were attracted to your mum – but I also knew her untidiness, her vagueness, her otherworldliness irritated him and they would be a hopeless match. I was confident he could see that, too.

'From the early days, he used to talk about seeing me with another woman. I told him I had no intention of sharing him, that I would find it degrading, but he said that wasn't what he meant. He only wanted to watch, he wouldn't join in.'

Abby shifted uncomfortably in her seat. She was getting images she didn't want to see.

'You get to that stage when you're teetering on the brink between fantasy and reality, don't you? We started to conjecture about people we knew, but Erin was the only one we could agree on. She was attractive enough but not so much that I felt threatened, and she had no family at the time. She was with your dad but I didn't think it was serious. I'm sorry, but you wanted to know. If you want me to stop, say so.'

Of course, Abby wanted her to stop, but she had to hear it. 'Go on.'

'I'm not sure what tipped it into reality. We were all renting a place together in Zaragoza, but Liam got an important contract and had to go back early. The three of us were on the rooftop drinking cheap champagne and smoking, watching out for shooting stars. Philippa was a baby – I'd got her off to sleep in the bedroom. We were all a bit high and we were talking about it in a theoretical way, and suddenly it was happening. She and I were kissing. He was watching. We went down into the living room, gave each other a massage, shared a smoke, played tricks blindfolded.

'I remember the music. It always gives me a bad feeling when I hear it.

Alan watched and pleasured himself. There was a strictly no touching rule. I expect you want me to spare you the details.'

That, at least, was a relief – although Abby suspected Sue wouldn't have spared her the details if she'd remembered them. She was still getting used to seeing her mother in a new light. It was making her wonder if she'd ever really known her at all.

Sue got up and went out to a kitchen at the back. Abby heard her running the tap and putting on the kettle. She came back carrying a glass of water, slid open a drawer in the desk, removed a bottle of tablets, and a swallowed a couple. 'Sorry, I've got a headache. This is all very unexpected.'

She sat down again.

'In the end, we all fell asleep on the floor. I remember feeling so surrounded by love, so safe and so happy. But in the early hours, I got up to go to the bathroom. When I came back they were having sex on the rug. I almost tripped over them as I came into the room.

'I stood watching. The feeling – I can't describe it. I'd never felt so betrayed. After everything we'd agreed. Alan didn't even notice I was there but Erin did. Her eyes locked onto mine but she didn't stop, didn't say anything. Her expression was so cold. There was a stillness, a silence. She just kept looking.'

Sue's dark eyes darted at Abby. Her voice hardened 'Don't look at me like that. As though I should have known better. You always were a censorious little bitch.'

'I didn't say anything.'

'No, but then you never did, did you?'

It took all Abby's strength to remain calm. There was nothing to be gained from storming out of there or venting her feelings. Sue had gone over to stand by the window. The sun glinted off the sea. People hurried past, their faces bright in the sun but their coats done up against the wind.

'When it was over, Alan saw me. I backed away. He came after me, hauling his trousers on, but I ran out into the street.'

She was addressing the window now. 'I ran across the square. I was sick just behind the cathedral. I sat by the fountain for ages not knowing what to do, trying to work out where it had all gone wrong. I felt so small, disgusting, such an idiot.

'Alan found me eventually. He said he had thrown Erin out. I told him he needn't have bothered, I was leaving anyway. He begged me to hear him out.'

She started wandering around the gallery, rearranging things, trying to look busy.

'He said he'd woken up and found her already doing things to him. He'd wanted to resist but he just couldn't help himself, he'd been so turned on. Somehow, he persuaded me to come back with him – although, at the time I was still thinking I would collect my stuff and go. When we got in, we had the biggest row we'd ever had. Hit each other, threw things, I think I threatened him with a kitchen knife at some point.

'I told him I hated him, hated her. He begged me to stay. Said she didn't mean a thing to him, it was purely physical, something he'd had to get out of his system. He didn't even like her; if anything, he despised her for letting herself be our plaything.'

Abby was not going to look at her. She stared past her aunt at the boats, the gulls, and the light on the water, trying to keep her breathing steady and reassure herself that there was a good world out there.

'It took a long time, a very long time, to get over it. We stayed away from her, never mentioned her name. But she was always there. That's when I started having the affairs. If you'd asked me back then, I'd have said I was trying to rebuild my confidence but I suppose the ugly truth is that I wanted to punish him. He couldn't say anything – if he did, I threw Erin back in his face. And he couldn't leave; he needed me in those days, needed the money. Perhaps that had always been the case, although he said he couldn't live without me.

'But we couldn't avoid Erin forever, not while she was still with my brother.

We met again at my father's funeral six months later – neither of us could get out of it. Occasions like that can be quite surreal. You think how short life is and how pointless these rifts are.'

Abby nodded. That part at least made sense.

'We didn't mention Zaragoza. The only way we could go on was to act as though it hadn't happened. After all, Liam knew nothing about it. I remember him telling me Erin was pregnant but that wasn't the reason they were getting married. The way he looked at her, he was so full of love, I couldn't tell him.

'Alan had a theory she'd had her own agenda all along – she'd wanted to get pregnant in order to persuade Liam to marry her.'

Abby felt her breath constrict in her throat.

'She and Alan avoided each other as much as possible. It was awkward when the three of us were together, but they were able to put on a show of polite indifference in front of Liam.

'I wouldn't say we forgot about it, but we pushed it to the back of our minds. It was years later that she told me her side of the story. I was staying at your house, perhaps you remember? You were in bed; your father was working away somewhere – it was when he was working on that shopping centre in Kent. Erin and I shared a bottle of wine, we got talking, got careless, one of us brought up Zaragoza. Once the name was out there, you couldn't ignore it any longer.

'She said she woke up and found Alan messing about with her and she tried to stop him but he wouldn't. When she saw me standing there in the doorway, she thought we had planned it all along and that I was watching for gratification.'

Sue turned and smiled. 'Did you think you were conceived out of love? Well, it doesn't matter, does it really in the end?'

It was almost too much to take in. Abby had to move away, to put some distance between her aunt and herself. She got up and walked to the back of the shop, picking things up pointlessly, trying to control the shake in her hands.

'She said she'd grabbed her things and run, got the first flight back to England. She saw a doctor, took the morning-after pill. I'm sorry but it's what happened. Only it didn't work. She was horrified, expected you to be born with some awful deformity.

'She never told my brother. She didn't want to hurt him. She couldn't bear the pain of him finding out, looking at her differently. But you were born. You were perfect – she couldn't believe you weren't damaged. She had to live with the guilt, the way you'd been conceived, the way she'd deceived your dad. I think it contributed to her depression. I'm not proud of it, but I was a bit glad about that.'

Abby's hands curled into fists, the nails digging into her skin.

'You had her looks so it was easy enough to fool Liam. But she was always looking for signs that you'd inherited some of Alan's nature. You would always remind her of him. She was determined to make it up to you. Perhaps she over-compensated in some ways. Made you too dependent. Clingy.

'Neither of us heard Liam come in while she was telling me this. The first thing I was aware of, he was just standing there in the middle of the room. I could tell by the look on his face that he'd heard every word.'

Abby's heart detonated.

'He was very calm. He asked me to leave. I don't know what went on between them that night, but he'd never have Alan in the house again. They stayed together but I don't suppose he saw Erin in the same way after that. But he never took it out on you. It didn't change the way he felt about you. You were always his little girl.'

Abby felt the anger creep up her body into her face. She fought against it, she must hold it back.

'Perhaps, like me, he had the affairs out of revenge. She couldn't do a thing about it. Except for that final act. I think the suicide was to punish all of us. It's often a selfish act, isn't it?'

Abby gripped the edge of the table. Her eyes were burning. Sue repositioned a picture on the wall.

'When you saw me with Marco that time, it felt like

retribution – as if Erin had sent you. The way our eyes met. History repeating. I felt haunted by you from the moment you appeared. You look so like her.'

'And you hated me for that?'

'I'm telling you how I felt. I'm not saying it was right.'

'You're unbelievable.' She could barely bring herself to look at her aunt. 'You don't think any of it was your fault, do you?'

'No I don't, not really.'

'And Josh? Are you going to justify that little episode, too?'

Sue turned to another picture with a sigh. Outside, the clouds had slid over and a few drops of rain landed on the window.

'Josh. You might not believe me but I thought he was older. He certainly gave that impression. He worked at the garage where I used to fill my car up. One day he slipped me a cheeky note with the change. It happened a few times, and then one evening I told him to get in the car if he meant it. We found a layby – well, you can guess the rest.

'We'd been seeing each other a few weeks when I got a job at the school he was at. It wasn't as if he could hide from me there. It was a shock. I tried to end it but he'd become very attached.

'It was never anything serious, as far as I was concerned. I've already explained my reasons for having affairs. I told Josh he shouldn't be getting involved with me, encouraged him to find someone else, and I was relieved when he said he was seeing a girl of his own age. It never crossed my mind it was Philippa. When I found out, I went mad of course. It was a shock for him, too – he hadn't known we were related. Only found out when I picked up his blazer after lovemaking and the pictures fell out – one of those strips from a photo booth. Of them together, smiling, serious, pulling faces, kissing.'

She stopped and closed her eyes.

'I ended things but he kept coming back. Said it wasn't serious with Philippa, she was too young, it was just a crush. He promised to let her down gently. But then events overtook us.'

She wiped a smear from the glass front of the picture with her sleeve. 'Someone spotted us holding hands on Brighton Pier. We'd always been so careful, but we were so far from the school we thought it was safe.

'That evening I got a phone call from the Head. I was given a choice – to be fired or resign. I took the opportunity to go quietly before the scandal broke.

'Alan had been trying to persuade me to move abroad for some time. It was his dream. He jumped at the chance, although he started to suspect something was up so I had to tell him. He asked if it was over and I told him it was. He was furious but agreed to stay with me. He still loved me, you see. I can't think why – it made me behave badly. I'd discovered he was much sweeter when he felt insecure.'

Abby shook her head. 'You're despicable.'

'I didn't love him much by then, but what choice did I have? I wasn't just thinking of myself. If I'd stayed in England, the news would have got out and the school would have been closed down. All those people would have lost their jobs.'

A laugh escaped Abby. 'So, that was big of you.'

Sue gave her a cold stare. 'Anyway, it was a new start for all of us. I thought it might work. I wanted to try and get back my relationship with Philippa. She'd been so difficult lately.'

'*Difficult?* How did you expect her to react to knowing her mother was sleeping with her boyfriend?'

Her aunt carried on as though she hadn't heard. 'It seemed to be working. It was such a relief to finally settle somewhere after months of travelling. The villa was a wreck but the surroundings were spectacular. It was all we'd ever dreamed of.

'When Liam asked if we could have you to stay for a few weeks when he was on honeymoon – he begged actually – I knew it was going to be difficult, but I couldn't think of a reason to say no that would have made any sense to him.'

She looked exasperated. 'I wanted to like you Abby. I wanted to be able to atone for your mum's death by being nice to you, by making you happy, helping you find your voice again. But you made it very difficult. You weren't easy to like.'

Abby's hand jerked and cut across the table, sending pots and trinkets onto the floor. Sue sprang back. While she was trying to understand what had just happened, Abby's eyes fell on a rock with a painted scene on it. She could pick it up and throw it at her aunt and it would all be over. She wouldn't have to hear any more.

'Sometimes I think Erin sent you,' Sue said. 'You certainly got your revenge on all of us, didn't you?'

Abby's fingers strayed towards the rock but then withdrew. In the end, what good would it do?

Looking up, she saw Sue follow her thoughts. 'You needn't bother. Nature's taken care of it.'

Abby grabbed the small dark bottle on the desk containing the tablets Sue had been taking. She read the label. Her breath caught.

'How long have you got?'

'A month, perhaps two.'

'I'm sorry.'

'No you're not.'

'Does Mina know?'

'No, and I don't want her to. Not until after. I want her to get on with her life, make a new start. She'll be quite well provided for. Always has been – the English house was in my name. I paid for Mina's schooling and a lot of her care. Now she'll have this place, if she wants it. And now, if you don't mind, I want to be left alone.'

Wordlessly, Abby walked over to the door, turned the Closed sign back to Open, and left.

Chapter Forty-Two

'A baby's been kidnapped,' said Mina, rushing in from the shop. 'In broad daylight. Everyone's talking about it out there. He was taken from his house. *Signora* Nardini. You know, the one with the canaries? In one of those houses in *via dell amore*. I just met Angelina – she said the police called on her. They're calling on everyone.'

'Terrible,' said Alan. 'The poor parents must be worried sick.'

'I'd better see if there's anything we can do,' said Sue.

Abby looked at her plate. Blood roared in her temples. The fear was so bad she thought she would have a heart attack. They would come here. They would find the baby. Someone must have seen her.

'Are you okay, Abby?' Mina's voice was sickly sweet. *She knows*, thought Abby. She managed a shrug and a smile but she couldn't think about eating.

As soon as she dared, she went back down to the tower. Philippa still looked battered and exhausted, but she smiled at her. Abby recoiled at the sight of the baby suckling Philippa's breast. *Couldn't he tell that she wasn't his mother?* At last there was a popping sound and Philippa lifted him up and laid him in the chest. There was no sign of the gun.

The more Abby looked at him, the more she realised he looked nothing like the first one. He was bigger, stronger, with a larger head and less scrunched-up features. Surely Philippa could see that? Was she just pretending not to? Perhaps she was biding her time, waiting for Abby to admit what she had done. But then it struck Abby that Philippa had refused to look at him last night. She didn't know what

238

he looked like.

'When are you going to tell your parents?' Abby asked.

'I don't know. Why do you always have to spoil everything?'

'We could say it was Luca's.'

Philippa looked exasperated. 'No, we couldn't.'

The baby hadn't been asleep long when he coughed a few times, and then started crying, quite quietly at first but soon very loudly, balling his fists and arching his back. They tried shushing him but it had no effect. Footsteps outside the door, Philippa closed the lid of the chest with a bang, and the crying stopped.

Mina stood in the doorway, a triumphant look on her face. The crying started again, muffled but distinctive.

'What have you got in there?'

'Don't you dare,' said Philippa, as she followed Mina's eyes.

Ignoring her, Mina sprang to the chest and lifted the lid. 'It's the missing baby,' she whispered.

She reached to pick him up.

'Don't touch him. Stop her, Abby.'

How was she supposed to do that?

'Did you hear what I said? She'll ruin everything. She'll tell the others. For God's sake, don't you see what will happen? She'll run and tell like she always does, and they'll take the baby off me and they'll send you away. They've never wanted you here.'

But it was already too late. Mina ran to the door and screamed, 'They've got the baby – the missing baby!'

In a few moments, Sue arrived, breathless and dishevelled. She stared at the baby in disbelief.

'How did he get here?' she asked. And then, her voice rising gradually, she said, 'What were you thinking of? He'll suffocate in there. You've got to take him back to his parents.'

But Philippa shook her head. 'He's mine. He's my baby.'

For the first time ever, Abby could see fear in Philippa's eyes. Her voice was unnaturally high, breathless, as though she might start laughing or screaming at any moment. The baby's crying was nothing like the other baby's feeble cry.

'He's mine,' Philippa repeated. 'This is Francesco.'

Her mother was looking at Philippa as if she didn't know her. Then she knelt down on the floor but made no move to come any closer. When she spoke, her voice was calm, measured, a teacher reasoning with a volatile pupil, but with a note of barely suppressed hysteria.

'This is not your child. He belongs to a family in the village and he was taken from his pram this morning. They're out looking for him right now. The police are calling on all the houses. They'll be here soon. Philippa, this is very, very serious.'

Philippa started to laugh quietly. 'No. No, this is my baby. I should know. I gave birth to him.'

'You did not.'

'I did. I had him last night. Nine months, Mum, and you didn't even notice.'

Sue looked as though she had been slapped. 'Don't be so stupid,' she said. 'Philippa, that baby is not newborn. I can see that from here. I don't know what game you're playing...'

'It's not a game. Ask Abby.'

Abby felt Sue's hard eyes on her. She looked down fixedly.

'Well, come on then?' Sue's face was tight, her eyes full of light.

Abby felt her throat tighten, as though being choked from the inside.

'Tell her,' Philippa demanded. 'Tell her what happened last night, Abby.'

Sue gave a short laugh. 'Oh yes, please do.'

Abby looked from one to the other.

'Tell her,' Philippa shouted, but Abby was playing over the events in her head, everything from watching the birth yesterday to lifting the baby out of its pram that morning.

'For God's sake, just open your mouth and say something, you fucking freak!'

240

It was like a catch springing open. Somewhere between watching Philippa close the lid of the trunk and hearing her call her a freak, she realised she no longer cared about her approval. The look Philippa gave her was pure contempt. She looked a mess, slumped there, her face swollen with tears, but she still thought she could make Abby feel worthless.

Later, perhaps Abby would look back and think how random things really were, how a few seconds, a couple of words, even a look could change the course of your life. Abby had done something so terrible she didn't want to think about it. She could own up to taking the baby, but she would never win Philippa back now and she realised she didn't even want to. She was the same as everyone else; she had just been better at hiding it. Everything seemed so clear now.

She shrugged, holding Sue's glare. Her throat burned but she forced out the words.

'I don't know what she means,' she said in a whisper.

Philippa started. 'Abby, please. Tell her it's my baby. Tell her I gave birth to him last night. You were there. You helped me.'

Abby shook her head slowly.

Sue looked at her. 'Well?'

'I don't know anything about it.'

'Thank you.' Sue's voice was like an ice-cold blade as she turned back to Philippa. 'I think I might have noticed if you were expecting a baby, don't you? So, how did it get here?'

Philippa moved swiftly, grabbing a handful of Abby's hair and yanking it. 'Why are you doing this?' she shouted. Then she saw Sue moving to pick up the baby.

'Don't touch him. I don't want your hands on him. I don't want him contaminated with your filth.'

'Philippa, you're not well.'

'I'm fine. I've never been better. Do you want to know who the father is?'

'Don't,' said Abby.

But there was no way she could get through to Philippa now.

Her cousin's mouth spread into a malicious grin. 'It's Marco. Your Marco – except he isn't really yours, is he?'

Sue looked stunned. 'What are you talking about?'

'You heard. It was easy. What are you going to do about it? Tell Dad how I stole your lover just like you stole mine? Because if you don't, I will – he deserves to know that you're cheating on him. Again.'

A slap rang out. Philippa gasped. She staggered backwards, almost dropping the baby. She slumped over him, catching her breath, moaning and cooing, trying ineffectually to soothe him.

Abby put her hands over her ears, trying to block everything out.

'Why are you doing this?' Sue demanded. 'I don't believe a word of it. None of it makes any sense.'

'In your world, perhaps not.'

For some moments, they stared at each other. It was as if a film had stalled and restarted.

'Okay, yes. If that's what this is all about, yes, I am in a relationship with Marco. And I suppose you found out that we are leaving together. Abby told you, of course. She would, wouldn't she?'

She rounded on Abby. 'This is your fault. You told her everything. You're a scheming little bitch. Listening at keyholes and spying through cracks. Look what it's done to my daughter. For someone who barely speaks you've caused an awful lot of trouble.'

Abby still blocked her ears to the sound of the baby crying and Sue shouting. She wanted to be far away before anyone discovered the truth about the baby. He was still crying furiously, clenching his fists and shooting his legs up and down.

Sue appeared to come to her senses. 'For God's sake, we've got to get this little one back to its parents. We can fight later.' She held out her hands for the baby but Philippa took a step back.

'What's happening?'

No-one had heard Marco opening the door. He must have come looking for Sue and heard the commotion from outside. Abby held her breath.

Sue took him by both hands and pulled him inside. 'My daughter says this is your baby,' she said, her voice high and hysterical, almost laughing. 'You're going to tell her that's impossible, aren't you?'

Marco took one look at the baby and stopped.

'This is Gabriele. Where did you find him?' He lifted him out of Philippa's arms. She tried to stop him, but he shook her off. 'Is this a joke? I'm taking him back.'

There was a moment of silence as Marco walked towards the door. The baby stopped crying, secure in his big arms. A scrape of metal made Abby swing round. Philippa was holding the shotgun, pointing it directly at Marco.

'Give him back.'

He looked for a moment as though he was going to laugh, but then thought better of it. He knew she was a pretty good shot, despite the fact that the gun was waving from side to side because she was so worked up. She was breathing audibly through her mouth.

He said softly, 'You're not going to shoot me while I'm holding the baby, are you? So, put the gun down, let me put Gabriele down safely, and we can talk.'

She refused, still waving the gun involuntarily, her shoulders jerking with the tension.

'His name's Francesco.'

She was very pale, Abby noticed. She saw that the dark patch on her jeans had spread right down her legs to the knees. She swayed slightly as she stood. Her teeth were chattering and a spasm of pain crossed her eyes, but she held firmly to the gun, just as she had to the baby.

Slowly, maintaining eye contact the whole time, Marco laid the baby down on the floor in front of Abby.

'Take him back,' he whispered.

She made to pick him up. 'Don't move,' Philippa shouted. Abby froze.

243

'You want me to apologise for that night, is that it?' Marco said. 'Okay. I apologise. Although I seem to remember it wasn't my idea. But what's it got to do with this? This isn't your baby.'

Sue's face was contorted with pain and confusion. 'Why?' she asked him, shaking her head. 'I really, genuinely thought…'

'Let's talk about it later.' He turned back to Philippa. 'Please. This isn't fair. He doesn't have anything to do with this.'

He took a step towards her. She let out a scream. He kicked the gun upwards and threw himself on top of Philippa, grappling with her, but she still had hold of the gun. The baby was on the floor, screaming. Marco had his hands around Philippa's throat to make her drop the gun. She threw it down. It clattered onto the floor.

'Abby!' Her eyes were pleading. Abby knew what she wanted her to do but it was hopeless. She had never used a gun and was afraid to even hold it.

Would you kill someone for me? That's what she had asked her once. That was what she wanted now.

Chapter Forty-Three

Abby stepped off the plane into driving rain. She picked up a hire car and found her way onto the motorway, and then along a series of smaller roads. She had booked a hotel in the town because she didn't know how she would react to seeing the village. She would work up to it gradually.

On the plane, she had read in the paper that there were calls for James to resign. Someone at the school had leaked the news that the education secretary had taken his children out of school during term time for 'family reasons', provoking outrage among parents who had had their requests denied for holiday or, in one case, a wedding. The head teacher refused to be drawn on the precise circumstances and pointed out that his children had a one hundred per cent attendance level, but the tone of the article was indignant about what it described as the cabinet minister's 'breathtaking hypocrisy'.

Taking her phone out of airplane mode, Abby found several missed calls from James – presumably attempts to warn her too late about the furore, or perhaps blame her for the situation even though she had had nothing to do with the decision to remove the girls from school. She decided she didn't have the energy for another confrontation. Besides, she needed to stay focused. She deleted the calls and put the phone on silent.

The hotel was a fin de siècle building, faded grandeur, dated facilities, but with a pleasant view of a park. In the evening, she sat on the balcony looking up at the village high above. Villa Leonida, in its resplendent new guise, looked down at her from its commanding position, daring her to come closer. She looked back at it that first evening,

245

biding her time, plucking up courage.

She spent the next morning revisiting the squares and towers in the town, and tried to find the shop where Philippa had suggested taking the baby. Later, she drove out to the coast, walked along the promenade where they used to eat ice creams and play on amusement machines. On the way back, she stopped off along the river, walked up over the bridge, and found the beach where she and Philippa had lain on the rocks. But this morning, enjoying a freshly squeezed orange juice on the hotel terrace in the early sunlight, she realised she couldn't delay her appointment with the village itself any longer.

Santa Zita was disturbingly familiar. A bit cleaner, better cared-for, but essentially the same. Garish red factory-made tiles had replaced some of the old terracotta roofs, and some of the houses that she remembered in bleak grey had been painted in cheerful lemon, pink or peach. Some of the trees had been felled to form vineyards or install swimming pools. The houses were starting to creep up the hill now towards Villa Leonida, making it seem less remote and imposing, but she had no difficulty recognising the place.

She had left the car in the car park just outside the village, noting with relief that cars were now banned from the square. She hadn't fancied negotiating the narrow arch even in that tiny vehicle.

Now she was here at last, she wasn't sure what she felt. She had thought that being here would bring her closer to past events, but really, she was seeing it all with new eyes. The little piazza was busier than she remembered. People were sitting at the tables outside the bar – Armando's bar, as she thought of it – and congregating around the fountain, taking selfies and playing on their phones.

She headed for the path in the far corner, and followed it up from the piazza in a daze. The views were as beautiful as she remembered – the hills, each a different shade of green, folded into each other.

Perhaps it was a trick of the light, but she saw a small person walking up the path ahead of her, a girl with tight

French plaits, combed at perfectly even intervals, clutching a notebook as though her life was contained in it. She recognised this figure as herself, but at the same time knew she had nothing to do with the person she was now. She watched the child push the chained gates. They melted, and the girl walked through them along the path towards the house.

The adult Abby stood watching. She wanted to follow the girl inside but she could see that the gates were locked and the land taped off, which was in a way a relief. Someone else was standing at the gates looking in, his hands in the pockets of his coat. He was forty-ish, scruffy, with hair in a ponytail. Her heart missed a beat as he turned towards her. Marco. But, of course, it couldn't be. Marco would be in his sixties now. What was he doing here? Were some people's lives so empty that they came here just to look?

Onto the gates were tied dozens of bunches of flowers with little notes. Studying them, she felt ashamed of her anger. It was touching that people like this man had bothered to come all this way and leave flowers for people they didn't even know.

She stood there, taking it in. But there was no sign of Philippa here. No giggling, whispering, burping, singing, crying, swearing. Living. Just a silence buzzing in her ears. Not even the cicadas' relentless screech. Perhaps it was too early in the year, but there should be *something.* She turned to go.

As if in reply to her thoughts, the sound of a baby crying made her stop, her heart lurching. There wasn't one to be seen. Was she imagining it? It sounded so real, cutting through her. Cautiously, she turned towards the noise, following the path back down towards the little church.

She hovered outside, disbelieving, and yet…

But before she could open the door, she realised the cries came from further away. She walked on down the path and saw a young family walking through the piazza below, the baby in a papoose on her father's back, a floppy pink hat on her head. The top of the papoose was folded down around her face like petals. The couple looked at the menu outside the restaurant and, after a short discussion, decided to eat there, manoeuvring the pram around the knot of other diners. An elderly man came out and showed them to a table.

Her throat suddenly dry, she walked back into the piazza and headed for Armando's bar, which looked exactly as she remembered. She pushed the door open, wondering what she would find inside. It had changed very little; she even recognised some of the posters on the wall – faded now – of the bridge, and the hills, and the bar itself in the previous century. But the air was no longer thick with smoke. A man who looked a little like Armando was serving, and she guessed it was probably his son.

She took a seat, surrounded by strangers, but seeing familiar faces and hearing old voices. *Did any of it really happen?*

She looked at her watch and was surprised to see how much time had gone by since she had arrived at the gates of the house. How long had she stood there? What had she been doing? It surely couldn't have taken her that long to walk up to the house and back? Another of those memory lapses that had dogged her life.

An elderly, gaunt-faced woman sitting by the fridge met her eyes in the gilt mirror.

I remember her. Who is she?

'On holiday?' the barman asked, bringing her to her senses.

'Actually, I'm looking for someone,' she said, reciting the little speech in Italian she had rehearsed on the plane.

'Someone who used to live in this village many years ago. His name was Luca. Do you know him?'

The barman pulled his mouth down into a horseshoe. *'Giornalista?'*

She shook her head. 'No, I'm not a journalist. I'm a doctor.'

He rubbed the side of his face.

248

'*Luca? Comercialista? Notaio? Il figlio di Ferdinando? Quello con l'occhio difettoso?*' He pulled down the corner of one eye.

She gestured helplessly. He went into the back and shouted for someone, talking in rapid Italian. A voice yelled something she couldn't catch, and the barman wandered back through the bar and called to someone else across the piazza.

'He is coming. He speaks English,' he said, going back to polishing glasses.

A few moments later, a man of around seventy, with grizzled hair, came in and was pointed in her direction.

'Hello, my name is Carlo. I speak English. My wife's American. How can I help you?'

She explained again who she was looking for, but this time was also able to convey that Luca had been a teenager in 1992.

Carlo also wanted to know if she was a journalist.

'We've had so many reporters and police up here since they found the bodies.'

She was beginning to glimpse why Philippa's identity had remained a secret. The villages were closing ranks against the outsiders, protecting their own.

'No. A friend sent me. I wanted to give him a message.'

In a protracted and at times heated discussion with a cluster of people standing at the bar, they narrowed the search down to two Lucas of the right age – one who had moved down to Bari, the other a dentist still living in the area.

'And there's the Luca in Montebello,' said Carlo. 'He works for the paper industry. It's about twenty minutes from here. If you like, I can give him a call.'

She felt a jolt of alarm, not at all sure what to say but he was already keying in a number.

'It's been so busy since the bodies were found,' he said. 'Some people come just to look, sometimes they have a theory about what happened. Occasionally they're looking for someone they've lost. There was a man here earlier, looking for his father. He thinks one of the bodies might be his. His father walked out on them when he was still a boy and hasn't been seen since. They thought he had gone off with another woman – he'd done it before. But when he saw the news about the bodies, he started to think there might be another reason for his disappearance. He remembered his father had done some work at the house shortly before.'

It fell into place then - the man at the gates of Villa Leonida she had thought was Marco. It must have been Nino. She had a sudden memory of Philippa in dressing-up clothes calling him over, putting the camera into his hands and ordering him to take their picture.

'Usually people are just curious,' Carlo was saying. 'They are moved by it. Who knows if they'll ever find anything?'

The voices at the bar rose again. One appealed to Carlo and he shrugged. 'It's always been a strange place. It was abandoned after the war and was a ruin when I was growing up. My mother told me it was cursed. She banned me from going there when I was young – of course, that made it more exciting.'

The excitable man was off again. 'He's saying it's the perfect place for a murder. Hidden by trees in summer and mist in the winter.' Carlo shook his head, wading into the debate and then withdrawing. 'He says it should be pulled down. But Matteo here says it's good for business.'

Carlo laughed at something the man said and shook his head. 'Tourists at my restaurant keep asking which house it was. They always look surprised when I point up there. That lovely pink house, they say? As if horrible things can only happen in horrible places.

'Something terrible happened in this village during the war – that's why the villa and a lot of the other houses were left empty for years. There were very few children left afterwards, and those of us who grew up here felt guilty playing in front of people who had lost their own children. We were like shadows.'

She waited for him to expand but he seemed lost in

thought. He swallowed his drink and stared into the distance. She took her chance. It might not come again. 'I remember my friend telling me something once about a baby who went missing.'

Her heart beat fast. Carlo threw the question out to the people at the bar. More discussion, shoulders hunching, heads shaking. One man's voice rose above the others.

'There was something,' Carlo translated. 'Gabriele. He's an architect. He's moved down to town, but he visits his mother here quite often. I'll see if he's about.'

Chapter Forty-Four

'My mother told me about it as soon as I was old enough to understand.'

Gabriele Nardini showed her into his garden. She recognised at once the magnolia tree under which the pram had stood all those years ago. He was in his mid-twenties, pale, skinny, with thinning blond hair and round glasses.

'Because of what happened she always fussed over me, worried about my health and every sort of danger. They found me in the church – in front of the altar. She went there to pray and there I was. To her, it was a miracle.'

A vision crept into Abby's mind of the vengeful Madonna in the painting beating off the Devil with her club. Gabriele's mother would have looked up into those eyes as she lifted her baby up from the floor. No wonder she thought a miracle had occurred.

'There were stories that I had been carried off by wolves or bad spirits of the forest. People really used to believe things like that. She was sure I was returned for a purpose – that puts a lot of pressure on you when you're a child. You feel you have to achieve enough to justify being given that second chance.'

'What do you think happened?' Abby forced herself to ask.

'It was the hawkers,' he said without hesitation. 'It happens from time to time. There was a woman down south who tried to smuggle a child off a beach under her big skirt.

'This lot had been round earlier, a man and a woman, trying to sell linens. My mother was reluctant, because she'd already bought some a few days before and they were terrible quality, but she gave them some money because she was afraid they would put a curse on her, otherwise. They did that sometimes.

'She could see the woman peering past her into the house, having a good look at what was inside. My parents weren't well off but these people would take anything they could sell. My father came home and saw them off, and she thought they'd gone.

'Anyway, after a feed she put me out here while she was preparing the lunch. I always slept better out of doors. Once I was asleep, she could pretty much guarantee I would stay that way for a couple of hours, which gave her time to get on with the household tasks.

'That day, she looked at the time and was surprised that I hadn't woken. She went outside and saw that the pram was perfectly still and there was no noise. She tiptoed up to have a look. It was empty.

'All sorts of things went through her head – she checked all around in case I'd somehow fallen out or been attacked by foxes. There was no sign. Someone must have climbed over this wall here. We didn't have the railings in those days.

'She stood there screaming, and neighbours dashed round to see what was going on. No-one could believe it. The police organised a search. Everyone joined in. They scoured everyone's land. My father said one of the worst aspects was that any one of those people looking might have been the abductor. He didn't know who he could trust.'

He looked at Abby. 'Do you have children, *signora*?'

'Yes. Two girls.'

'Then I think you can imagine how it feels.'

She nodded. Her heart squeezed at the thought of her two girls. She had thought about the baby every time she had lifted her own babies out of their cots or left them to sleep. It was the reason she had been so against leaving them with anyone they didn't know well, why she would never trust a teenage babysitter, and why she had sometimes got up in the night to check they were still there.

'What state were you in when they found you?'

253

'That's the funny thing. I didn't seem harmed. I had blood on me, but it wasn't my blood. Must have been some sort of ritual. I was found in front of the altar. But my mother always swore there was a psychological effect. I was an anxious baby. I'd just started to sleep through the night, but after the abduction I went back to waking every couple of hours. And she was an anxious mother – never let me out of her sight, even though they'd caught the man who did it.'

'Caught him?'

'Some of the villagers caught the hawker. They tried to beat a confession out him. I'm ashamed to say that in their frustration they got carried away and the poor man died. But I suppose if they hadn't, I wouldn't have been brought back. Who knows what life I would have had?'

Her heart dropped. So, that was the third body – the latest line of enquiry.

He turned his mouth down. 'The police found the body hanging from a tree some weeks after I'd been returned. They suspected my father. Made his life difficult for a while but they couldn't prove anything. To be honest, I think they sympathised with him. My parents were good people. They never asked for any of this to happen. No-one was going to betray my father for what happened, or his friends who were just trying to help.'

So many emotions surged through her. On the one hand, the relief was enormous. The baby she'd taken had not only survived but had also grown into an attractive, apparently well-adjusted young man. The fear and guilt she'd had for Gabriele all these years were lifted. But yet another person had been killed as a result of her actions – something she hadn't even considered before.

And, of course, it still left the other baby – Philippa's baby, the one Abby had replaced with Gabriele. No-one seemed to know anything about a second baby. And yet someone must have taken him from the church that first night. If he had been dead and they'd taken him to bury, it was odd that nothing had been recorded. There was no grave in the cemetery, no mention anywhere of a mystery baby. That left, as the most likely explanation, that someone had taken him and brought him up as their own. She hoped so much that this was what had happened. But then as Gabriele said, what kind of life might he have experienced?

For all she knew, she might have already passed him in the piazza. He could be any of the young men drinking prosecco in the evening sun. Perhaps she would know when she saw him. A glint of red hair, Philippa's infectious smile, her glacial green eyes. She would probably spend the rest of her life looking.

Chapter Forty-Five

Luca met her two days later in the bar. He worked as a sales rep for an international paper company so his English was good enough not to need Carlo's translation services.

Looking at the photograph of the girls in their dressing-up clothes, he went quiet.

'You know it's her, don't you?' he said quietly. 'The body at the villa. I'm glad she never got old. I'm sorry, that's a very bad thing to say. I'm not glad this thing happened to her. I just mean, she was lovely and that's the memory I want to keep. Do you understand?'

She nodded. 'Yes, of course.'

'I loved her. We were young, very naïve. We weren't thinking about the future. I just wanted the present to stretch on forever. I knew I'd never feel that way about anyone again.

'But something happened. I sensed a change in her. She started to pull away. I didn't know what I'd done wrong. I thought she must have changed her mind about us. We fell out over silly things. She started picking fights. I didn't understand why she wouldn't let me touch her any more.

'Her father was strict. He had a terrible temper. I thought perhaps he had found out about us and told her to stay away – although, knowing Philippa, if he had said that she'd have been all the more determined to be with me.'

Abby smiled. He must have understood Philippa better than she'd thought.

'Eventually she told me she was pregnant. I didn't handle it well. I was fifteen. I panicked. I didn't understand it – we'd been so careful, I hadn't thought it was possible to get pregnant doing what we were doing. I was scared for what my parents and her parents would say.

'My family is very traditional. They would have never forgiven me. They wanted me to marry a local girl. My father had seen Philippa around, and he said she was heading for trouble.'

Luca looked over at the bar, where several people were shouting out orders at once and the coffee machine was roaring. 'It never crossed my mind that anyone else might be the father.'

He wiped a hand over his face. 'I told her I couldn't deal with it. I heard from friends about a woman in another village who girls went to when they wanted to stop a pregnancy. I told her to go there. We had a big row.

'After that, she refused to talk to me. She had a friend to stay so she wasn't around as much. I assumed she had gone to the abortionist because she didn't look like she'd put on weight. But she looked ill, she looked different, that wonderful vitality had gone. I thought it must have been a terrible experience for her. It played on my mind. I felt so bad about what she must have gone through.'

Abby started to get an inkling he knew more about it than he was admitting. 'Do you know what happened to Philippa?' she asked.

He flinched. 'I went to see her, that's all. I just wanted to apologise, see how she was. I swear to you, that's all.'

From the back of the bar there was a shout and a clatter of coins as someone scooped up their winnings from the slot machine. Abby could remember standing around those machines with Philippa, watching her punch the air with excitement, inviting everyone else to join in her celebration. She used to have all sorts of theories about how to win, and on the rare occasion she was successful she seemed to forget all the times she hadn't been lucky.

'When? What happened?'

She recognised something in his eyes. The old struggle of trying to keep something back.

'Nothing. They'd moved away.'

The blinking, the little darting glances to the side as

though he was trapped, looking for a way to escape, gave him away. Her pulse quickened.

'I don't believe you.'

He shrugged, said he couldn't remember, but she kept pushing gently.

'When was this? Did you see her?'

He met her gaze for a moment. She saw it, the fear masked by defiance. He gripped the sides of his head, cast a look up at her.

'All right, I saw her, saw all of them. And I saw you. You were there that night.'

Abby felt as though her chest was being stamped on. He had thrown the fear right back at her. She swallowed. 'What night?'

He leaned in. 'You were the friend, weren't you? How else would you know about it?'

She felt the blush creep up her throat. He could see through to her thoughts just as she could see his.

'I went up there to see her, ask her to forgive me. I'd tried many times but I was determined she wasn't going to send me away this time. I went to the tower where Philippa and I used to meet. I saw you. You were carrying something.'

He had known. All these years he had known. She felt sweat break out on her forehead.

'I couldn't believe what I saw when I went in that place.' He shook his head. 'Oh God, it was terrible.'

His hands were shaking as he lifted his glass. He turned his head so she couldn't see his eyes. 'My beautiful girl, she was dead. Slaughtered like a pig.'

Without realising she was doing it, she placed a hand on his arm. He closed his hand over it. He gripped so hard it hurt.

'There were two other people lying there. Her father and the builder, Marco Mungai. I understood it then. It was Marco's baby. I'd heard rumours but I'd never taken them seriously. Her father must have found them together and shot Marco. Philippa must have got in the way. Alan must have been devastated and turned the gun on himself. Or perhaps Marco retaliated, I don't know, but they were all three lying there.'

Except that it wasn't possible for Alan to be one of the bodies – not if he was still writing his books. She held her breath, looked at the table, didn't dare put thoughts in his head.

She found herself asking, 'Why didn't you tell anyone what you saw?'

He closed his eyes, pressed his forehead as though trying to push it all back inside. 'I heard a noise. That's when I realised Marco was still alive. He couldn't speak, his face was all swollen and there was something wrong with his jaw, but he was pointing at Alan and looking at me, and I knew he was begging me to help him.'

Her heart thumped. 'And did you?'

Luca looked away, slumped back in his chair. 'I should have done. I know I should have. I did something I'm so ashamed of. I was so angry, so full of hate for him taking my precious girl and destroying her – and the baby inside her. I kicked him in the face. Then I walked away.'

He put his head in his hands. 'I still dream about it. Sometimes I'm not even sleeping and I hear him groan, see those eyes pleading. That's what it's done to me.'

Abby couldn't think what to say. None of this was what she had expected.

Luca wiped the sweat from his face. 'I ran. I'm not proud of it, but I ran through the woods. I threw up. When I looked up, he was standing over me.'

'Who, Marco?'

'No. The woodcutter. We stood there staring at each other.'

Abby digested everything. Yes, the woodcutter had been there that night, but what did he have to do with it? She had seen him and she had thought about that over the years, wondered if he'd seen her, if he'd heard the gunshots. It seemed incredible that he hadn't come forward when the bodies were found. He must have remembered. But perhaps he had been afraid to. Or perhaps he was protecting a young boy he thought was responsible.

'Did you move the bodies into the cave?' she asked.

'No. Marco must have done that. The next day I realised I'd lost my wallet. It must have fallen out of my pocket back at the tower. I had to go back. It was the last thing I wanted to do but I had no choice. The wallet had my identity card in it. The police would have come straight to me. They would have found her blood on my clothes, although I tried everything to get it out. I don't see how I could have persuaded them I didn't do it.

'But when I got there, the bodies had gone. At the time, I thought the woodcutter must have moved them. I suppose he thought the same about me, but lately since the story came out that they'd found two bodies not three, I've realised Marco wasn't as badly hurt as I thought. The blood he was lying in – it must have been Alan's and Philippa's. He must have moved the bodies before fleeing.'

So, the woodcutter thought Luca had killed the others. It was just conceivable that Marco had walked away, but if he had why wouldn't he have gone to the police? Unless he, like the others, thought he would be the prime suspect.

It was starting to sink in that without intending or wanting to, Abby might have committed the perfect crime – one for which everyone else felt responsible. Noise broke out in the piazza. A scraping of chairs, people running, someone shouting.

'Something's happened,' the barman said.

Abby stiffened. In the gilt mirror, her eyes met those of the gaunt woman. Someone stood in the doorway and shouted a garbled explanation, but it was too quick for Abby to understand.

A small child not more than six or seven burst through the doors, her waist-length golden hair forming a halo of light in the dark interior.

'Mummy, Mummy, I've just seen a real-live dead person,' she said in English.

Her mother, at the other end of the bar, looked up from

her iPad and waited for a few moments for a punchline. When none came, her smile froze. 'What do you mean, sweetie?'

'It's in the fountain,' the little girl said importantly.

Everything slowed around them. It was as if a plug had been pulled. The barman dropped the cloth he was using to wipe the glasses, and dashed outside. There was a murmur and scraping of chairs as people surged to the door. Abby followed.

'Can I help? I'm a doctor.'

The word *medico* went round. She was pushed to the front. A man shouted at everyone else to get back. A woman was screaming. People were leading their children away, shielding their eyes.

Abby saw the water before she saw the body – it was stained a vermilion red. The body had been hauled out. Someone was attempting resuscitation. The ambulance siren echoed around the hills as it made its way up from the valley, but it seemed unlikely they would be able to do anything.

Someone was ordering the crowd to give her space as she weaved her way through, bracing herself for what she might see. She found herself gazing at the body of a man in his forties, poorly dressed, olive-skinned, and with a six-inch gaping wound at the base of his neck. The blood was no longer flowing. She knelt down beside him and checked his pulse, but there was nothing.

The police arrived and taped off the area, appealing for witnesses to stay in the square and wait until they had given their statement, and for others to give them some space.

The inspector seemed to be asking the barman what had happened. The barman indicated that he'd been inside at the time.

'Qualcuno lo conosce?' asked the inspector. Heads shook. Nobody knew him.

Except for Abby.

Chapter Forty-Six

It had been easy to slip away from the piazza with all the confusion. After handing over to the local emergency service and the police, Abby wandered around for a while, trying to get her thoughts straight. She had gone back to the bar and had a drink, but it was chaotic in there now and she wanted to get away from all the people, be somewhere quiet.

The little church was exactly where she remembered it, screened by shady plane trees, perched if anything a little closer to the edge above the precipitous drop. She tried the door, expecting it to be locked these days, but it eventually gave with a sigh.

The first thing that met her eyes was the painting, the angry Madonna wielding the club. It had been restored in the intervening years and the colours were much cleaner, her robes a brilliant red and the eyes blazing gold. The Devil, still crouching in the shadows, looked less menacing than she remembered, more like a child's depiction with its horns and tail.

Her eyes fell on the exact spot where she had placed the baby years ago, in front of the altar. She pictured him lying there like a sacrificial offering, which of course he had been.

You were supposed to keep him safe.

There was a slight movement in the dark room. A figure with bobbed hair was sitting silently in one of the pews, with her back to Abby, and it gradually sank in who she was.

Mina turned slowly to face her. 'I knew you'd come,' she said at last, her expression a mix of triumph and contempt.

Abby eyed her warily, forcing herself to stay outwardly calm but making a mental calculation of the distance to the door was and how quickly it could be reached and opened. She stood there, her hand resting on a pew, hoping it looked like a casual gesture, but really it was providing essential support.

She began to feel the old tightening sensation in her throat but fought against it, keeping her voice steady. 'I came out here to try and make sense of it all. Is that why you're here, too?'

Mina made a noise that sounded halfway between a whine and a high-pitched giggle. 'They say the killer always comes back to the scene of crime, don't they? I recognised Marco out there, sitting by the fountain, like he didn't have a care in the world. It could only be him.

'I'd watched him make a fool of my father, and then destroy my sister and leave me like this for the rest of my life. Unable to cope on my own. Unable to do anything really except be a danger to myself and others.'

Abby thought of the scene in the piazza, the body dragged from the fountain. The same man she had seen outside the gates of Villa Leonida. She had thought it, too, for a moment.

'But it wasn't Marco. How could it be? He looked like Marco as we knew him then. Twenty-five years ago. That was Nino, his son. He came looking for his father when he heard about the bodies.'

She saw a glint of metal in Mina's hand and realised too late that she still had the knife she had used to stab the man. Abby tried to keep her talking, while moving back millimetre by millimetre towards the door.

'They'll understand,' she said. 'Diminished responsibility or something like that.'

'Oh, they'll understand. But will you? Will you ever understand?'

'I think I do.'

Mina scoffed and then continued as though she hadn't heard her. 'I don't blame him for *everything*. None of it would have happened if you hadn't come and divided us all, spreading rumours, recording people's conversations, drawing pictures of everything you saw. Filthy pictures of things that were only in your head, your twisted mind. Getting everyone to hate each other.'

'But…'

'We never liked each other, did we?'

'No, but…'

'For God's sake, stop interrupting.'

Abby took a step back.

After some moments, Mina continued, 'I wanted to like you but you made it obvious you wanted to replace me. You were more my father's daughter than I was. As soon as I saw you, I knew it was true.'

The hurt in her eyes was matched only by disgust.

'You never really believed that, did you?' said Abby.

Mina carried on as though she hadn't heard.

'It makes sense. Who knows who my father was? I don't believe it was Alan. That became more and more obvious the older I got – the more aware I became of my mother's habits. We had nothing in common, Dad and I, nothing at all. Most of all, I hadn't inherited his vast IQ and that seemed to anger him. It was as though it was the irrefutable evidence and he held it against me. My mother used me as a weapon.'

She looked vulnerable all of a sudden, and Abby felt a tinge of sympathy for her. She had always known things hadn't been easy for Mina, but she was only now letting herself see it from her point of view.

'My mother was a narcissist. She didn't really care about anyone else. She wanted to be at the centre, in control of everyone. My father adored her. He would do anything for her. That's why she stayed with him as long as she did.

'But a part of her despised him for allowing her to be the person she was. He knew she saw other men, but he wanted to believe that he was the only one she actually loved. He may have been right once. Philippa admired her for it. You could see she was going the same way. I hated her. I could see the damage it was doing to Dad.'

Mina was talking to her as though they were close now, as though she were confiding her feelings to a friend. Not for the first time, Abby felt a pang of guilt. But she couldn't forget that Mina had just stabbed someone and still had the knife in her hand.

'And because he was so obsessed with trying to keep her, he had no time for us. We were always in the way. Of his writing and his marriage. He was jealous of us, but especially of me. I suppose every time he looked at me, he saw someone else. Every time I did something he found alien, it was as if I had done it deliberately to hurt him and remind him.'

She took a step nearer. Abby took a step back.

'All I wanted,' she continued in a quiet voice, 'was for him to notice me, and love me. I knew I was different. He got angry with Philippa, too, but never like he did with me. I only had to look at him sometimes to make him angry. Can you imagine what that does to you, day after day, year after year?'

Abby shook her head.

'And just when I thought I might have won some kind of acceptance, he died.' She laughed again, a short, breathless laugh.

'But I thought your father was still alive,' Abby said, confused. 'He wrote another book. It must have been Alan who hid the other bodies. I suppose he did that to protect us.'

Mina laughed. 'I wrote the book. He'd left half of it unfinished. He had all sorts of notes and an outline. It was like painting by numbers, filling in the gaps. I knew him better than anyone, you see. I knew how his mind worked. I watched him plot everything out.

'I'd typed his work for him so often that I knew how he wrote, how he thought. We may not have been blood relatives but our minds worked in the same way. I got to know the stories really well, absorbed the style as though it was my own.'

265

Abby nodded. 'You understood each other.'

But Mina was not going to be knocked off course. 'The one thing, the *one* thing, I could do which pleased him was type his manuscripts. If he didn't, couldn't love me, I'd settle for his appreciation. You know, I cherished those moments, sitting in there with him for hours on end. I sometimes made suggestions. He hardly ever liked them, but just occasionally he agreed they made sense, and he let me into his world just a little bit.

'It helped me gain a little respect from him. I knew he needed me then. Mum wouldn't bother with anything like that and Philippa always had better things to do. But when he got writer's block and had nothing for me to type, I was out in the cold again and it felt even colder than before.

'I knew when you started listening at doors and peeping through keyholes that it would all fall apart. Those drawings. And then the baby.'

Yes, the baby.

'You see…' Abby began.

'No, I don't see. I've never seen.' Her voice went quiet, thoughtful. 'Why did we start that day like any other, getting out of bed, eating breakfast, doing all the normal things. And by the end…'

Abby shrugged helplessly.

'I remember Marco was throttling Philippa, trying to get her to drop the gun. Mum picked up a rock and brought it down on his head. There was a lot of blood but he still wouldn't let go of her. She dropped the gun. It clunked onto the floor. You picked it up.'

Abby swallowed. 'Yes.'

'You let her control you.'

Abby felt her heart in her mouth. She saw through a veil of mist her own childish hands picking up the gun, felt the smooth wood and cold metal in her hands, the weight of it making her arm ache. Not knowing what to do with it, seeing Marco shaking Philippa like a rag doll, blinded by anger and love. And then feeling the gun explode in her hands as the images exploded in her head. She was watching a silent movie, Philippa's face that wasn't there any more, Mina drenched in blood, screaming.

'I remember Philippa's face,' Mina was saying. 'She was telling you to get him off her, to end it. But you were hopeless, weren't you? You just stood there looking at the gun. You lifted it up, pointed it at Marco. And she realised you'd make a mess of it. She shouted "No!" She knew you were a hopeless shot.

'We could all see what was going to happen. I jumped across to take it off you.'

A memory slotted into place. Mina lunged forward trying to wrestle the gun out of her clutch. But Abby's hands felt stuck to it in a grip she couldn't loosen, she'd forgotten how to work them. Instinct made her cling on. She couldn't let Mina have the gun. Who knew what would happen to it in her hands?

'I was trying to stop you,' Mina said.

'I was trying to stop *you.*'

Sue was screaming, the gun was jerking up and down, Mina was pulling and pulling. Abby felt her breath on her face. A flurry of hair and clothes, the baby's cries, Mina's strength as she pulled. And then the explosion. Philippa reeling backwards. Philippa hurt. That spray of blood – so much of it, all over the wall, part of her head obliterated. Abby twitching and heaving. The silence roaring.

'You pulled the trigger,' said Mina. 'Missed Marco, just as I knew you would. Hit Philippa full in the face. In her beautiful face. It's never beautiful in my memories. All the blood and bits; I feel like I've never got them off me.'

Her voice was a whisper now. The air around them was so cold.

'It took a few moments to realise what you'd done. That awful, eerie silence. Mum sitting there in Philippa's blood, just looking at it spreading. Her face was like one of those horror masks.'

Yes, Abby remembered the silence – it was as though time had stopped and no-one knew how to restart it. The world had changed. It could never be the same. She couldn't take in that something so horrible had happened.

And yet Philippa couldn't be dead. That couldn't be the end. She was always okay. She would jump up any minute and say something like, 'You see? It's fake you idiot – it's just paint.'

No she wouldn't. She would never say anything. There was so much damage, you could never scoop up all those bits and put them back in.

Abby stepped towards Philippa's crumpled body but Sue screamed in her face, 'You did this. You did it. It was your fault.'

'I'm sorry, I'm so sorry,' she said over and over. The words were jerking out of her, but she was shaking so much she could hardly understand them.

'Marco ran at us,' said Mina. 'His face was twisted in rage and horror. I screamed at him to get back, get away. We swung the gun at him. He stopped and held his hands up, stepped back. I remember the way his nostrils flared and his chest rose. His lips were moving but he wasn't saying anything. I think he was praying. It made it easy then. We shot him.'

Abby remembered how to let go. As though the bones in her arms had melted. The gun fell. It bounced on the floor, the clatter seemed to go on forever. In the end, it was the baby who broke the silence. She had almost forgotten he was there, lying on the ground where Marco had put him. She remembered thinking the baby had been hit, too, but he hadn't. The blood on his face and body were Philippa's.

And Sue's voice: 'Get him out of here.'

Abby gathered him up and scrambled to her feet. She was trembling so much she thought she would drop him. She could barely remember how to walk. The simple act of putting one foot in front of another seemed alien. She had to step round the bodies of Philippa and Marco. Her eyes fell on her notebook lying there open on the floor. It had a bloody footprint on the page.

But someone blocked her way as she tried to get out of the door. She looked back at the others. Mina was curled in a ball, rocking. Sue was on her knees bent over the trunk, as though she was being sick.

'We knew it was hopeless,' continued Mina. 'We didn't know what to do, we were frozen from the horror of it all. Then my father was there. And this is what I don't understand…' Mina's eyes, red and swollen, were staring into Abby's, searching.

'Where had he come from? I don't know how he got there. He wasn't there before. He shouted. Suddenly he was falling. My dad was falling, clutching his chest. There was blood streaming out from between his fingers, waves of it. He was looking at me when he died, as though it was my fault, as though he would have expected nothing else from me. I've never forgotten that look.'

She shuddered, biting her lip so hard it bled.

'Marco was on the ground. He was still alive. We'd missed him. He called out to Mum. He crawled towards her and tried to grab onto her like a child but she kicked him away, her knee in his jaw. Do you remember that crack? He fell down and stayed there this time. We looked at each other and we knew it was over. There was nothing we could do. We had to get out.

'You see, I remember every detail.'

Abby felt tears escape down her face. She brushed them away but new ones appeared.

'Except for one thing. The more you go over something, the more complicated it gets. Do you find that? You see, I didn't fire the gun a third time. I've been over it so many times in my head, but I'm *sure* I let it drop to the ground after we shot Marco. And then I was curled up next to Philippa. I had my knees up and my hands over my face when I heard the shot. When I took them away, that's when I saw Dad looking at me and dying.'

Her voice had changed. She sounded vulnerable, confused again. A coldness crept over Abby. She wondered what was coming.

'But *you* were there, weren't you? You could have shot him.'

Abby felt a sweep of nausea. Yes, she had seen Alan. He had come through the door just as she had been about to take the baby back.

She heard his voice. 'What the hell's going on? I thought I heard—' Then silence as he stared at the scene in disbelieving horror. 'No. God, no.' And then that roar that was barely human. 'What the hell have you done? You've killed her.'

But then everything went dark. The film jammed again.

When Abby opened her eyes, it was worse; even worse than she thought. If that was possible. Philippa hadn't moved. She wouldn't move, not now. But Alan and Marco also lay motionless on the floor. There was a huge pool of blood. She was trying to work out whose blood was whose and decided it didn't matter. And then Sue was there, holding Abby's face in her hands and saying in that strange, kind voice, 'Abby, listen to me, you have to calm down. Breathe slowly.'

Had she been holding the gun? Did she pick it up again? Had she denied the truth for so long that some of it had become permanently detached? *It could have happened that way...*

Mina stared at Abby, waiting for her response. Eventually, she shrugged, and made that noise again, halfway between a sob and a laugh.

'His look was the same in any case,' she went on. 'The look he gave me when he realised he'd been shot. He just assumed it was all my fault, whatever the evidence before him. I don't know. I don't know which version is right any more. That's why I wanted to see you, for you to tell me. But you won't, will you?'

Abby brushed away more tears. 'I don't know,' she whispered. 'I just don't know.'

Sue sent the girls in two different directions – Abby to take the baby back, Mina to the house to fetch their passports.

Abby stumbled down the path with the baby. She

270

expected a crowd of people and the police to be waiting at the church. She had no idea what she would say. This was where it would end. Her mind was churning, she couldn't breathe. She just wanted someone to take over now, even if that meant spending her life in prison.

But the church was deserted, curiously peaceful. She placed the baby back on the mat in front of the altar where she had left the other one to be guarded by the ferocious Madonna. All the candles were flickering this time. She wiped as much blood off him as she could with her t-shirt, but some streaks had dried and she didn't want to hurt him by rubbing too hard.

Please this time, please look after this one. Keep him safe.

The eyes looking back at her were so hard, so angry. It seemed even less likely that Mary would help her this time. Abby looked round but there was no-one to explain to, no-one to help. She walked back although she didn't want to, hoping someone would stop her but no-one did.

When she got back to the tower, she thought for a moment that she had been abandoned, that she would be the only one left to explain everything. But Sue and Mina came crashing through the trees, Mina carrying Abby's backpack.

'Come on, Abby, we have to go,' Sue said in an unnatural voice that would have chilled her if she hadn't already felt numb with horror. They might as well be going to the shops.

'Leave her,' said Mina.

'We can't.'

She handed Abby her backpack, into which she'd stuffed some clothes and her passport and the bloodied notebook. She grasped Abby's shoulders and brushed her hair away from her face, and said in that frighteningly calm voice, 'Abby, this is your fault. You know that, don't you? You must never ever tell anyone or you will spend the rest of your life in prison, do you understand?'

Realising the chance wouldn't be offered again, Abby followed Sue and Mina down the terraces to the lane right at the bottom, where the car was parked.

'Quick!' said Sue. The three of them jumped in, Abby stealing one last glance behind her at the house.

Sue was cursing under her breath, her lips moving all the time, but what she said was hardly audible and she was rambling, it seemed to Abby. None of them looked at each other. Nobody spoke. She started the engine and they were gone.

The car careered down the track onto the lower road. Mina stared into space. None of them said anything. There was nothing to say that didn't raise more questions. They drove until it was dark, stopping at last in a lay-by somewhere. Abby thought about getting out and running away into the blackness, but what good would that do?

By morning, Sue seemed to have recovered some composure. She made a phone call at a service station in the early hours, and eventually they reached an airport where she bought Abby a ticket.

Clutching her ticket, she walked through the barriers, glancing backwards only briefly and not at all surprised to see that Sue and Mina hadn't waited to wave her off. She had no idea where they were headed but was certain it wouldn't be back to Villa Leonida. At that point, she just wanted to get away from them, from everything. She put on her earphones, listened to Take That on her Walkman, standing squarely in front of the departure board, watching the destinations flicker until she saw the flight to London, then followed the crowd of holidaymakers, showed her boarding pass at the gate, and took her seat.

***

'We shouldn't have taken you with us,' said Mina. 'But we couldn't leave you there to tell everyone. It was a split-second decision and I don't even know who made it. We should have had the courage to kill you. I've done it in my head a million times since.'

Abby nodded. She took another step backwards.

Mina's hand was in her pocket, holding the knife. 'Why didn't you suffer?' she asked. 'I had a breakdown. I told people – I told my teachers everything. They thought I was hysterical, had me shut up. I told the doctors; they just increased the medication. I rang the police; they cautioned me for wasting their time. So, then I came to you. And what did you do? Nothing.'

'What could I have done?' Abby asked at last.

'You owed me. We could have left you there. We could have killed you. You could have come to see me. All those years. You destroyed my family. So, I asked you to help me have a child, give me a chance of a new family, and you wouldn't even do that.'

Something in Abby snapped. Perhaps it was the realisation that she wasn't going to get out of there alive. Perhaps it was sheer incredulity that Mina should think herself capable of being a good mother.

'What did you expect?' she asked, surprised at the strength in her own voice. 'How could you ever think I would want to help you?'

'You're family. You owed it to me.'

'I don't think so.'

Mina looked at her sharply. 'Why didn't you suffer?' she asked again.

Abby shrugged and shook her head. 'I made myself forget. I can do that. I can do it again. I'll forget everything.'

But Mina laughed softly. 'No,' she said. 'No, that won't be necessary.'

She sprang from the pew with surprising agility. Abby saw the knife flash. She made a desperate attempt to fend her off, but she had never been involved in a fight in her life, not even a playground scrap.

She felt the knife rip through her sleeves as she held her arms in front of her, but didn't feel the pain yet. Mina kept striking away with all the zeal of the painted Madonna behind her.

Abby knew she had to do something or die there in that

little church. She kicked out, catching Mina in the stomach so that she doubled up, winded, staggering backwards. Another kick sent the knife flying out of her hand. Abby couldn't see it but she could hear it spinning on the floor.

She turned and threw herself against the door, twisting the ring handle desperately this way and that, but in her panic, she couldn't open it. A movement behind her. Mina had the knife again. Abby darted to the side. Now they had changed places, Abby retreating towards the altar, Mina's eyes alight with adrenalin. Those dolls' eyes, bright as buttons.

She launched herself at Abby, catching her on the side of the head this time. Abby ran but Mina followed. There had to be a way to cut her off. Abby grabbed the candle stand with all the flickering candles, and toppled it in Mina's path. There was a crash as it hit the stone floor. *As long as I keep moving, I can keep her at bay.* But she knew she didn't have the strength to go on deflecting the blows indefinitely, and Mina showed no sign of tiring.

A smell of burning filled her nostrils. The candles had fallen against the curtains. Flames were creeping up the fabric. Mina caught Abby's look and whipped round.

For a second, the knife stopped. Abby stopped flailing. She launched herself at the door again, a last desperate attempt to save herself. *I have to get there, I have to.*

She rattled the handle. She felt Mina's breath on her neck. The door sprang open. Someone caught her. But Mina was right behind.

'Miss Tempest?' the commissario said.

Both women were stunned by the interruption and the fact the policeman knew Mina's name. Mina took a step backwards. She retreated inside the church, holding the knife out in front of her, daring the inspector to come any closer. She slammed into the altar, knocking it back against the wall, still holding the knife.

The painting rocked. With a crash, it pitched forward onto Mina, the crazed Madonna bringing down her club. Mina screamed. Her hand holding the knife slipped.

274

Chapter Forty-Seven

The commissario rushed forward and Abby helped him to lift off the painting and stand it on the floor. Mina's face twisted in agony with a horrible expression of pain and surprise. She emitted a series of choking sounds. The policeman inspected the wound but didn't pull the knife out. He sighed and shook his head. By now, the body was twitching and blood was shooting from Mina's mouth, more appearing as fast as she could cough it up.

His colleague radioed for emergency help as he ripped the fire extinguisher off the wall and attacked the flames.

'Sit down, please,' he said to Abby. 'You need medical attention. And I'll need to take a statement from you.'

She walked slowly to a pew and sank into it, trembling, her eyes fixed on those of the *Madonna del Soccorso*. She sat for what seemed like hours but could only have been minutes. She heard the sirens clanging, coming up from the valley again. She felt a creeping sensation down her arms and down the side of her head, and only then noticed the pain. The wounds were probably superficial but she found it hard to stay calm, seeing all the blood.

'We've been keeping a close eye out for Miss Tempest since a man called Mr Mungai recognised her this morning,' said the inspector. 'He remembered her when she lived at the villa – he used to work there with his father, a builder.

'We looked into her history. She has a severe mental disturbance, a history of violence, and she hasn't been taking her medication. Unfortunately, we lost track of her before she stabbed Mr Mungai by the fountain. He knew she was following him – I imagine she wanted to stop him identifying her. The sad irony is the second body wasn't Mr Mungai's father at all, it was Alan Tempest.

'It seems Miss Tempest killed her father and sister – possibly over Marco Mungai. I believe she was in love with him and killed her sister out of jealousy and her father as he tried to protect her.'

The words swirled around Abby's head. He really had no idea who she was.

'You were very good to help Mr Mungai today. I know you did what you could. Unfortunately, she seems to have wanted to punish you for trying to save him. I'm sorry we didn't get here sooner.'

'Please don't apologise,' she found herself saying. 'I'm just so grateful you came.'

The paramedics arrived and did what they could for Mina, although it didn't seem there was much they could do. Abby's last sight of Mina was of her being stretchered out to the ambulance. There was no siren as they drove off.

'Are you sure the other body was Alan Tempest?' she asked.

'Certain. DNA tests have proved the two victims were related.'

Abby felt lightheaded as she was having her wounds patched up. In the doorway, she thought she saw a familiar figure silhouetted against the light. She must be hallucinating. She looked again, trying to make herself focus.

James smiled apologetically as he walked towards her. He held out his arms and she fell into them, forgetting for that moment everything that had happened recently. Despite the pain, she found herself breaking into a smile, relief mixed with utter bewilderment washing over her.

'What are you…? How did you…?' Not for the first time in her life, she was lost for words.

'Connal told me I'd find you here. I hate to admit he's right about anything, but he was.'

***

'It wasn't that hard to find, actually,' he told her later over dinner in the *Tre Fratelli* restaurant in the square.

The lights were just coming on and the sky was filled with bats and the first fireflies. Carlo brought them a plate of local cheeses with honey, and a dry white wine from the local hills. It all seemed so surreal.

A young woman with chestnut hair and an infectious laugh arrived at the restaurant with her boyfriend. She kissed Carlo, exchanged a few words, and came over to join the elderly couple at the table next to theirs. The young man embraced the gaunt woman whose face was much prettier when she smiled and then the elderly man. Carlo brought them prosecco. A family celebration on what to them must be an evening like any other – another reminder that the world carried on in spite of everything that had happened. Philippa had passed through like a comet and left a trail of destruction, but to the people sitting here smiling and drinking, she was invisible.

'I'd gone back to the house for some more stuff,' said James. 'A woman turned up, looking for you. She was very on-edge. I assumed she was one of your patients. She looked so desperate I asked her in so she could get herself together. I felt sorry for her.

'I said I had no idea where you were but she didn't believe me. She got more and more agitated. I worked out pretty soon she was Mina.'

Abby nodded quickly. She could picture it.

'She threatened me. I knew she was going to get violent. I was frightened for my life, to tell the truth. I only just managed to get her out of the door.'

Abby had noticed the scratch marks at the side of his face, a bruise up by his hairline. She could hardly believe what he was telling her. To think he could have ended up getting hurt. James, who had nothing to do with Villa Leonida and who had such an optimistic, generous view of other people.

'After she'd gone, I didn't know what to do. I knew she'd be looking for you. I couldn't ring the police. I knew

277

you wouldn't want that, so I rang Connal.'

He drank some wine.

'That was a tricky conversation. He wouldn't take my calls at first, but when he heard about Mina he agreed to talk. He said you'd have come out here; it made sense. He suggested the little church. Said it was the logical place for you to go. It's where you left the baby, isn't it? I'm sorry I didn't get there in time to be any help.'

'At least you came. Thank you. You didn't have to.'

She was touched, perplexed, and also incredibly grateful. Whatever had happened between her and James, it was humbling to know she could still count on him in an emergency.

Sitting here with him in this beautiful square made it almost seem as though none of it had happened and they were together on a weekend break. But she had to remind herself that he wasn't hers any more. She would think about that later.

'Of course I had to,' he said with a barely concealed note of irritation in his voice.

He dipped a wedge of pecorino in some honey and tasted it.

Abby drank some of the wine. She told herself she needed to keep a clear head, but it helped dull the pain from her cuts and took the edge off the horror of recent events.

'I got the next plane out and arrived this afternoon. I thought I might see Mina on it, but she must have got on an earlier flight. By the time I made my way up here, she had already arrived.

'I saw her coming out of the restaurant kitchen just before all the commotion. She pushed past me, didn't seem to recognise me. I was having a beer at that table over there. The next thing I knew, someone screamed and everyone was pushing back their chairs and rushing over to the fountain.'

'You were here?'

'I knew she had done it then, that she really was unhinged, so I went to the police. I had to. Turned out, they were already looking for her. I told them about the church. Then we saw the flames.'

A surly waitress brought out some pasta dishes and plonked them down in front of them. Abby twirled her fork in the *tagliolini* but didn't raise it to her mouth. For one thing, her arms hurt a lot now the adrenalin had worn off. For another, she just didn't feel like eating.

'The problem is, the more I think about it the more I wonder if my recollection is any more accurate than Mina's. I know we were fighting over the gun and it went off and that's how Philippa died. I know she shot at Marco and missed. After that, I blank out. I took the baby back. Then we're running for the car. What happened to Alan? I just don't know. I guess that's her revenge, isn't it? Planting that seed of doubt so now I can never be sure.'

She looked down. *What are you doing here with me?* she thought suddenly. 'But when I think about Alan, I remember how I felt about him. I was so angry that he might be my father. And I suppose I thought everything that happened there in some way related back to him. I can't help wondering if that anger took me over.'

The familiarity of James's hand on hers was unbearably painful.

'You could be right,' he said at last. 'I don't know – it's all way out of my experience. She certainly wants you to think that. And everyone else. That's why she wrote the book.'

'What book?'

'The seventh one. The one she left on the step. I've been reading it to Lucy – I'm sorry, I didn't know the connection between Hal Storm and Alan.

'To be honest, I could have guessed it wasn't her father's work. It starts off brilliantly but the ending's forced. And I can see now, it's a thinly veiled account of her version of what happened. Of course, she sees herself as a force for good and you're clearly the evil goblin.

'Look. I've no idea what happened but I could hazard a guess. From what you've told me, I don't think it could have happened the way she says. For one thing, you said you were holding the baby when Alan came in. You wouldn't have been able to shoot someone with a baby in your arms.

'But supposing you put the baby down. How much do you know about guns?'

Abby shrugged. She knew what they did. She knew what someone looked like after they'd been shot from a few metres away.

'What type of gun was it? A pump-action? Semi-auto?'

She threw her hands out. 'I don't know. Alan had it for hunting – birds, rabbits, I suppose. It was long, quite heavy.'

'Did it have a magazine attached? Did you pull a handle back towards you before each shot?'

She tried to cast her mind back, but it was useless. She put her head in her hands. 'It was twenty-five years ago.'

'Draw it for me.'

He reached inside his jacket for a pen. With painful effort, she sketched it out on a napkin.

'Something like that. I really can't remember.'

He stared at it and nodded. 'So, it had two barrels? Side by side like this, not one over the other? Sure?'

She shrugged helplessly. 'I think so, yes.'

'It's important.'

'All right then, yes.'

'Right. So, it sounds like a pretty standard double-barrel shotgun, probably 12 gauge. And yet, two cartridges had already been fired – the one that hit Philippa and the one that missed Marco. You'd have to have reloaded before firing again. Would you have known how to do that?'

'It's pretty self-explanatory, isn't it?'

'Is it?'

She rubbed her temples, forcing her mind back. 'Wait. I remember seeing Philippa reload that time she shot the rabbits,' she said at last. 'So, I suppose I would have known. She broke the gun in half and fed in the cartridges.'

'And where were the cartridges kept in the tower? Could you have reached them and reloaded in the time you had, without anyone stopping you? Do you remember doing it?'

She thought back. 'No, I don't remember. I think I would remember. I suppose Philippa would have kept them in the trunk with the gun, but I wasn't near the trunk. I was on the opposite side of the tower.'

James said, 'My guess is that the mother – Sue, is it? – killed Alan. She'd have had plenty of time to reload and she'd have known how. If the cartridges were stored in the chest, she would have seen them when she saw the baby in there.'

An image slid into Abby's head – of the blue velvet hat and the orange tubes nestling in it. And another of Sue bent over the trunk while Alan was shouting at Mina. He probably hadn't even realised Sue was there. She'd thought Sue was being sick, but perhaps she could have been rummaging for something.

'Sue could have shot Alan to stop him attacking Mina when he realised she'd killed Philippa.'

Abby considered this. It was a possibility. Alan adored Philippa, and if he thought that Mina had shot her he would have flown at her. And that would be the hardest thing for Mina to deal with later – the knowledge that he would have killed her if he had been able. She would find it impossible to forgive Sue for killing him, even if Sue had saved her life.

'But how could Sue kill her own husband?'

'It was a choice between husband and child, wasn't it? She'd just lost one daughter. And from what you've said, she didn't love Alan. She was going to leave anyway, with or without this Marco, wasn't she?'

Abby nodded slowly, feeling tears prick the back of her eyes. 'It's no surprise Marco hasn't come back. He wouldn't have wanted anything to do with Sue after it all, anyway, and he would be the obvious suspect. He must have spent his life on the run, with Nino always believing his father would come home eventually when he'd tired of his other woman.'

'Look, whatever happened,' James said, looking at her

steadily, 'there is nothing you can do to change it. And it's so easy to say, but I guess you just have to accept that now so you can move on.'

Move on where? She had wanted so badly to find out what had happened and prove that she hadn't been to blame for it all, but where did it leave her now? She had never allowed herself to think beyond this point. The future stretched out in front of her, bleak and uncertain.

'You're right, I know. But the fact remains that nobody would be dead if I hadn't taken the baby, and I'll never know what happened to him.'

'No, I guess you won't.' James ran his fingers lightly over her arms.

Her skin tingled at his touch. If things could only go back to how they had been, but they couldn't, could they?

'You've no idea how much I've missed you,' he said.

'You had Petra,' she said, before she could stop herself.

He looked appalled. 'For God's sake, there's nothing between me and Petra. She took me out to cheer me up because she could see I was miserable. We went to some awful club, sank a few bottles of wine between us. We could barely stand, that's the only reason we had our arms round each other in those photos.'

Laughter rose from the table behind them. The young couple studied the menu, their hands interlocking. The man made a remark and his girlfriend reached over and ruffled his dark, springy hair. Such a short time ago, Abby and James's relationship had been like that – or, at least, it had appeared to be like that.

James rubbed his eyebrow. 'I didn't know what to do with myself. I didn't understand why you hadn't told me – and yes, I was jealous of Connal knowing more about you than I did. I think I've always been jealous of him. These past couple of weeks without you have been hell. I don't want to be apart again.'

His knees were pressed against hers under the table. It felt familiar and right, but at the same time there were things they had both said and done that couldn't be easily forgotten.

'Neither do I. But it's not as simple as that. I've hated these weeks, too, but so much has happened and I don't know if we can get back to being the people we were. I know I kept all this from you and you'll find it hard to trust me again, and nothing compares with that. But you've hurt me, too. The way you spoke. And taking the children away from me. I never thought you would do that.'

'I thought it was better for them.' He sighed. 'No, all right, I did do it to hurt you. I never really believed you were a danger to them. It was petty and I'm sorry.' His eyes glinted with tears.

'It was such a shock, especially the way you told me, it was so unexpected. I didn't know how to react. But I should have had more faith in you. I should have realised it wouldn't have happened the way you thought. I know you better than that. And now I think about it, I should have realised a long time ago that there was something about your past, some part of you I didn't have access to. Maybe I always knew and I chose not to ask. Do you remember those dreams you used to have when I first knew you? The way you cried in your sleep? You used to laugh it off in the morning, gave it some medical term, and I think I let you convince me because deep down I was afraid to find out more.

'I just wish I could have been there, wish I could have done something, kept you safe. And I wish I could have been more supportive when you told me, instead of reacting the way I did.'

After a while he added, 'I'm not saying everything can be the same as it was. But that doesn't mean it's hopeless, does it? Why don't we stay out here for a day or two, away from the pressures, and the press, and all day-to-day stuff, so we can talk, see where we might go from here?'

She bit her lip. 'What about the children?'

'It's only a couple of days. They're fine with Trix.'

'Can you get time off at such short notice?'

'I don't need to. I've resigned.'

Her glass froze halfway to her lips. 'Resigned? Why? Because of taking the children out of school?'

He smiled grimly. 'No, although that wasn't my finest hour. Because it's not the way I want to live my life. All the aggravation and the press intrusion. I want to concentrate on more important things.'

Her heart beat faster. 'But what will you do?'

He shrugged. 'I don't know yet. What matters is getting my family back. Look, we don't have to make any promises. Just tell me you'll think about it.'

It was tempting – but to stay here surrounded by those memories? They were more vivid now than they'd ever been. But looking at James, she realised she wouldn't be facing them alone and would never have to do so again. His eyes were bright with hope. She thought how lovely his face was.

'No promises?'

'No promises.'

'All right, thank you, yes.'

Her eyes strayed to the family on the next table. The old man's face was pouched and wrinkled. His skin had that leathery look that showed he had spent a lot of time outdoors. His breathing was laboured but his arms still looked strong. Something about those meaty forearms was familiar. And then it came to her. She had seen them stacking logs and carrying the chainsaw. All these years he had hidden the truth about what he must have seen, although for Luca's sake, not hers.

Or was there another reason for his silence? The young man reached across the table and handed his girlfriend a small package wrapped in tissue. She frowned and laughed, making a show of trying to guess the contents, prodding and shaking it. Finally, she ripped through the layers. For a moment she was silent. She scooped up the chain and held it up, examining it in delight. The older couple stared, their faces frozen in fear. They looked at each other and then away. Abby wasn't sure if it was intentional, but for a second the gaunt woman's eyes seemed to rest on her.

The girl was protesting, saying she couldn't possibly but the young man insisted. He fastened the chain around her neck for her while his parents looked on helplessly. The old man started to cough. His wife scraped her chair back, must have been saying they must get back, it was late. She helped her son's girlfriend on with her jacket although the girl was protesting she wasn't cold.

As the four made their way out of the restaurant, the evening sun caught the girl's necklace– a shooting star-shaped pendant with diamonds on the tail. Abby's hand crept to her own throat where the pendant had once hung, but she no longer felt it. The weight had gone.

THE END

Fantastic Books
Great Authors

CROOKED CAT

Meet our authors and discover
our exciting range:

- Gripping Thrillers
- Cosy Mysteries
- Romantic Chick-Lit
- Fascinating Historicals
- Exciting Fantasy
- Young Adult and Children's Adventures

Visit us at:
www.crookedcatbooks.com

Join us on facebook:
www.facebook.com/crookedcatbooks

Printed in Great Britain
by Amazon